PEPPER
PIKE

"A corker of a whodunit ... Gritty, grim, humorous, sentimental—a perfect 10."
                    —*Chicago Sun-Times* (*The Duke of Cleveland*)

"The characters are vivid, and the plot goes in unusual directions, but ultimately it's Cleveland that captures our hearts."
                    —*Pittsburgh Post-Gazette* (*The Duke of Cleveland*)

"Roberts affectionately weaves in the history and rich ethnic mix of Milan Jacovich's Cleveland turf." —*Publishers Weekly* (*Collision Bend*)

"Roberts is a wordsmith of high order, and *Collision Bend* is a terrific novel of the mean streets."   —*Meritorious Mysteries*

"Roberts certainly creates a sense of place. Cleveland rings true—and he's especially skillful in creating real moral and ethical choices for his characters."   —*The Plain Dealer* (*The Cleveland Local*)

"Jacovich [is] one of the most fully realized characters in modern crime fiction ... Roberts is a confident writer who knows his character well and who has made him complex enough to be interesting."
                    —*Mostly Murder* (*The Cleveland Local*)

"[Roberts] tells his tale in spare and potent prose. His Cleveland stories get better and better, offering far more than regional insights and pleasures."   —*Publishers Weekly* (*The Cleveland Local*)

"A series that gets better and better ... strongly recommended for those who like their detectives cut from the classic mold."
                    —*Booklist* (*A Shoot in Cleveland*)

"[Milan Jacovich] is a hero one can't help but like. Roberts's polished prose, inventive plots, and pleasantly low-key style add extra appeal to his long-running series."   —*Booklist* (*The Best-Kept Secret*)

"Page turner of the week ... narrative comfort food ... a nifty spin on a classic P.I. formula."   —*People* (*The Indian Sign*)

"Brilliantly plotted, with a powerhouse climax."
                    —*Booklist* (*The Dutch*)

"[A] roller coaster ride of a mystery ... Roberts speeds the reader through an investigation offering plenty of delicious twists and turns without ever compromising credibility."
                    —*Publishers Weekly* (*The Irish Sports Pages*)

PEPPER PIKE

A MILAN JACOVICH MYSTERY

LES ROBERTS

GRAY & COMPANY, PUBLISHERS
CLEVELAND

Gray & Company, Publishers
1588 E. 40th St.
Cleveland, Ohio 44103
www.grayco.com

Library of Congress Cataloging-in-Publication Data
Roberts, Les.
Pepper Pike : a Milan Jacovich mystery / Les Roberts.
p. cm.
ISBN 1-59851-001-0 (pbk.)
Originally published: New York : St. Martin's Press, 1988.
1. Jacovich, Milan (Fictitious character)—Fiction.
2. Private investigators—Ohio—Cleveland—Fiction.
3. Advertising executives—Fiction. 4. Cleveland (Ohio)—
Fiction. 5. Missing persons—Fiction. I. Title.
PS3568.O23894P4 2005   2005011145

ISBN 1-59851-001-0

Printed in the United States of America

10 9 8 7 6 5 4 3 2 1

To Joe Sordetto
the Godfather of Burbank and
my favorite straight man,

To Jim Peck and Jim Peck Jr.
for the use of the hall,

and

To Bill Balaban,
whose picture should be in the dictionary
next to the entry "Friend."

PEPPER PIKE

CHAPTER ONE

A couple came into the bar and sat down next to me. They both had that kind of unremarkable, unmemorable face that you couldn't identify ten minutes later, and the only reason I noticed them at all was that his head got in the way between me and the TV set at the far end of the bar. That bugged me because this was an important moment in my life and I wanted to see every bit of it. Twenty-seven million dollars was nothing to shrug off, and it was going to be mine. I could sense it. The ticket felt right in my hand, the numbers seemed to dance on the paper, to tell me that they were winners. Of course I knew that already. I had picked them carefully. My birthday, my mother's birthday, my father's, my two kids', even my ex-wife's birthday: eight–eighteen–nineteen–eleven–thirteen–twenty-eight. The same numbers I'd been playing for the last five years, every Wednesday. But on this night we were talking about real money, no paltry million. Tonight the Super-Lotto Jackpot was worth twenty-seven million dollars. And it was going to be mine.

I took a big swallow of beer as the Lottery Lady's smiling face appeared on the screen, and I edged forward the better to see around my next-stool neighbor's big head, but everyone at the bar at Vuk's was leaning up a little in anticipation. They all had tickets, some of them ten and twenty, all spread out across the bar top and curling where their edges hit a beer spill. Every eye in the place was on that TV set, watching those little Ping-Pong balls with the magic numbers. My numbers. Everybody's numbers. Everyone in Vuk's had a winning ticket. Everyone in the state of Ohio had one. We were all just waiting for the announcement, for those six little Ping-Pong balls to come up with our numbers.

The TV lady was still smiling and saying something about the jackpot being worth twenty-seven million, and I lit a Winston and waited. I knew how much the jackpot was; you'd have to have spent the last five days fifty feet under the ground in a Zambezi diamond mine not to know. It was the big news, the biggest jackpot since the lottery had started up in Ohio.

The first ball popped into the air lock and the lady turned it with her fingers so the number showed. It was eleven! All right, I had one of those. Twenty-seven million, here I come. And then the second ball.

"Twenty-one," the lottery lady said. "Thirty-four. Thirty-three. Fourteen. Twenty-six. Two. The winning numbers tonight are . . ."

I crumpled the ticket in my hand and looked down the length of the bar. Disappointed murmurs made Vuk's sound like a swarm of bees had been let loose at the back bar. No words were discernible save an occasional "Shit!" Just a disillusioned hum, low-key and inner-directed as if everyone were mumbling to himself alone, unwilling to share his disappointment with his neighbor; it was the sound of dreams crashing and burning. The wadded-up lottery tickets were hitting the floor like hailstones where they sat sadly in the sawdust between the legs of the stools, mute testimony to failure.

Vuk, the bartender and owner, who had served me my first legal drink of alcohol when I'd come of age, noticed my beer was gone and came down to where I was sitting. Automatically he emptied the ashtray in front of me.

"Another one, Milan? Drown your sorrows?"

"There's not enough Stroh's in all of Cleveland, Vuk. Not twenty-seven-million worth."

"You'll get 'em next week," Vuk said. A Slovenian philosopher. No one was much in the mood to watch *Wheel of Fortune*, even to see what outfit Vanna was wearing, so Vuk switched on ESPN. There was a replay of a golf match in progress, and I've often felt that watching golf on TV is akin to watching someone read. Besides, I don't like a sport where the announcers have to whisper. It's a lot better when they yell: "Wow, he hammered it! The left fielder's going back—to the track, to the wall—it's gone!" Spectator sports are supposed to relax you and help blow off steam and ease tension, not make you feel like you were at High Mass.

I threw a five and two ones on the bar and climbed off my stool. A few of the old regulars waved goodbye, but most of the younger guys didn't know who I was. Over the years I'd been drifting away from Slavic Town, the neighborhood where I was born and had grown up, and was spending my days south and east of there in Cleveland Heights, where I now lived. It made me feel sad that I was something of a stranger on my own turf, but ever since my divorce it was just easier to stay out of Slavic Town most of the time. Too many memories.

I walked out onto St. Clair Avenue and around the corner to the vacant lot on East 55th Street that served as the unofficial parking lot for Vuk's Tavern. The snow from the blizzard a week ago had melted and then refrozen so that it crunched pleasantly under my size twelve shoes. It had been one of the mildest winters old-time Clevelanders could remember, which is to say it probably would have killed a Californian or Floridian, but for us natives it had almost been a vacation. Here it was, mid-February, and there had only been three really serious snowstorms.

I climbed into my slate-gray Chevy Caprice wagon, a car I roundly hated. It was big enough to rent out the backseat to a family of Puerto Ricans, and because it was square-backed and looked like a hearse, people would take their hats off when I drove by. I'd taken the car in lieu of payment for a job I had done a few months earlier, so I figured to drive it for a while before trading it in on something I really liked. I checked my watch. It was a quarter till eight. The Cavs were playing on TV tonight—the Celtics at Boston Garden. Something masochistic in me made me want to watch the slaughter. Besides, I didn't feel sociable this evening.

I'd been divorced from Lila for over a year now, and it was okay, I was getting used to it. But once in a while when the night was cold and the air was clear and crisp, the loneliness bit hard and held on. Tonight was one of those nights.

I headed south on 55th Street, hung a left on Euclid, negotiated the crazy traffic pattern at University Circle, and headed up Cedar Hill to where I maintained my office and apartment. It was nothing fancy, but there was a big front room I used for my business, a small parlor where I did most of my living, a closet-sized kitchen with a postage-stamp dining alcove, and two good-sized bedrooms. I kept twin beds in the smaller one for when my sons came to spend the weekend, and I slept in the larger one with the big bay window looking out over the triangle where Fairmount and Cedar come together at the top of the hill, right across the street from the Mad Greek and the fancy food market and the drugstore.

The apartment was empty. No surprise there, it always was. Every other weekend I'd get the kids, Milan Jr. and Stephen, but in the middle of the week it was lonely and cold as a tomb. I turned on the steam heat in the parlor, got a Stroh's out of the fridge, and switched on the TV just in time for the tip-off. The crowd at Boston Garden was as rude and noisy as ever, and they had a lot to yell about. The Celts got the tip, Ainge took it down court and passed it off to Bird, who hit a three-pointer when the game was less than twelve seconds old. A demoralizing beginning. I got a fresh pack of Winstons out of the drawer and ripped it open. I didn't really want a cigarette. I never did. It was just something to do.

Boston scored on the Cavs almost at will, and at the end of the first quarter they led by fourteen. Lenny Wilkens looked as though he'd been hit with a ballpeen hammer, kind of the way I felt. I turned the game off, stripped, and got into the shower, where I stayed until the hot water began to fail. I toweled dry, put on a terry robe, and went back into the parlor and got down a book. I'd read about two pages when the telephone rang. It sounded loud and harsh in the quiet. I picked it up on the second ring before it frazzled my nerves any further.

"Is this Milan Jacovich?" a male voice said, and I allowed as how I was, but corrected his pronunciation. It's Milan with a long *i*, and the *J* in Jacovich is pronounced like a *Y*.

"You do security work?"

"Yes, sir."

"I need a bodyguard. For twelve hours. Then tomorrow morning I want you to drive me someplace at nine o'clock, wait for me about half an hour, and drive me back. I'll give you a thousand dollars, which I'm sure is more than your usual rate. Is that all right?"

I turned my book face down on the table, which my mother had always told me never to do. "It's more than all right," I answered. "Who'm I talking to?"

"My name is Richard Amber. I live in Pepper Pike. I've asked around and they tell me you're completely trustworthy. Is that true?"

"I'd like to think so, Mr. Amber."

He was breathing hard as though he'd been interrupted in the middle of sex, although I had to remember it was he who had called me. "How fast can you get here?" He gave me an address on S.O.M. Center Road.

"It'll take me about an hour."

"Break the speed limit. I'll pay for the ticket. And you can spend the night here."

"All right," I said, jotting down the address. "Can you give me an idea what this is all about, Mr. Amber?"

"Not on the phone."

"I won't do anything illegal."

"This is perfectly legit, I can assure you."

"All right, then."

"And I can count on you?"

"I'm leaving in five minutes," I said.

"Good. And Mr. Jacovich? Are you licensed to carry a firearm?"

"Yes, I am."

"Bring it," he said.

• • •

Pepper Pike is a high-rent district, a relatively new suburb out
on the eastern edge of Cleveland. The big money used to live in
Shaker Heights, but as the wrecking ball flattened the downtown
area the denizens of the inner city moved a bit too far eastward for
the landed gentry, who in turn fled a few miles farther away into
the brand-new homes and subdivisions of Beachwood and Pepper Pike. In a town where a three-bedroom house with a quarter-
acre of land and a two-car garage can still go for around sixty-five
thousand dollars in Cleveland Heights, Pepper Pike real estate
was very inflated, into six figures and averaging out at about three
hundred thousand. For whatever reason Richard Amber wanted
to pay me a thousand dollars for twelve hours' worth of babysit-
ting, I wasn't going to feel badly about it. He could afford it.

I didn't break any speed laws. The suburban cops don't have
much to do in the way of tracking down armed robbers and rap-
ists, so they fill their idle hours by nailing motorists who go three
miles an hour over the speed limit. Though Amber might be willing to pay for my ticket, I doubted he'd pay the increase in my insurance. So I was careful. Doubly careful because I was carrying
a .357 Magnum in my armpit. I was licensed for it, but I didn't
particularly want to have to stop and explain to the law why I was
wearing it. I owned a smaller weapon, a .38 from my days in the
Cleveland Police Department, but the .357 had a lot more stop-
ping power, and if you're going to shoot some poor bastard you
might as well make it stick.

The more I traveled eastward the higher the snowdrifts were
piled at curbside, because for some strange reason the East Side
always got a lot more snow than the West. This phenomenon was
referred to mysteriously as "the lake effect" by TV weathermen,
but no one ever bothered explaining it to my satisfaction or anyone else's. It's one of those things you accept when you live here,
like each year's disappointments over the Cavs and the Indians,
or jokes about the river catching fire.

I swung onto Shaker Boulevard at Richmond Road and drove
down the darkened street past homes I'd never be able to afford,
finally turning a few blocks south at S.O.M. Center Road. I found

the house easily, a sprawling Cape Codder, white with black trim and shutters, set well back on a sloping lawn now covered with virgin snow that was beginning to go a little gray. It was a two-story with an attached garage and a driveway that climbed up one side of the slope to the garage or else, if one preferred, curled around to the front door and then down the other side of the slope to the street again. The driveway was neatly cleared of any snow or ice, and was dry. I parked directly in front of the entrance and got out, turning up the collar of my car coat and hunching my shoulders against the cold, whistling wind. The temperature was in the low teens, the kind of evening you want to stay home with a good book, which had been my original plan. A thousand dollars, however, makes it worth going out in the cold.

The porch light was on, rather brightly, I thought, and I found the doorbell easily. I heard it chime inside and waited for about forty seconds, then rang it again. No answer. I stamped my feet on the mat to keep the circulation in my toes and looked around. There were no lights on inside at the front. After ringing fruit-lessly for the third time, I walked around the side of the house, sinking ankle-deep into the snow. When I got to the back there was a light on behind a sliding glass door, and I peered in. It was a study, obviously a man's room, with wood paneling and a thick dusky rose carpet. There was a large walnut desk, and a few occa-sional chairs and a nut-brown leather sofa. I slipped off my glove and knocked on the glass door and called out something dumb like "Anybody home?" It was obvious there wasn't. I vacillated between annoyance and concern, and finally concern won out. I walked clear around the house looking for signs of occupancy, but it seemed completely deserted. No lights were on at all up-stairs. I wound up at the front door again, stupidly ringing the bell once more before sticking one of my business cards into the door handle and driving away.

It was just past ten o'clock. I headed for a little bar down on Chagrin where a journeyman piano player was banging out golden-oldie show tunes for middle-aged patrons to sing along with off-key. I hung up my coat and went to the phone booth and dialed Richard Amber's number. An answering machine, in a soft feminine voice, told me that no one was home but that she'd be ever so pleased if I waited for the tone and left a brief message.

"This is Milan Jacovich, Mr. Amber. It's . . . ten past ten o'clock. I was just at your house and there was no one there. I'm at . . ." I looked at the number of the pay phone and read it off to the tape. "I'll stay here until midnight, and then I'm going home."

Back at the bar I ordered a beer and listened while a fat, bald, gray-bearded customer who thought he was Robert Goulet massacred a few songs from *Camelot* and came on as strongly and gracelessly as I'd ever seen to a fiftyish woman wearing a white blouse and a blue-gray skirt slit up to her crotch. Having to stay and listen was cruel and unusual punishment, and I took some sort of perverse satisfaction when she put on her coat and went home right in the middle of "I Loved You Once in Silence." Everybody strikes out sometimes.

By the time midnight rolled around the bar had pretty much emptied out—it was a Wednesday evening, after all, and most of these folks had to work in the morning. I was pretty annoyed. Not only had I wasted an evening and half a tank of gas, but I'd lost an easy thousand dollars. It wasn't much compared to the twenty-seven million I'd missed out on from the lottery that evening, but in my head I'd already banked the thousand, and I was very out-of-sorts. I went back to the phone, called Amber's number, and waited patiently through the recording again.

"Milan Jacovich here," I said after the beep. "It's twelve o'clock and I'm going home."

I headed west on Chagrin and got stopped by a Beachwood cop for going five miles over the speed limit. I nursed some bad feelings about Richard Amber the rest of the way home.

CHAPTER TWO

I woke up around seven o'clock, still tired. I don't sleep much these days, which is not to say I don't need the sleep. It just doesn't come, somehow. Maybe it's the empty-bed syndrome after a lifelong marriage; maybe it's just that I'm pushing forty and not terribly pleased with where my life has taken me. I'd gone to Kent State and played some football—defensive guard—and then Uncle Sam had arranged for an all-expense-paid tour of Southeast Asia, where I'd functioned in the military police, maybe because of my size or maybe because I would have done just about anything to stay out of the infantry. After my discharge I figured I'd capitalize on what the army had done with me and spent four years with the Cleveland P.D. But I'd had enough of saluting and spit-shining, so after a few years I quit and opened Milan Security Service. I call it that because I get awfully tired of people mispronouncing Jacovich.

I married my high school sweetheart. Trite? I suppose it was. Lila was a pretty kid, of Serbian descent, and as we grew older she developed that Serbian aggressiveness that just didn't mesh well with my Slovenian mild manners, and we finally called it quits, fourteen years and two kids later. We're still good friends—I suppose we'll always love each other in a very real way—but we're better off apart. The marriage had been a flop but the divorce was a big success.

I made some instant coffee, then got into the shower. After I finished, I saw with dismay that a clump of hair was clogging the drain in the tub. I ran a brush through my hair; it was growing thinner by the day. The curse of the Slovenes, or one of them anyway. There's an old Yugoslavian homily that if you put three Serbs together you had a regiment; put three Croats together and you got a parliament; put three Slovenes together and that made three Slovenes, because no one had ever been able to classify and label us. And I guess that was part of my current malaise. I was a private cop with a temperament and personality more suited to teaching history; a blue-collar neighborhood guy with a master's degree; a devoted family man living alone in an apartment. I had yet to find the pigeonhole in which I'd be comfortable.

I was on my second cup of coffee and well into the newspaper's reports on the remainder of the Cavs game when the phone rang. The voice on the other end was familiar, and it pronounced both my names properly.

"Is this Milan Jacovich? This is Judith Amber." I realized I'd heard the voice twice last night on Richard Amber's answering machine. "You left messages for my husband last night? And a card in the front door?"

"That's right, ma'am. Your husband and I had an appointment, but I was stood up."

"I wonder if you could drop by the house at your earliest convenience."

"Is your husband there now, Mrs. Amber?"

"No, he isn't. Would eleven be convenient?"

"It would if you'll promise to be home when I get there."

"I'll be here," she said. "And I'll make last night up to you. The trip will be well worth your while."

I made another cup of coffee, which tasted even worse than the first two, and vowed to buy myself a real coffee maker. My old one was just one of many things I didn't get custody of in the divorce settlement. I cooked up a few scrambled eggs and toast and four rashers of bacon. The Ambers were starting to pique my curiosity. First Mister offers me a thousand dollars to hold his hand all night and doesn't show, and then Missus says she'll make it worth my while just to talk. I decided to do a little homework before I left.

I called Ed Stahl at the *Cleveland Plain Dealer* and asked him if the name Richard Amber tinkled any bells.

"Richard Amber, the advertising guy?" Ed said.

"That's what I'm asking you."

"The only Richard Amber I know is a VP with Marbury-Stendall Advertising in Shaker Heights. Big bucks, and veddy high so-sigh."

Ed Stahl had been a mainstay of the *PD*'s city desk dayside for more than fifteen years and was blessed with two things that make a great reporter: an encyclopedic memory and an insatiable curiosity. Tucked away somewhere in a musty old drawer along with half a bottle of Jim Beam and a lifetime supply of Tums was a Pulitzer Prize for investigative journalism. I figured if anyone was anyone in this town, Ed would know about him without having to look it up.

"What's the skinny on Amber? Any funny stuff?"

"If being a benefactor on the Playhouse Committee and a patron of the Symphony and on the board at the Art Museum is funny stuff, I guess so," Ed said. "He's got connections at City Hall and in Columbus, and for all I know in D.C. as well. He hasn't missed a Browns game in eleven years, and to make it even more complete he's high-church Episcopalian. Now, what's up"?

"Put your pencil down, Ed. Nothing is up, or at least not yet. When there is you'll be the first to know."

"I'd better be," he said darkly. "When are you going to spring for lunch?"

"I lost out on the lottery last night, Ed, so I'm a little short."

"There were three winners, you know," Ed said. "A cool nine million apiece."

"Who were they? A couple of slobs living in a trailer park in Lima?"

"An elderly couple from Youngstown was one, and an unemployed auto mechanic from Marysville was another. The third one hasn't shown up to claim the bread yet."

"I wish I could be that go-to-hell about nine mil," I said. "I would've camped out on the lottery's doorstep all night with my ticket in my sweaty little hand."

"That's because you are a materialistic, greedy, penurious Slovenian," he said. "No class at all."

"You can tell from who my friends are. Thanks for the dope, Ed. Lunch next week?"

"If I'm still alive. If not, the week after."

I'd first met Ed Stahl when he was a cub and I was a beat-walking rookie. I'd slipped him some information on a series of robberies and the resulting story won him a raise and me a dressing-down from my captain, the first of a series that had finally helped me make the decision to turn in my blue suit and badge in favor of private practice. Ed was one of the good guys, and one of my best contacts in town. A private detective without contacts is like a prima ballerina with a prosthetic leg.

The drive to the Amber manse was more pleasant in the sunshine. Bright sunlight in February in Ohio usually means cold temperatures, and the day lived up to its public relations, with the thermometer hovering at around twenty above. There wasn't much wind, though, so it was bearable. The Ambers' home looked even better in the daytime. The box hedges that surrounded the house were snow-covered, but I could see they'd been impeccably trimmed, and on the white facade there was not a blemish, as though it had been painted the day before yesterday. Behind the house and almost dwarfing it was a stand of birch and cottonwood in almost military rows, bleak but proud in their winter nudity. The windows were shiny clean and there were white shades drawn in each of them, also spotless. Even the doormat was clean and new-looking. The only footprints I could discern in the snow were the ones I had put there the night before. It was the kind of house that made you feel no one who lived in it ever went to the bathroom.

The woman who answered the door was short and slight, delicate-looking, with soft blonde hair shag-cut around her ears, blue-blue eyes, and skin so fair it was almost transparent, showing the faint tracery of blue veins beneath.

"Mr. Jacovich? I'm Judith Amber. Come in."

She led me into the living room, which was painted white with a light blue trim. The furniture was, as I had expected, expensive and feminine-looking, all in whites and off-whites and delicate shades of blue. Judith Amber was in blue, also—baby blue knit with white stitching at the neck and hem, almost as though she had color-coordinated her outfit to match the room. She was by far the most patrician-looking woman I'd ever seen: Romanesque nose and high brow and full mouth that looked as if it didn't smile much. Her saving grace, which made her somehow sexy, was one slightly crooked tooth.

Indicating with a royal gesture that I should sit on the sofa, she perched across from me in a wing-back oyster-white chair and crossed her legs demurely; it hardly occurred to me at all to peek at her knees. She moved with the air of a supremely confident woman, the confidence being that she would get anything she desired. She looked at me for too long a moment in an evident attempt to make me ill-at-ease. It didn't work.

"What can I do for you, Mrs. Amber?" I said, ruining her moment.

She didn't budge. After looking at me for another fifteen seconds or so, she finally said, "You left my husband messages last night, and you must have been here at the house to leave your card in the front door. I'm prepared to pay you to tell me why.

"You already know why," I said. "I told you on the phone. I had an appointment with your husband last night and he never showed up."

"According to your card you're a sort of private detective or a security specialist."

"Both," I said.

"Were you working for my husband?"

"Not yet."

"Then you wouldn't compromise your professional ethics by telling me what he wanted of you."

"I don't know what he wanted."

"Did it have something to do with me?"

I tried to sit up, but the sofa cushions were so deep I only succeeded in looking like a big awkward bear. "I don't know," I said.

She waited a few seconds, then stood up and went to a table by the window where her purse was. She took out a leather checkbook and turned to me. "I want to hire you," she said.

"For what?"

"To find my husband. He didn't come home all night, and his car is still here. I find that rather peculiar."

"That does happen sometimes, Mrs. Amber. I think it's a little premature to be overly worried. Have you called the police?"

She smiled faintly. "My husband is very prominent in the community. I'd like to avoid going public with this until we find out what's going on. Besides," she said, "the police aren't interested in missing people until at least forty-eight hours have elapsed. They feel the way you do." She unscrewed the cap of a fountain pen and began writing a check. I was impressed. You hardly ever see fountain pens anymore.

I was even more impressed when she handed me the check. A thousand dollars. The Ambers seemed to think alike when it came to money.

"Will that do for a retainer?" she asked. "Or do you want more?"

"That'll do just fine." I folded the check and put it in my wallet. "I'm sure there's a simple explanation for your husband's absence, Mrs. Amber, but we'll find him in any event. He'll probably show up this morning sometime."

She went back to her chair. "Now that you're working for me, you can tell me what my husband said to you on the phone."

"He called at about nine and said he needed an all-night bodyguard. Then he wanted me to drive him somewhere in the morning. That's all. When I got here at ten, there was no one around, so I went to a local pub and left my first phone message, which I guess you heard on the machine. At midnight I called again. That's all I know."

Her brows knitted ever so faintly, as though a full-out frown might damage the perfection of her face. She put a long red fingernail between her teeth, but didn't bite down. Finally she said, "I see," very quietly.

"I'll need some information from you, to give me a place to start looking. Where does your husband work, who are his friends, what does he look like, what was he wearing last night, things like that." I took out my notebook and a pen. It was a fifty-nine-cent Bic from the drugstore. I felt embarrassed using it.

"Well," she said, "Richard is senior VP of Marbury-Stendall Advertising, which is one of the biggest agencies in the state. They're over on Warrensville and Chagrin. But he didn't come in to work this morning. I've called three times."

"Who do I talk to over there?"

"John Marbury is chairman of the board, but the actual running of the agency is done by Jerry Stendall, John's nephew. I suppose Jerry is as close to Richard as anyone."

"How about friends?"

"Richard is an account executive, Mr. Jacovich. Everyone is his friend. That's his job, to make the right friends. You might say the governor is his friend, and the mayor, and most of the top business people in Cleveland and Columbus. But if you're talking about real friends, pals, confidants . . . he was too busy to have any."

She sucked on her fingernail again for a while, deciding whether to release the next bit of information. When she did, her blue eyes went dark and icy cold. "There's an actress down at the Playhouse by the name of Karen Wilde." There was more than a bit of Bette Davis in the way she spat out the name. "I suppose you might call her a friend."

"When was the last time you saw your husband?"

"Yesterday morning before he left for work. I went out at about six o'clock, before he got home. If he got home."

"Why would you think he didn't?"

"I don't," she said. "Sometimes he comes home for dinner, sometimes not. He knew I was going to be out last night, so he might not have."

"Couldn't you tell? Wasn't there any sign of his having been home? Dirty clothes or something?"

She smiled dimly. "My husband is a very meticulous man, Mr. Jacovich. I can count on the fingers of one hand the times he's left his clothes lying around or made any sort of mess in the bathroom. Of course he did call you last night, but who knows whether it was from the house? One can only assume—"

"Let's not assume anything for the moment. Mind telling me where you were last night?"

"I went out to dinner and then to Severance Hall. They were doing an all-Mozart program."

"You went alone?"

Her eyes met mine challengingly. "Is that important?"

"Mrs. Amber," I said, "you suggested that the call from your husband to me might have had something to do with you. Would you explain that?"

"Mr. Jacovich, you aren't investigating me."

"Is there anything to investigate?"

I could see the blue vein in her throat pulsing. "If you must know, Richard and I have been married for nine years. For the last two it has been . . . little more than a convenient arrange-ment. For both of us. Do I make myself clear?"

"Crystal," I said. "Mrs. Amber, I hate to give up a thousand dollars, but under the circumstances it does seem logical for Mr. Amber to stay out all night, doesn't it?"

"It's not his pattern. He always comes home eventually. Be-sides, he'd never miss work without calling in. He had some sort of meeting scheduled for ten this morning—and he'd cut off an arm before disappointing a client."

"Who was the client? Do you know?"

"No," she said, "he didn't talk to me about his work."

"Didn't?"

The color crept into her face. "Doesn't," she corrected. "I meant doesn't. Look, don't make a big thing out of a slip of the tongue."

"Mrs. Amber," I said, "it sounds to me like you don't really give a damn if your husband comes back or not. Forgive my saying so."

She stood up. The interview was over. "No," she said, "I don't think I will forgive your saying so. I'll expect to hear from you this evening one way or the other."

"Will you be home?"

That didn't go over too well. I could tell from the way her eyes widened. "Do you disapprove of me, Mr. Jacovich?"

"Do you care whether I do?"

That stopped her for a second, and then she laughed, really relaxing for the first time. She had a nice smile when she wasn't playing lady-of-the-manor. "I quit," she said.

"I will if you will. By the way, I'll need a description of your husband, just so I have an idea of who I'm looking for."

"I suppose that would help. Let's see . . . Richard James Amber. Fifty-two years old, a Leo, about five foot ten, one hundred eighty pounds, more or less. Dark brown eyes and hair." A faint smile twitched at the corner of her mouth. "Appendectomy scar." She recited the statistics as though reeling off significant dates in American history.

"And what was he wearing when he left?"

"I'm not sure. But his loden coat isn't in the closet. It's tan with light brown leather trim."

"You wouldn't happen to have a recent photograph?"

"I think so," she said. "Excuse me."

She went upstairs, and I took advantage of the alone time to give the living room a more careful scanning. I had the feeling no one ever came in here. Despite the expensive furniture and rich carpeting, it was a cool and lonely seeming place. There wasn't an ashtray in sight, but that didn't surprise me. Smoking in here would be like firing up in the Sistine Chapel.

Judith Amber came back with a five-by-seven color photograph and handed it to me. "This was taken about four weeks ago," she said. "You may keep it; it's a copy."

The picture showed two men in dark business suits. One had an arm around the other's shoulders and both were smiling those knowing, masculine, old-boy smiles into the camera. It seemed to have been taken at one of those dreary parties that were always held in the *second*-largest banquet room of a commercial hotel.

The man on the right fit the description she'd just given me of her husband. He had a brandy snifter in his free hand, and was collar-ad handsome, radiating self-assurance and power and affluence, as though he were accustomed to having his picture taken frequently. Yet around his eyes there was a marble hardness, and the smile was just a bit too hearty to seem totally sincere.

The tall, thin man in the photo with him was the governor of Ohio.

CHAPTER THREE

The offices of Marbury-Stendall Advertising were in one of those gigantic buildings all faced with mirrored glass that were beginning to spring up in former cow pastures all over the far East Side. They threatened the suburban residential dwellers with ugly traffic snarls, high-tariff expense-account–luncheon restaurants, and a proliferation of tanning salons and exclusive beauty shops, boutiques, and software stores. The agency had seemingly taken over the third floor, as almost every door had the company name affixed to it on a silver-colored plaque. I went in the front entrance and told the pretty black receptionist that I had an appointment with Mr. Stendall. She asked me to wait a moment while she did some strange things with a computerized telephone system and then announced me, after which she told me Mr. Stendall's secretary would come and get me. I used the time to examine the framed Clio awards and self-congratulatory framed pictures that covered most of the reception area's walls.

A nice middle-aged lady came to fetch me and led me through a Byzantine maze of corridors, past glassed-in cubicles where graphic artists toiled over slanted drawing tables, past copying machines and fax machines humming with the business of business, past small offices where sweater-clad copywriters doodled on yellow pads and stared out the window, past larger offices where junior account executives seemed anatomically fused to their telephones. Finally we arrived at the executive suites; the carpet was thicker and the framed awards and posters were replaced with signed lithographs by Klee and Picasso and Ben Shahn. She paused in the doorway of a large airy office, piloted me in, and announced, "Mr. Jacovich," mistakenly pronouncing the *J*.

Jerry Stendall was in a comfortable upholstered executive chair behind a large, low, round glass coffee table on which was a telephone and personalized notepad and a few big abstract pewter sculptures. He shook my hand and indicated one of the chairs on the other side of the table. He mispronounced my name, too, but him I corrected.

"Sorry," he said with little conviction. "What can I do for you?"

Stendall was about forty, well-built and trim, even though he couldn't have been more than five foot seven. He boasted an artificial suntan and was having less success in the battle with hairline fallout than I was. He was without a jacket, but his shirt, light blue with a white collar, was immaculately pressed and starched, and his tie was midnight blue with almost microscopic yellow fleurs-de-lis sprinkled in a careful pattern. He tended to blink a lot and rarely looked at me when he spoke.

I said, "Thank you for letting me take your time, Mr. Stendall. I'm trying to locate Richard Amber."

"So am I," he said earnestly. "It isn't like him to do this."

"When's the last time you saw him?"

"Around closing time last night, five-thirty or six. He stuck his head in to say good night. Now, let me understand this. You're a private detective?"

I gave him one of my cards, and he examined it the way one might a hundred-dollar bill suspected of having spurious origins. "And you're representing Judith?"

"She's naturally worried about her husband, yes."

"I see." People who say that usually don't. He swiveled around in his chair and put my business card on a shelf jutting out from the wall, right next to a cluster of photographs of his ugly children. "I can't imagine how I can help you."

"Maybe by telling me what kind of day Mr. Amber had yesterday. Who he saw, where he went, what he did."

"Hell, I'm not his keeper. He's the senior vice president of this agency. He doesn't punch in and out like a typist."

"Of course not. Did he spend most of the day here in the office?"

"That's right," Stendall told me. "He went out for lunch but that was it."

"Do you know who he had lunch with?"

"Like I say, I don't keep tabs. You'll have to ask his secretary."

"And what's her name?" I asked, taking out my notebook. "Rhoda Young. Richard's office is right next to this one, so his secretary is in the cubicle just outside his door."

"I'll speak to her on the way out. He didn't have any visitors, any meetings yesterday that you know of?"

"You're not listening, Mr. Jacovich." At least he got it right that time. "Richard's time is his own. We chatted a bit yesterday afternoon right here in this room, and other than that I've no idea how he spent his day."

"Mind telling me what you chatted about?"

"I mind like hell," he said defensively. "I can assure you it was agency business, though."

"Okay. Mrs. Amber said he had a meeting scheduled for this morning. Can you tell me about that?"

"Since he didn't show up, I'm not sure it's that important."

"How about letting me decide?"

He crossed one ankle over his knee. His shoes must have cost two hundred dollars. "I don't mean to be hostile," he said. "I'm just not used to private detectives coming in here and grilling me."

"This isn't grilling, Mr. Stendall. We're just talking."

"Okay, okay. He had a meeting with a client for this morning. Our biggest client, as a matter of fact. Walter Deming of Deming Steel and Alloys here in Cleveland. It was pretty damned embarrassing when Walter showed up here and no Richard, I can tell you."

"Mr. Amber is the executive on Deming's account?"

He touched his tie at the knot, sticking his neck out like Rodney Dangerfield. "He *is* the Deming account. About four years ago, Marbury-Stendall—well, it was just Marbury Advertising then—bought Amber Advertising. Richard came with the package, and so did Deming Steel. We were delighted to get him—and to get Deming, too, of course."

"And was Richard delighted as well?"

Stendall smiled. It was a smarmy smile. "He's still here, isn't he?"

"What connection does this agency have with the governor's office in Columbus?"

He sat up a little straighter. "We handled all the TV spots for the governor's reelection campaign."

"Was Mr. Amber the exec on that campaign, too?"

He nodded. "He's known George—the governor—for a lot of years. They went to Ohio State together."

"So, in effect, Richard Amber brought a lot of business into this agency?"

"That's why we pay him the big bucks. Look, all this is a matter of public record. I'm not telling you any secrets."

"I appreciate that," I said. "Is there anyone in the office that Mr. Amber is especially close to?"

"Well, he works pretty well with everyone. That's what account executives do, for God's sake. But three of his people came over with him from his own shop when we merged. Rhoda, his secretary. Jeff Monaghan, our head of creative services. And one of our TV producers, a real old-timer name of Charlie Dodge. He's known all of them a long time."

"Do you get along with Mr. Amber, Mr. Stendall? I mean, personally."

He laughed. "What do you think, that I spirited him away in the night? So I could look like a holy ass in front of a client this morning trying to explain why he never showed up? Be real, Mr. Jacovich."

"I'm trying. Do you have any idea where he might be? Any at all, no matter how far-fetched."

He fingered the edge of his nostril gently, as though it were a pearl beyond price. "I'm being indiscreet in saying this, but . . . what the hell! Richard's been seeing a woman for some time now."

I consulted my earlier notes. "Are you speaking about Karen Wilde?"

His eyebrows shot up. "You know about her?"

I nodded. "She's in the rep company over at the Playhouse."

"Where'd you hear about Karen Wilde?"

"It's not important," I said.

"No, probably not. But how come you get to ask all the questions and I don't?"

"Get yourself a PI license and ask all the questions you want. Now, about Karen Wilde?"

"Richard's had a few . . . extracurricular ladies in the past few years, but they never interfered with his work. He never missed meetings or took days off. He's one of the top admen in this state, in the whole Midwest. He's not going to jeopardize his reputation—or an account that bills over six million dollars a year—to spend a leisurely day screwing."

He looked over my shoulder, and his face changed. He got to his feet, not exactly scrambling out of his chair, but he was pretty quick about it, and I looked around to see why.

A very tall old man was standing in the doorway. He wore glasses, but they only emphasized the keen, quick intelligence in his pale gray eyes. He looked from me to Stendall and back again.

"Come in, John," Stendall said unnecessarily, because John already had. "This is Mr. Jacovich. He's looking into Richard's . . . uh . . . whereabouts."

"John Marbury," the old man said in a wavery voice that reminded me of Beulah Witch on *The Kukla, Fran, and Ollie Show*. I remembered the landmark Supreme Court decision *Marbury v. Madison*. John Marbury looked old enough to be the fellow it was named after. His face was a disaster area of fine lines and wrinkles and pouches, and the skin of his hands was stretched tight over the bones and had the texture of ancient papyrus. He carried himself, however, with the assurance of a much younger man, and his handshake was surprisingly firm. He sat down in one of the chairs, and only after he had done so did Jerry Stendall resume his own seat.

"I can't understand it," Marbury was saying. "Richard knows how important Deming is to this shop. He should've called. Inexcusable to behave in such an irresponsible fashion."

I tried to remember if I'd ever heard anyone use the word "fashion" in that way in conversation, but the memory wouldn't come to me. I said, "I don't suppose, Mr. Marbury, that you'd have any idea where Richard might be?"

"If I knew I'd be reaming his ass right now," Marbury said. It took me aback, although it shouldn't have. Often we tend to forget that an elderly person can swear the same way he did when he was younger.

"Well, if you hear anything, I'd appreciate your contacting me." I gave Marbury one of my cards, too, just for the fun of it.

"Yugoslavian name?" he said, glancing at it. When I affirmed that it was, he nodded his head. I wasn't sure if the nod was in approval of my heritage or whether it meant he now understood my lack of class and my boorish behavior. I didn't care which.

Stendall said, "And you'll call us if you find him, won't you?"

"That's up to my client, not me. Thank you for your time, gentlemen."

Stendall rose to his feet to shake hands when I left the room. Marbury just waved tiredly. When you're as old as he is, I guess you don't have to be polite. Or when you're as rich.

I walked down the corridor to the next office and stopped at the cubicle just outside it. "Miss Young?"

"*Mrs.* Young, yes," said the woman at the desk. She was in her late thirties, Mediterranean-looking with a slight bump in her nose. A lot of attractive people have bumps in their noses, big ones, too, that no one ever notices. Her black hair was frizzy and worn shoulder-length. She wasn't really pretty, but her looks worked.

I introduced myself and explained why I was there.

"I just can't understand what happened," she said. "I'm just sick about it. It's not like Richard . . . Mr. Amber."

"Everyone seems to think he's a model citizen," I said. "I figure his secretary would know him better than anyone else."

"You'll never hear a discouraging word from me about Richard Amber. He's a wonderful man. A very nice man. And a talent. He's been great to me."

"Do you happen to know who he had lunch with yesterday? Is it on your calendar?"

She looked, then shook her head. "If he did have a lunch appointment, he didn't tell me. He just left. Was gone about an hour and a half, and then he came back."

I smiled at her. "If I may call you Rhoda, you may call me Milan."

She bobbed her head in assent.

"You've worked for Mr. Amber how long?"

"Let's see . . . five years at his own shop and four here."

"Right. Now, Rhoda, was he acting unusual lately? As if something were bothering him?"

"No, not at all. He has a lot on his mind, but then he always does. I mean, like he practically carries this agency on his back. Without him . . . I don't know. But he always manages to be cheery and pleasant, no matter what. The perfect boss."

"And a good friend?"

She smiled. "When Marbury bought Mr. Amber's company, Richard said that I had to come along, too, or there'd be no deal. He made more than a million dollars when he sold, but he would have let it go on a principle. He's just that kind of man."

Her dark eyes gleamed while she talked about him. Another case of unrequited love and/or hero worship in the executive suite. Rhoda Young would die for her boss, that much was clear. I gave her one of my cards. I was passing out a lot of them today. "Please call if he should get in touch with you."

She read it with interest. "Did she hire you? Judith?"

"That's right," I said.

A short, sharp breath came out of her nose as if she were trying to clear her sinuses like a welterweight.

"What?" I said.

"Nothing. I'm just . . . touched by her concern."

I cocked my head and looked at her. She flushed. "I shouldn't have said that. Sorry."

"No, go on."

"I shouldn't."

I waited. Sometimes waiting is the most effective form of asking questions.

"She's just such a cold, calculating bitch. I'm surprised she even cares." She looked up quickly, agitated. "Don't tell her I said that, will you? Don't tell Richard, either."

"I wouldn't want to cost you your job."

"It's not that. But it would hurt him very much if he knew that's how I felt about her."

And it would scare Richard very much, I thought, if he knew how she felt about *him*. Funny how you can see someone every day for nine years and not know anything about them. I smiled at her gently. "Your secret is safe with me."

"Thanks. I guess I'm just a little emotional about this whole thing," she said.

"It's okay. Rhoda, tell me where I can find Jeff Monaghan and Charlie Dodge. I'd like to talk to them, too."

She took a deep breath, composing herself once more into the perfect amanuensis. "I'm afraid you're out of luck. Charlie went to Detroit last night to shoot a TV spot, and Jeff called in sick."

"Nothing serious?"

"I didn't talk to him, but the rumor mill says he has a hellacious cold."

"It's the season. Thanks so much for your help, Rhoda."

"Look, I'd do anything if it would help Richard Amber," she told me unnecessarily. "Anything you need."

"I'll remember that. Thanks again."

It was not quite three in the afternoon when I got to the shopping mall closest to Marbury-Stendall and found a telephone. I called a banker friend of mine, Rudy Dolsak, a neighborhood kid from St. Vitus's parish who'd made good and was now some sort of high-muckety-muck in the financial world.

After the hellos and the what's-going-ons I said, "Rudy, I need a favor."

"Forget it, Milan. With your credit rating, Christ Almighty couldn't get you a loan approved."

"Thanks, but it's nothing that drastic. I need a credit check run on somebody."

"Aw, Milan," he said, "I'm getting too old for this cloak-and-dagger shit."

I didn't want to hear that. He was my age.

"It's all on the up-and-up. Rudy. Be a pal."

He took a deep breath and blew it out. Through the phone it sounded like Hurricane Hattie. "Go," he said.

"Richard J. Amber of Pepper Pike."

He whistled. "Heavy hitter."

"Would I ask for a credit check on a cabdriver?"

"You'll have to give me till tomorrow. I do have a few things to do around here, you know? For the bank?"

"Bull," I said, "I know about you bigwigs."

Rudy said softly, "Is Amber in some kind of jam?"

"I don't know. I might be trying to keep him out of one. I'm just covering all the bases."

"Okay, Milan. Be secretive and see what happens."

"Now, you know I can't tell you client secrets."

"Yeah, yeah, the Code of the West. I know."

"Rudy, I owe you one."

"As a matter of fact," he said, "you owe me about five."

Since I was at a public phone anyway, I took the opportunity to look up Jeff Monaghan's address and number in the directory. I was in luck. He lived in University Heights, which was almost right on my way home.

CHAPTER FOUR

The man who came to the door of the large red-and-white cottage was wearing faded blue jeans with a rent in one knee, moccasins, and a red-and-black flannel shirt buttoned up to the neck, and was sporting a very red and sore-looking nose. He had a wad of Kleenex the size of a softball in one hand.

"Look," he said, "I'm really sick today and I don't want to buy anything."

"I'm not selling, Mr. Monaghan," I said. I showed him a copy of my PI license.

"Jesus, I've never met a real private detective before," he said, and sniffed mightily. "But what I said still goes. I'm not feeling very well, and I don't want company."

"I'll just take a minute."

"All right, but for God's sake come in so I can shut the door."

He led me through a cluttered living room into a small den. A Jackson Browne tape was playing on the stereo. He sat down in a big overstuffed chair, pushing aside a faded blanket. Next to him was an economy-size Kleenex box and the dregs of a cup of tea. The room smelled like Vicks VapoRub. Monaghan had a sandy beard that matched his hair. He was in his late thirties, I imagined, and from the packed bookshelves that lined the walls I could see he was a habitual reader. Most of the titles had to do with advertising, media, and pop psychology. On one wall was a poster from *Casablanca* in a cheap frame.

Monaghan blew his nose painfully. "What's up?"

"One of your co-workers seems to have disappeared. Richard Amber."

"You've got to be kidding! I saw him yesterday."

"So did a lot of people. But no one has since. I was wondering if you might have heard from him?"

"Hey, man, I didn't even know he was missing."

"You've worked with him a long time, haven't you?"

"About seven years," he said. "He's a great guy. I hope nothing's wrong."

"What could be wrong?"

"I don't know, like an automobile accident or something. I mean, have you checked the hospitals?"

"It's unlikely he would have been without ID."

"That's true," he said. He put a hand on his chest as though he were having trouble getting air.

"Nasty cold," I said.

"Yeah. My first one of the winter, too. I thought I was going to get away with it."

"With what?"

He looked at me strangely. "With not having a cold all winter. Look, I don't think I've got much to offer you. I didn't even know there was a problem until you walked in here two minutes ago."

"Well, maybe you can fill in some background for me. Was Mr. Amber into anything that might be considered chancy or dangerous or possibly illegal?"

"I don't follow."

"Did he gamble? Speculate on the market? Use drugs? Any hidden vices?"

"Oh, Christ. He didn't use drugs at all that I know of. He's been known to bet a few bucks on a Browns game now and then, but doesn't everybody? As for the stock market, well, we never discussed that."

"What about women?"

He didn't answer, so I prompted, "Besides Karen Wilde?"

"I'm not sure I want this conversation to go on any further. I mean, I don't know you from Adam, I don't know what you're doing here, and I'm not going to go into personal and embarrassing details of my friend's life just because you flash me a license."

"Suit yourself," I said, "but your friend may be in trouble, and if I find out everything about him that I can, I may be able to help him."

He chewed on the corner of his lower lip and thought about it for a while. "Okay, so Richard likes to chippy around a little. No big deal, lots of people do."

"It happens in the best of families," I said. "Can you give me any names?"

"I don't know any. He's had a thing going with Karen for quite some time now. Before that there was no one special. Not that I can remember, anyway. Oh, yeah, there was Mary . . . God, I can't remember her last name, even. She works down at Channel 12 in sales. Mary . . . Soderberg, that was it. Mary Soderberg."

I wrote the name down in my notebook.

"But that was two years ago or so, you know? And it didn't last for very long.

"How long?"

"Six, eight weeks. I didn't pay much attention. I have enough to worry about getting laid once in a while myself."

"And how did it end? Happily?"

"I'm not sure I can define that. He was married, she knew it, so I suppose neither one of them had any great expectations. They still do business together—I mean Marbury-Stendall still buys time on Channel 12. But I don't think there's anything else going on anymore."

"One more question."

"I hope so. I feel like shit."

"If *you* were looking for Richard Amber, where would you go first?"

"I can't imagine him bugging out on work like this, but I suppose if I were looking, it would be someplace where Karen Wilde was. That's about all I can tell you."

It was enough. After he closed the door behind me and I was

walking down the steps of his house, I heard him blowing his nose again, hard. It sounded like a rogue elephant in rut.

I went to a pay phone outside a liquor store on the corner and called every taxi company in town to find out if any of them had picked up a fare in Pepper Pike between nine and ten last night. Two of them told me to get stuffed, but Red Top Taxi's regular dispatcher was a friend of mine, an ex-con who had done me a few favors, and he looked up the records for me. There weren't that many to look through—Cleveland, unlike New York and Chicago, was not a taxicab town. Al told me there had been no pickup anywhere near Pepper Pike during that hour last night. So if Richard Amber had indeed called me from his home, he had left there in someone else's car or on foot.

It had been a long day and looked to be longer as I made my plans for the evening. I had spent most of the day talking to strangers, most of whom didn't give a damn about my existence. I needed a hug.

Lately I get a funny feeling walking up the walkway to my house, or my ex-house, as is more precise. I had lived there for a long time. It was known to the folks in the neighborhood as the Jacovich place. Lila and the kids still lived there. But it was no longer the *Milan* Jacovich place, and I hadn't yet come to terms with that.

My younger son, Stephen, was wandering around in the front yard, tossing a football up in the air and catching it, or at least attempting to. At eight years old, he reminded me a lot of myself at that age. He had the same unruly brown hair, the same pale blue eyes, and from the size of his shoulders even at this tender age he was going to be a big man like me. His older brother, Milan Jr., more resembled his mother's side of the family, the Serbian side, with dark hair and eyes and olive complexion, and the Serbian temperament, too. But little Stephen was all sunshine and laughter and effervescence.

"Hey, pal," I said as he passed me the ball.

"What are you doing here, Dad?" he said, and I'm sure he didn't mean for it to hurt me as much as it did.

"I was in the neighborhood." I put my fingertips on the laces. "Go out long and cut left."

He did, running a jerky, little-boy pass pattern, and I threw him a spiral. It squirted out of his fingers.

"Aw, come on!" he said, going to retrieve the ball. He threw it back and trotted to within ten feet of me.

I said, "Play action, go right," and he ran off almost to the curb and I threw him another pass, which he dropped.

"Shoot," he said.

I waved at him and went up the steps to the porch and rang the bell. I hated ringing the doorbell in my own house, but then it wasn't my own house anymore.

Lila was wearing a pair of light-colored jeans and a dark blue wool shirt with the top three buttons opened. She looked wonderful.

She also looked annoyed.

"Milan, I wish you wouldn't just drop over."

"I was in the neighborhood," I lied again, "and felt like having a cup of coffee."

She looked at her wristwatch and frowned. "Okay, but just for a minute."

I followed her into the kitchen. I smelled stew cooking. Lila's kitchen was so full of plants and potted palms it looked like the set for a Tarzan movie. I sat down at the table, noting that I had picked the chair with the uneven legs, and I rocked back and forth on it while she poured me some coffee.

"I'm on a case," I said.

"Well, that's good."

"It's very good. I got a thousand-dollar retainer."

"Good for you, Milan." She sounded very disinterested.

I sipped the coffee. Lila always put a few sprinkles of cinnamon in the grounds before the water went through, and it tasted terrific. I said, "Stephen's getting so big."

"Kids do," she said.

"Uh . . . I have to go to the Playhouse tonight. They're doing *A Streetcar Named Desire*."

"It's supposed to be a good production. I read the reviews."

"I have to interview one of the actresses."

"Why?"

"The case."

"Oh."

"So I thought I'd take in the show while I was at it."

"That's a good idea."

"Want to come with?"

She moved away, back to the range, and poked a wooden spoon into the pot. The stew smelled wonderful, but then Lila always did have a way about her in the kitchen. "No, thanks."

"Come on," I said. "You'll enjoy it."

She turned to face me, looking pained. "Milan, I can't." Her dark hair was taken up at one side with a red barrette. She looked fifteen again.

"Okay, just asking." I drank some more coffee. Then I said, "Where's Milan Jr. ?"

"I don't know."

"For God's sake, Lila, I don't like the kid just running around all the time when you don't even know where he is."

"Milan, he's twelve years old and he's with his friends someplace." She got that serious, flat tone in her voice she always used prior to getting really angry. "And I don't appreciate your coming in here and telling me what a lousy mother I am, letting my kids run loose."

"I never said that."

She thought it over and I guess she realized I hadn't, which I would never do anyway because Lila is the best damn mother I've ever seen, and her frown softened a little as she went back to the range and stirred some more, a pensive look on her face, and then she looked at her watch again.

"Is Joe coming over for dinner?"

"Milan," she said, and it was a warning.

"Okay, okay, just trying to make conversation. But I thought that if he wasn't, and if you were free, you'd like to come to the play with me. You always liked going to the theater."

"Not tonight, Milan."

"All right," I said, nodding my head like one of those fuzzy boxer dogs in the back window of a Mexican's car, and I took another slug of coffee, hoping to hide the look on my face and ease the pain inside at the same time. I failed on both counts.

"Milan, let's not start anything, okay? Let's just be friends. I'll always be your friend."

"Hey, me too. No problem."

We talked like the friends we were for about five more minutes and then I said I had to go.

"Okay," she said. "I hope you enjoy the play.

"Thanks, I'm sure I will."

"Let me know if it's any good."

"Sure," I said. So you and Joe can go see it together. In a pig's ass I'll tell you. But aloud all I said was "Sure."

When I got to my car Stephen came running around the side of the house and threw his arms around my waist. "Dad! Dad!" he said. It was the hug I'd been needing.

"Hey," I said.

"You staying for dinner?"

"No, pal, I'm not."

He tried not to look sad. "Why?"

"I gotta work tonight," I said.

He handed me the football and ran a few yards away from me. "One more try," he pleaded.

"Okay. Go straight and long."

He began running, then turned and stopped, not the NFL-approved method of catching a football. I pumped once, eluding imaginary linebackers, and let the ball go in a high, lazy arc, and he shifted his feet to get under it. It floated into his outstretched arms like a piece of newspaper on the wind, and the impact made him stumble backward, but he held on and kept his feet, clutching the ball to his chest like something precious and dear.

"Gee!" he said in wonderment and pride, and the smile of triumph that illuminated his beautiful little face cracked my heart.

• • •

A Streetcar Named Desire is one of those plays in the American repertory that either works brilliantly or becomes ludicrous, depending on the skills of the director and actors involved—especially the performers playing Blanche and Stanley. The Playhouse production worked, but as good as the leading players were, it was the actress in the supporting role of Stella who caught my eye and attention, and it wasn't because I had come to the theater to talk to her in the first place. Karen Wilde had a remarkable stage presence, a luminous glow about her that was impossible to ignore. She didn't need the lighting man to hit her with a spotlight. She carried her own with her. Her performance was alive, real, dynamic, and hurt like truth.

The audience was enthusiastic, even though there were quite a few empty seats. I guess *Streetcar* is pretty heavy going for a generation raised up on *Porky's* and *Police Academy*. After the curtain calls I went around to the stage door and sent my card in to Karen Wilde, asking for a few minutes of her time. After a while the stage-door keeper came back and told me Miss Wilde would meet me in the Playhouse Club in fifteen minutes.

The lounge was crowded when I arrived. Just about everyone who had been to one of the three shows at the complex and was planning a post-theater toddy was already there. I explained to the bartender that I was waiting for Karen Wilde and he grudgingly agreed to serve me a drink.

I noticed I was the only one there alone. It didn't bother me much. I was getting used to it. Slowly. The crowd seemed to be in a good mood, and I marveled once again at how the people of this town support cultural activities like theater and music and art much more than those in larger cities like Los Angeles, which have more to offer in terms of sheer volume. Cleveland is a pretty good place to live, I guess, if you don't mind the weather. An awful lot of people do, though.

Karen Wilde made a rather theatrical entrance into the club and graciously acknowledged the smattering of applause. She looked around a bit, and I got up and went over to greet her. Her smile could warm up the northern Ohio winter considerably. I led her to the bar, to an empty stool next to mine, and she ordered a Campari and soda. Not my kind of drink. I'd just as soon have a Pepsi.

I said, "I really enjoyed the show tonight. You were marvelous."

Her eyes sparkled. For any actor, praise is a drug. "How nice of you to say that," she said. "I must admit your card puzzled me. I assume you didn't want to talk to me just as a fan."

"No," I said, "I didn't. I'm doing some work that involves a friend of yours."

"Oh?"

"Richard Amber."

She was good. I had to admit she was good. The talent she showed as Stella DuBois was nothing to the artfulness with which she fielded that one. A slight widening of the irises was the only indication she gave that the name meant anything to her at all. Her smile never varied. "Oh, yes, Richard," she said. "Well, I should tell you, Mr. Jacovich . . ."

She mispronounced it, but I didn't have the heart to correct her. She was small-boned and delicate-looking, which was the direction in which Richard Amber's tastes ran. She seemed to have brittle bones that would shatter with rough treatment. What was a hard *J* among friends?

"I have a real problem with gossiping about my friends to strangers. So I'm afraid you've wasted a trip."

"No, it was hardly a waste, because I enjoyed the show, and you, so much. Perhaps if I tell you what I'm doing—"

"I hardly think it will matter."

"Richard Amber has been missing for twenty-four hours."

She wasn't *that* good. "What do you mean?"

"He disappeared from his home last night and hasn't been seen or heard from since."

She said carefully, "Why come to me?"

"I understand you and he are . . . close."

She nervously pulled out a cigarette, a More menthol. I lighted it for her. "May I ask on whose behalf you're making this inquiry?"

"Mrs. Amber."

She rose quickly. "I'm afraid you'll have to excuse me. It's been a long and arduous evening and I'm feeling a little drained."

"Wait, please."

"If that woman sent you here to snoop—"

"It's not like that."

"He's probably not even missing at all."

"I assure you he is." I had stood up, too, and I put my hand on her arm. I towered over her—she couldn't have been more than five foot two. It's probably why, with her talent, she was still working in Cleveland and not in New York or Los Angeles. Gently I pressured her elbow back toward the bar, and she allowed me to guide her onto the stool again. The color had fled from her face, even under the makeup.

"How . . . how can I help?"

I was relieved. "Tell me when was the last time you saw him."

She took a moment deciding whether to cooperate. Then the gravity of the situation made up her mind for her. "Monday," she said. "We usually spend Monday evenings together. We're dark Mondays. That means there's no show, my night off."

"Have you talked to him since?"

"We speak every day. Except today. He didn't call today."

"What time did you talk to him yesterday?"

"Last night. Just before eight. We have an eight o'clock curtain."

"Wasn't that a bit unusual? Calling you right before a performance?"

"I suppose so, although he's done it before. Usually he calls during the day—from his office. But last night he seemed very agitated, very excited."

"About what?"

"He didn't say. He was being mysterious. But . . ."

I waited while she fought with herself about whatever she'd been about to say. Then she said softly, "He asked me to marry him."

Before I could reply the bartender came over and looked at us expectantly, and I indicated he should bring two more. She said, "Wait a minute, Bud. Bring me a vodka rocks."

Apparently Campari and soda wasn't going to be enough to get her through the rest of the conversation. I waited until the new drinks were served before going on. "Are congratulations in order, then?"

She shook her head. "I'm not sure. Richard and I have known each other a long while. We care about each other. But I was happy the way it was. I've been married before and I'm not anxious to do it again."

"So what did you say? When he asked you?"

"I told him we needed to talk."

"Have you any idea why, after all this time, he suddenly called you a few minutes before you were supposed to go onstage and proposed?"

"No, I don't. It really messed me up for the show last night, though. I blew two lines. I *never* do that."

"How did you leave it? The proposal?"

"Just like that. I said we'd talk."

"And he didn't call you today?"

"No. I thought it was strange but I figured he was busy. He's a very busy man."

"Normally not too busy to call you every day."

"It's happened before. Not often, but it has happened. Look, Mr. Jacovich—"

I couldn't stand the mispronunciation anymore. "Why don't you just call me Milan?"

"Milan, then. I'm beginning to get worried."

"So is Mrs. Amber. That's why I'm here."

"Did she tell you to see me?"

I ran my thumb alongside the Pilsner glass, making a streak in the condensation. "Your name was mentioned."

Karen Wilde laughed. "I always thought she knew. Richard swore she didn't, but I always thought so."

"Why?"

"Richard is a very prominent man here in town, and being an actress I'm fairly well known. I suppose someone saw us together."

"Does it bother you that she knows?"

She shrugged her narrow shoulders. "Not really. She isn't exactly a saint, you know."

"Oh?"

"She plays around as much as Richard. More, I should think."

"Any idea with whom?"

"Frankly, my dear . . ." she said, letting me fill in the rest of Rhett Butler's closing line.

I let half a minute tick by, and then I said, "Do you think you'll marry Richard Amber?"

"If he ever shows up again, you mean?"

"Yes."

She took a long pull on her vodka and blinked as it went down. Then she looked at me.

"No," she said.

CHAPTER FIVE

First thing in the morning I phoned Judith Amber and told her how yesterday had gone. She didn't seem pleased. I don't know what she had expected. I thought I'd done a good bit of work in twenty-four hours. She suggested I should call the airlines and see if her husband had taken a flight out of Cleveland, a possibility that had occurred to me already. But that process would take the better part of the day, and after I thought about it I was sure it would be a waste of time. Richard Amber had not taken his automobile and no cab had picked him up that I knew of. And why would he have asked me to come out and guard him if he were leaving town in less than an hour? I simply thanked Judith Amber for her suggestion. Rhoda Young was right—Mrs. Amber was a pretty cold cookie, and despite the similarities in look and build I could see why Richard might prefer the warm vivaciousness of a Karen Wilde to the unscalable perfection of his wife.

I couldn't face the day without having breakfast, especially since dinner the night before had consisted of coffee at Lila's and a few beers elsewhere. I dressed quickly and drove up Cedar to Corky and Lenny's delicatessen and had some matzo brie. By the time I'd read the newspaper and gone back home it was almost nine, and I decided to make some phone calls. Two incoming calls interrupted me.

The first was from an old high school chum who'd gone into

law enforcement about the same time I did, but had stayed with it after I broke away. His name was Marko Meglich, but he'd quietly Americanized it some years before to just plain Mark and had recently added a Lieutenant to the beginning of it. Marko never lost an opportunity to remind me. I probably could have made lieutenant, too, if I'd hung around. He just didn't understand. Marko was a guy who thrived on routine and regulation and structure, and it was hard for him to comprehend the needs of people like me who prefer living out of their hats.

"Well, Milan," he began. He'd been a policeman so long he was beginning to sound Irish. "Looks like you're playing in the big kids' league these days."

"What's that supposed to mean, Marko?" I still called him Marko because it bugged him.

"Got a phone call about you the other night."

"What other night?"

"Night before last, it was. Someone wanted to know if I knew you and if you were reliable, dependable—"

"Clean, reverent, and obedient," I finished. "Why didn't he call the Boy Scouts?"

"He was looking for a trustworthy bodyguard. I recommended you."

I doodled a gallows with an empty noose on my yellow pad. I'd always doodled that, even when I was a kid. If my parents had been a little more hip they might have worried that such a doodle showed a dangerous morbidity of thought and had me checked out by a shrink, but Louis and Mirijanna Jacovich didn't know much about child psychology back then. The most that had ever been said about it was my father's terse "You're gonna hang *yourself* one of these days!"

I said to Marko, "You wouldn't be talking about Richard Amber, would you?"

"Ah, he got in touch with you? I'm glad you got the gig, Milan. Outstanding."

"What time did he call you, Marko? Remember?"

"Oh, around eight, I guess. No, more like eight-thirty. It was my last night shift for a while—I had yesterday off or I would have called you."

"What did he say?"

There was a pause. "Why don't you ask him?"

"I'm asking for a reason, Marko."

I could hear him lighting a cigarette. He blew the smoke into the mouthpiece of the phone and said, "He just told me he needed someone for a twelve-hour bodyguard job and did I know anything about you. And he mentioned one other agency, to be honest. He'd gotten both of you out of the Yellow Pages. I told him you were a personal friend of mine and that you were the best."

"That's all he said?"

Marko said, "What's going on, Milan?"

I took a breath. "Mr. Amber's pulled a vanishing act."

He chuckled. "These rich people, man, they're really something else."

"Yeah."

I felt I'd gotten out of that one pretty well. I dislike lying to the police, but Judith Amber had emphasized confidentiality when she'd hired me and I didn't want to tell Marko Meglich what I was doing. If he wanted to take the information that Amber was missing as some kind of rich man's practical joke, it wasn't my fault.

My second incoming call of the morning was from Rudy Dolsak, telling me he'd gathered some information about the Ambers' financial dealings.

"Richard and Judith Amber," he said, "hold two thousand shares of Deming Steel and another thousand shares of Marbury-Stendall Advertising as joint tenants, along with various other stock holdings amounting to another three hundred thousand dollars, all in blue chips. They also jointly own a summer cabin in Wawassee, Indiana, purchased in 1981 for thirty thousand with a current equity of about twelve thousand seven hundred."

"How about cash?"

"A joint checking account with a balance of nine thousand two hundred and seven, and another twenty-three grand in a money market account they can't touch until July of next year without taking a big bath on the interest. Amber also has a personal checking account with a balance of around three thousand, which he pretty much maintains at that level. And Mrs. Amber has a personal checking account with a balance of fourteen thousand something."

"What about the Pepper Pike house?"

"Purchased nine years ago for one ninety-five, now appraised at three seventy-five. The equity in it is about one eighty and change. However, the house is in the name of Judith Marie Amber. Period. Nowhere does Richard Amber's name show up on the papers."

"A little unusual, isn't it, Rudy?"

"Not when you get the rest of the picture. The aforesaid Judith Marie holds another twenty thousand shares of Deming Steel in her own right, as well as a personal stock portfolio that would gag a hippo. She also has various savings and money market accounts and CDs stashed at several banks around northern Ohio, including two here at Ohio Merk, that add up to about two hundred and twenty thou."

"Wow," I said, scribbling.

"Now that isn't counting her trust fund, Milan. It's a living trust, set up years ago by her late father. The principal was six million something, and she's pretty much left it alone all these years except for an occasional dip into the interest. It's worth more than eight now. She also has a twenty percent interest in several housing tracts up in the Lake communities—Ashtabula, Geneva, Fairport Harbor, etc. And those tracts were all built by a firm called North Coast Developers. I don't have the exact figures, but her twenty percent ought to come to something well over a million, maybe two. Want me to get the real numbers?"

"No," I said, scratching my chin with the eraser end of my pencil. "But I would like to know who the principals are in North Coast Developers."

"So would I," Rudy said. "There was a holding company listed, but no names."

"What holding company?"

"Boot."

"What?"

"That's its name—the Boot Corporation. Listed in Columbus."

I wrote that down. "What this seems to boil down to, Rudy, and correct me if I'm wrong, is that Richard Amber without Judith Marie Amber is worth approximately seventeen and a half bucks."

"That's what it says here," Rudy Dolsak said. "Don't forget he makes a pretty good salary at Marbury-Stendall. I mean, no one's running any benefits for him. But the real money in the Amber family is tucked neatly into the top of Judith Amber's stocking."

"Any idea where it came from?"

"Judith Marie Amber is née Judith Marie Deming, if that helps you any."

"Deming as in Deming Steel?"

"Daddy was Donald Deming, brother and partner of Walter Deming."

I wrote DEMING on my pad in block letters. "Rudy, I understand Amber is pretty well connected in Columbus."

"That is also due to his lady. Deming Steel was the second-largest producer in Ohio at one time, and she got to know a lot of people in high places."

"What do you mean, at one time?"

"Don't you read the papers? Other than the sports page, I mean? Steel is in deep shit right now, and Deming is hurting. They're on the ropes. They've been looking around for a government bailout for the past year, but no dice. There've been massive layoffs at the plant, and rumors have been flying like Canada geese that they're just about belly up."

"I guess I did read something about that, but I'd forgotten."

"If you were a stockholder you wouldn't have forgotten. The stock has dropped faster than the Indians' team-batting average."

"Didn't Marbury-Stendall buy up Amber's own ad company a few years back?"

"That's right."

"Well, what happened to all that money?"

"Ah," said Rudy, "this is where the cheese really gets binding. Nine years ago Judith Amber gave her husband the money to start up his own company—no, not gave it, invested it. Under the terms of the agreement she was the sole owner of Amber's shop. In effect, she was her husband's boss. So when the company was sold the money went directly into her pocket."

"And what did she do with it?" I said.

"She didn't confide in me," Rudy said dryly. "But I'd imagine it was wisely invested. She's a pretty canny lady."

"Sounds like it. Hey, Rudy, thanks a lot. You've been a big help."

And he had been. Rudy and I had played ball on the streets when we were kids, and our friendship had lasted a lot of years. I guess when you come from a real neighborhood like ours you don't lose track the way you might when you're brought up in some upper-income suburb and go off to college a thousand miles away and then relocate. Rudy, Marko Meglich, Alex Cerne, Matt Baznik, Sonja Kokal—we'd all stayed in touch, even though our lives had taken different directions. Rudy was a banker, Marko was on the police force, Alex went into dentistry, Sonja was a psychologist. And Lila, of course. Lila Coso Jacovich. Soon to be Lila Coso Jacovich Bradac, as in Mrs. Joseph Bradac? I wondered.

So now I had a wealth of information on the financial health, or lack of it, of the Ambers, Richard and Judith. How I was going to utilize it, or what bearing it might have on Richard's disappearance, I didn't know. But I usually find that in a case of this kind, every little piece eventually fits together, including the fact that Richard had checked me out with Marko Meglich at around eight-thirty Wednesday evening, soon after he'd called Karen Wilde with his sudden and uncharacteristic proposal of marriage. But when you're putting a jigsaw puzzle together you usually look first for puzzle pieces with one straight edge so you can build the frame for the rest of the picture. I didn't have any straight edges yet, or at least they didn't look straight to me.

• • •

Channel 12 was about ten minutes from my place, downhill all the way in more ways than one. The city has done an incredible job of urban renewal in its downtown area and on both banks of the Cuyahoga, making the central city a good place to live and work. However, just east of the financial district and Cleveland State University things begin to change. Every urban center needs its slums, and when you tear down or rehabilitate one, another pops up somewhere, and in Cleveland the most recent had popped on the near East Side. Euclid Avenue was one long stretch of sixty-year-old office buildings that looked their age, gutted one- and two-family dwellings whose survival against the winds of winter was a source of wonderment to me, structures that looked as though they should have been torn down, and old warehouses. Most of the inhabitants of the area were black welfare families, and the sidewalks were choked with men permanently down on their luck, with tired old ladies dragging wire shopping carts along the ice-caked pavements, and with sad prostitutes shivering from the inadequate insulation provided by their thigh-length miniskirts. It was in this area that Channel 12 had established its headquarters, in a white brick building that had long since faded to off-yellow, with a too-small parking lot in the back and a brave sign with the station's call letters and the boast "We're #1 in Cleveland!"

The interior, painted an institutional yellow, was sadly in need of touching up from the scuffmarks of two decades of heels and rolling mail carts and furniture dollies. The offices were laid out claustrophobically in rabbit-warren fashion off narrow corridors, having been designed and decorated an entire generation before they began making the workplace look like a surgery. On the second floor I found Mary Soderberg, behind a glass door marked Sales.

Mary Soderberg was one attractive number, though she didn't fit the Judith/Karen mold of Richard Amber's small and fine-boned women. She was about twenty-six or so, tall and lithe and full-figured, blue-eyed and fair, ruddy-cheeked with long straight yellow hair. She wore an argyle sweater vest over a white tailored blouse, and a rust-colored pleated skirt that couldn't quite hide her terrific legs and hips. She was the type of girl who would have been a cheerleader in school and dated the captain of the football team, with those Scandinavian/All-American looks that men often fantasize about but rarely get to touch. Charming lines at the corners of her eyes crinkled and deepened when she smiled, and she seemed to smile a lot. All in all, I was glad I'd come.

"The last time I saw Richard was at the Marbury-Stendall Christmas party," she told me after I'd introduced myself. "He pretty much works only on the Deming account, and they don't do their commercials locally."

"Is there anyone here at the station who worked more closely with him, who might have seen him more recently?"

She shook her head. "I do most of the talking to the agencies, because I'm the one that sells them time. I'm in pretty close contact with the Marbury media buyers, but hardly ever with Richard." She smiled up at me winningly. "Why would you think I would be, Mr. Jacovich?"

Bless her heart, she got it right the first time.

I felt myself coloring slightly, very unlike me. "I understand you and Mr. Amber were good friends at one time."

She laughed heartily. "My, you are a gentleman," she said. "Yes, we were. But that was a long time ago."

"And you haven't been . . . close . . . since?"

"No," she said with mock solemnity. "We haven't been close . . . since."

I didn't say anything, which prompted her to continue. "It was what it was for a very short time, and then it wasn't any-more. No big deal."

"Any hard feelings?"

"None at all," she said. "I was new in town and on the job, and Richard seemed pretty glamorous. After a few weeks I decided I didn't like the setup and I broke it off. My first and last married man."

I said, "Where are you from originally?"

"Boston."

"You don't sound like it."

"Because I don't say pahk the cah? I was a speech major at Boston College and worked really hard to get rid of the accent. Since the Kennedys left power it's not very fashionable anymore." Her smile was a dazzler. "I guess I succeeded."

"Very well," I said. "Ms. Soderberg—"

"Why don't you call me Mary? If I can call you . . ." She checked my business card. "Milan?"

"Milan is easier. Okay, Mary. Mr. Amber has been missing for thirty-six hours now, and Mrs. Amber is naturally worried. I thought maybe you might be able to point me in the right direction."

"I couldn't even begin to speculate," she said. "As I told you, I haven't seen or spoken to him since the holidays. Richard isn't much for hanging out, you know. No favorite cocktail lounge, no athletic club, at least not when I knew him. I assume you've checked out his office?"

"Oh, yes."

"And his current . . . friend?"

I nodded.

"Well, I'm at a loss, then. I hope nothing's wrong. When all is said and done he's a pretty nice guy." She brightened. "Oh. He and his wife have a summer cabin someplace in Indiana. On a lake." She scrunched up her eyes, thinking hard. It gave her a cute pussycat face. "Wawatosa or someplace like that."

"Wawassee."

"That's it. I was never there, because Richard was hardly ever there. They used to rent it out during the summer. It was mostly an investment thing."

"Why did you mention it, then?"

"It was the only thing I could think of, frankly. But it was probably a lousy idea."

"Why?"

"Look," she said, "Richard would never go on a holiday in the middle of a business week. He hardly ever takes time off, not even for getaway weekends. He's too into his job." She smiled again, a bit ruefully. "They call my generation Yuppies, and say we're too hung up on material things. But Richard is as money-obsessed as anyone I've ever known. Making it, keeping it. Maybe because he never had any real money of his own. It's all hers."

"Does that bother him?"

"Wouldn't it bother you?"

"I don't know," I said. "I've always been pretty happy being in my own skin."

"I can see why," she said. "It's pretty nice skin." My ears flamed. "Anyway, it's a summer cabin. You'd probably freeze your buns off there in February."

"Did he ever talk about his work to you?"

"Never. Not after we started seeing each other. That's how the whole thing started, of course, because of business. Marbury was producing some commercial spots for the governor, and they shot them here in the studio. That's how I met him. He was supervising the spots."

"He produced them?"

"No, Charlie Dodge was the producer. But Richard was always there to make sure everything was going smoothly, and to hold the governor's hand. That's his job, and he takes it very seriously."

"I take mine pretty seriously, too, Mary, so you'll have to forgive me if I get too personal."

"Get as personal as you like," she said kindly. "I'll let you know if you cross the line. Hey, did you ever think about advertising locally on TV? We could put a pretty low-cost package together for you. And there's no competition. There are no other private detectives advertising on TV in Cleveland."

It was my turn to laugh. "I see we all take our jobs seriously."

"Mary's the name, selling's my game."

"I can see it now: 'Wife run off with the milkman? Husband fooling around? Partner dipping into the till? Just call Milan Security and we'll make it all okay again."

"I love it," she bubbled. "You'll be a bigger celebrity in town than that used car dealer who looks like a gorilla."

"I think I'll pass for now," I said, "but I'll give it some thought. Mary, thanks very much for your time."

"Sure," she said, and stood up as I did. She was nose-high to me. Taller than Lila. We shook hands. Her hand was soft and warm.

I said, "Can I call you again if I need more information?"

"Are you married, Milan?"

"No."

She nodded, assimilating the information. "Then why don't you call me anyway?"

I felt my face getting unattractively red, and I was at a complete loss for words.

"Was that brazen?" she said.

"Not at all."

"You have laughing eyes. I like that."

I liked it, too, or at least liked it that she thought so. No one had ever told me that before, certainly not recently. I hadn't had much to laugh at in the past year or so, and was very much aware I was in danger of becoming a real drag. Maybe she thought my eyes were laughing because that's what they did when they looked at her. Maybe. At any rate, I'd had to park about two blocks from the station, and on the walk back to my car I hardly felt the biting wind blowing through my sheepskin coat.

I hardly felt the sidewalk under my feet, either.

CHAPTER SIX

There wasn't much of a crowd at Vuk's during the noon hour. Most of the regular patrons brown-bagged it and stayed around wherever it was they worked for lunch. About the only ones hanging out in a bar before five o'clock were unemployed steelworkers in the neighborhood and retirees, mostly guys from the old country, who spoke a strange mixture of Serbo-Croat and English that only they seemed able to understand. When I got there the TV was on—it was always on in Vuk's, from *A.M. Cleveland* first thing in the morning to the national anthem just before closing. Nobody watched it very much, but it was part of the atmosphere, like traffic noises in New York or the sound of the surf in Malibu. Not that Vuk—Louis Vukovich was his name but no one ever called him Louis except his mother—gave much of a damn about atmosphere.

The name on the plastic illuminated sign that hung over the door was VUK'S TAVERN, and that's what it was. It was not a cocktail lounge or a saloon, or even a bar in the commonly accepted sense. It was a tavern, the kind you find only in the Midwest anymore, a workingmen's hangout where few ladies ever ventured and if they did they were treated just like one of the guys. No pretensions, no bullshit, and the closest anyone ever came to a mixed drink was a seven-and-seven. Most of the people had known each other twenty years or more. It made me melancholy.

But it wasn't that far from Channel 12 to Vuk's, and I had a hankering for a sausage sandwich, the good klobasa fried in peppers and onions served with horseradish on thick, dark rye bread. I washed it down with a couple of Stroh's. A soap opera played on the tube, and glancing up at it made me wonder where they ever found so many beautiful young men and women who could act. Real people didn't look like that.

Well, most real people didn't. Mary Soderberg did, and that was something I needed to think about for a while. I hadn't really dated since becoming single, giving the lie to the carefree, profligate life of the urban bachelor. It was by choice, I suppose. I didn't have a lot of experience with women, because I'd gone with Lila more or less steadily since I was seventeen. The mere idea of dating was threatening to me, and that included Mary Soderberg. But I was smart enough to realize I couldn't go on the way I was indefinitely, the loneliness, the solitary drinking, hanging around Lila's like a whipped puppy hoping for a bone. I suppose it was time to dip a tentative big toe into the water.

None of this was getting me closer to finding Richard Amber, however, and that had to be my priority. I wasn't joking when I told Mary I took my job seriously. I asked Vuk for some phone change and went and called Judith Amber, but the line was busy. I waited ten minutes and called again, this time with success.

"Mrs. Amber, why didn't you tell me Walter Deming was your uncle?" I said after the hellos.

There was crackling silence on the other end and then she said, "I don't know. You didn't tell me your uncle's name either."

"You said your husband had a meeting set up yesterday morning but you didn't know who it was with. It was Walter Deming."

"I *didn't* know about it," she said. "My uncle and I talk maybe once a month, and Richard never tells me anything."

"I'd like to talk to Mr. Deming, if that's all right."

"I can't see what good it would do."

"Maybe none, maybe lots. I won't know till I try."

She said, "He doesn't know anything about this. I mean, he realized Richard didn't show up at work, but he doesn't know he's been gone for two days."

"Why don't you call him and explain it?" I said. "Then when I call for an appointment he'll know who I am."

She sighed a martyred little sigh. "Very well. I'll call him and call you right back."

I looked around at my surroundings, Vuk's phone being right between the two rest rooms, and said, "No, I'm on the go. I'll call you back in fifteen minutes."

I went and had another beer, and thought about Walter Deming. I had never seen him, but his picture had been in the *Plain Dealer* hundreds of times. He was known to be tough, every bit as much as the streetwise union bosses he faced across the bargaining table every few years, as much as the senators before whom he appeared in the course of committee hearings and investigations, as much as the puddlers and smelters who sweated on the floor of his mills. He had been born wealthy, but he'd learned early the value of being tough and had built his inheritance into a vast fortune. It was too bad the steel industry was in trouble, but I was sure Walter Deming would somehow land on his feet, fists clenched, when the smoke cleared.

Vuk came down and wiped automatically at the top of the bar. "So what's going on, Milan? Twice in one week, when I haven't seen you in months? I'm honored."

"I don't know, Vuk, it just laid out that way."

"Get tired of drinking with those pantywaists in the Heights?"

"Maybe I just got hungry for your klobasa."

"Seen Lila?" he said offhandedly.

"Yeah, just yesterday. She's fine. I'll tell her you asked about her."

He wiped the counter some more. "You know, Joe Bradac comes in here every once in a while."

I didn't answer.

"I hope there's no hard feelings there, Milan. I mean, I like you and I like Joe, and—"

"I'm not going to start a fight with him and bust up your tavern, Vuk. If I want him I know where he lives. Okay?"

"Yeah, sure, Milan," he said. Together we watched *As the World*

Turns for a minute, not really caring if it turned or not. Then Vuk said, "Didja hear they still haven't had anyone claim that nine million from the lottery?"

"Probably slipped the guy's mind," I said.

"He's prob'ly been busy."

"He'll go pick up his nine million when he's got a minute."

"Right. Maybe on his lunch hour at the factory."

"Must have had to straighten out his sock drawer and just couldn't get away."

"Busy man," Vuk said.

I looked at my watch. It had been nearly fifteen minutes. "Me, too," I said, and went back to the phone.

"My uncle will take your call," Judith Amber told me, "but he can't see the need for it either."

"I'll call you this evening and give you a report," I said.

"No!" And then, softer, "That won't be necessary. I mean, I won't be home this evening. Call me in the morning."

"All right," I said. I hung up and fished in another pocket for more phone change, shaking my head. The lady was paying me a lot of money to find her missing husband, but in the meantime she was going out for a festive Friday night. Rich people!

I reached Walter Deming without too much trouble. I only had to go through three other people.

His voice was brusque, gravelly, as though he needed to clear his throat but had too much class to do so where the common folk might hear him. "Jacovich, this is a bad day for me. My calendar is full."

It always rubs me wrong when someone uses my last name without a Mister in front of it. Maybe it comes from my days in the military, but I don't like it. Call me Milan, call me Mister. Call me Hey-You. But not just Jacovich. It's disrespectful, and I think Deming knew it. Just his charming way of keeping the peasants in their place. Screw him.

"I'm available anytime," I said. "How about tomorrow?"

"Tomorrow's Saturday," he explained as though I were men-tally deficient.

"It'll be a workday anyway if Mr. Amber is still missing."

"Well, look here, I'm going to be at my club tomorrow. You could come there."

"What club?"

"The Valley Gun Club," he said.

I was supposed to be impressed, I guess. Anyone in Ohio, in the whole Midwest, would have lifted an eyebrow at the Valley Gun Club, one of the most prestigious exclusive private clubs in America, a place where you don't ask to be a member but where they come and find you and invite you in if they want you. Mere millionaires need not apply. Multimillions were the ticket at the Gun, as it was called in tonier circles than I traveled in, though the place didn't have guns at all. They had horses and hounds and a lot of riding and yoicks-ing and tally-ho-ing through the woods, and a lot of drinking of eighty-year-old cognac at the bar, and a lot of deal-making and old-boy networking in the reading room. A couple of times a year they'd drag the scent of a fox through the nearby woods, and they'd have a big ceremony across the street at the little clapboard Episcopal church and bless the hunt and all that while the members stood around looking silly and uncomfortable in their pinks and the horses crapped on the church lawn, and then they'd let loose the dogs—one of the finest packs of blooded foxhounds in the country—and the valley would ring with the hoofbeats and the shouts and the hounds giving tongue (an expression that has always sounded more than a little obscene to me, but then we're not much into fox hunting over on St. Clair Avenue), and every once in a while some fat cat would fall off his horse and break a leg, but most of the time the chase was uneventful, and everyone would go back and drink some more cognac and warm their bruised butts by the fire and make some more deals. It didn't sound like it would be much fun, but then I didn't have ten million in the bank, and I had to take my fun where I found it.

"I could come out there, yes, Mr. Deming."

"Fine, around three o'clock. You know where it is, of course."

I almost laughed out loud at that. "Of course."

"Oh, and Jacovich," he said. "There is a dress code. Please wear a jacket and tie."

"I'll wear the outfit I had on at my cousin's wedding," I told him. I barely managed to stop myself from asking if he preferred any particular color.

I hung around Vuk's until it was well past the hour anyone might still be out to lunch, and Vuk stayed down at the other end of the bar for the most part, playing Horse with three of the regulars. Then I drove out to Marbury-Stendall again. The girl at the front desk recognized me and rang Rhoda for me. She came out about a minute later.

"Any news?" There were dark circles under her eyes, as though she'd slept badly. I felt sorry for her. She was taking Richard Amber's disappearance hard.

"Not yet," I said, "but I'm on top of it. Has Mr. Dodge gotten back from Detroit yet?"

"Yes," she said, "he came in this morning."

"Could I talk to him?"

"I guess so," she said. "He's editing."

"Editing?"

"The tape he shot yesterday in Detroit. Come on, I'll take you back."

I followed her into the bowels of the agency, and this time our route took us the other way, past Jeff Monaghan's office, where he sat doodling on a yellow legal pad. I stopped and stuck my head in.

"Feeling any better?"

He looked up through bloodshot eyes. His nose was tomato red and there was a box of tissues on the desk at his left hand.

"No," he said, "but one day out of the office is all I can spare. You want to see me?"

"I may swing by in a few minutes if you're not busy."

"If I'm not busy," he said. "A comedian."

"But seriously, folks," I said, waved, and followed Rhoda to a small room full of audio- and videotape equipment and speakers and monitors and mysterious-looking hardware. It was also full of Charlie Dodge, who had his hair dyed a silly reddish brown and was wearing a sporty turtleneck of nondescript beige over shockingly loud plaid pants. He sat before a TV monitor and was running a tape in the SCAN mode, so that the figures moved in a herky-jerky silent-film way and the soundtrack on the tape sounded like Alvin and the Chipmunks. Dodge looked a bit like a chipmunk himself, with little fat round cheeks that seemed ideal for storing nuts.

After Rhoda left us, he took off his glasses and said, "You're the private cop trying to find Amber?"

"That's right," I said.

He carefully stacked a bunch of well-worn papers, white and yellow, on the table next to the TV monitor, as if his entire existence was chronicled in the stack. He had stopped the tape in freeze-frame so that the actor on the screen was suspended with a very stupid smile on his face, his eyes half-closed, and his tongue partway out of his mouth as if he were in mid-word. "Well, I was out of town yesterday, so I can't tell you much."

"Did Mr. Amber phone you in Detroit?"

"Why in hell would he do that?"

"I don't know. Did he?"

What seemed to be a flicker of annoyance lighted his eyes. "I thought I already answered that."

"I guess maybe you did. You've been with Richard Amber since before he joined this agency, right?"

"Right."

"Ever known him to do anything like this before?"

"No," he said, and then amended, "Well, maybe once before. A long time ago."

"When was that?"

"Right after we came over here to Marbury. He just took off for a couple of days."

"Where'd he go?"

"That place of his in Indiana is what he said."

"Wawassee?"

"Yeah."

"Why did he go? Any reason?"

Dodge looked around for hidden eavesdroppers, highly unlikely in a ten-by-ten room. "Pull that door shut, will you?" I did.

"Marbury-Stendall signs my paychecks, but my loyalty is to Richard Amber, if you catch my drift."

I nodded.

"Richard had a big beef with Jerry Stendall that time. He got pissed off and he split for a couple of days until he cooled down."

"What was it all about, do you remember?"

"I can only conjecture. But Richard ran his own shop for a lot of years, and when he came over here Jerry felt it necessary every once in a while to remind him who the boss is. Or who the nephew is, I guess I should say. Jerry's name is on the door, but John Marbury calls all the shots here, and when John tells him to squat, Jerry squats. Sometimes he even squats on his own, just to show his sincerity. That makes Jerry pretty mean to people who work for him."

"You, too?"

"Most of the time, I don't have that much to do with him. But yeah, he's ragged on me a few times. He's not the pleasantest of guys at best. Add scared to that and you really fuck up Main Street."

"What's he scared of? His uncle?"

"His uncle, his shadow, the wind blowing. But scared is a condition that we live with in this business. Look, John Marbury built this company up over the last thirty years. He was a holy terror in his day, but he's in his seventies now and can't go on forever. The only one he has that's family to take over the business is Jerry Stendall. Oh, the agency pisses around with a lot of little accounts that keep the doors open, but the thing that makes the money these days is Deming Steel."

"And the Deming account is Richard Amber's?"

"With a capital *R* and a capital *A*."

"Other than that argument a few years back, Amber and Jerry have gotten along?"

"They've had to. When the old gentleman found out what happened, you could hear the reaming he gave Jerry out in Geauga County. Then Marbury drove out to Wawassee himself and begged Richard to come back. Since that time Jerry hardly says peep to Richard, but there's tension there."

Which explained, I thought, why Stendall had no idea of Richard's comings and goings in the office. I was beginning to get a clear picture of Amber's life, but as yet I still couldn't explain or trace his disappearance—unless it was to his little cabin in Indiana again. I said, "There was no problem with Richard and Jerry recently? Like earlier this week?"

"Not that I know of," Dodge said, "but the jungle drums rarely reach into my office. I'm not part of the big social life in this firm. And as I said, I was in Detroit."

"When did you leave for Detroit?"

He tapped a fat finger on the pile of papers in front of him, deciding whether to answer me. Then he said, "After work Wednesday. Checked into the Holiday Inn up there. You can verify that."

"That's all right. And you didn't notice anything funny about Amber's behavior Wednesday?"

"Didn't see that much of him. I was getting ready for my shoot. But from what I could tell he seemed okay."

"You wouldn't know who he had lunch with Wednesday, would you?"

Dodge shook his head. "I never have lunch. I'm not a lunch eater. I have my big meal of the day at breakfast, and then just a light snack in the evening. Look, I'm as anxious to find Richard as you. More, maybe. I don't think they'd put up with me ten minutes around here without him."

"Why do you say that?"

He looked down at his hands for a minute. They were wrinkled and dotted with age spots. "I've been in the business a long time," he said. "New York, Chicago—I go all the way back to Dave Garroway and *Studs's Place*. I'm a nuts-and-bolts guy, I leave the creativity to Monaghan and Amber. I'm kind of dull, I suppose, and I know it. I'm also older than most of the people in the business these days. Richard has been carrying me. Without him, well . . ."

He raised his hands in acceptance of a cruel fate. "So anything I can do to help you, let me know. Richard's been damned decent to me."

I stood up and shook his hand. The dyed hair wasn't fooling anyone, I guess, especially not Dodge himself.

I stopped by Jeff Monaghan's office on my way out.

"If I make it through the day without expiring right here on my desk, it'll be one of my major triumphs," he said. He really looked miserable. "Any headway in your search?"

"Maybe," I said. "Did Richard have any arguments with anyone on Wednesday? Or anytime early in the week? Any problems?"

"Advertising is a business that runs on emotion, and problems are the reason we're here. Screaming at each other is a way of life. You even scream good morning at people."

"Anything beyond that?"

"Clarify, please?" he said.

"You understand me perfectly, Mr. Monaghan. Anything that might be construed as a heavy-duty argument?"

"Richard fought with Jerry Stendall almost every week. This week was no exception. I wouldn't call that unusual or heavy-duty."

"Not like four years ago when he went to his cabin for a few days without telling anyone?"

"Heard about that, did you?"

"It's my job."

"Well, no, nothing like that. Just your ordinary bitch session. They don't like each other very much."

"Jerry Stendall looks at Richard as a threat? Or the other way around?"

Monaghan blew his nose. "My God, you're like an old lady looking under the bed for prowlers! No one is a threat to anyone else around here. Jerry is the agency's president and Richard is the senior VP and account exec, which more or less means they need each other. The fact that they aren't exactly best friends has nothing to do with it."

"An old lady looking under the bed," I said. "I'm going to have to remember that."

He slumped back in his chair and sighed, and the sigh turned into a wracking cough that doubled him over. I waited until the spasm had passed. "You ought to try a shot of whiskey with some warm water. That'll knock it out of you."

"Thanks, Doctor," he said, his eyes running.

I was wandering the halls trying to find my way out of the agency when I ran into Jerry Stendall.

"Back again?"

"I just wanted to check a few things out."

He ran his hand nervously through his thinning hair. When Jerry Stendall walked, he bent his upper body forward as if he were struggling into the teeth of a gale wind. I don't know, maybe he was. It's rugged sometimes, being a nephew. "Mr. Jacovich, no one wants to clear this mess up as much as I do, but we really can't have you wandering through the office upsetting the routine. I mean, Richard Amber or no Richard Amber, this agency has a responsibility to its clients."

I leaned against the wall of the corridor. We were back in peon territory so there was no flocking on the wallpaper. "You mean I can't come back here and talk to your employees?"

"I just wish you'd check it out with me first," he said. "Charlie's got a commercial he has to have done by Monday, Jeff missed a day of work and is falling behind, and Rhoda's got to handle everything that comes across Richard's desk while he's not here. So just give me a ring first before you come back, and I can schedule your appointments."

"You're the boss, Mr. Stendall," I said.

I noticed he stood up just a little bit straighter when I said that.

I had my notes on the Amber case spread out all over my desk and was trying to make some sense of them, but nothing seemed to work for me. None of the pieces had that straight edge I was looking for, no matter how I shuffled the three-by-fives. I always transfer the information from my notebook onto index cards at the end of my day so I can play with them, rearrange them, and see if there is a way of putting them together that would turn on an illuminating light bulb. I stacked the cards and set them to the side. Then I looked at my watch. It was just past four P.M. Scared silly, I called Mary Soderberg at Channel 12.

"Well, hello there," she said, sounding surprised but not unpleasantly so.

"I . . . uh . . . you said to call you anyway, so . . . uh . . ." I was doing this quite clumsily. I'd never been any good at it, and by now I was so out of practice I felt as though I were speaking in a foreign tongue.

"Well, I'm glad you did," Mary said. And then she must have sensed my nervousness because she made it easy for me. "Did you have something you wanted to ask me?"

"Well. Yes. I was wondering . . . if you were free . . . if you'd like to have dinner with me tonight?"

"Tonight?"

"Yes. If you're free. I mean, I know it's Friday night and I figured you'd probably be busy, but I thought I'd give it a try anyway. Maybe some other time."

"No time like the present," she said. "I can get out of my prior commitment. You want to meet somewhere?"

"Well . . . "

"I live out by Shaker Square, so it'd probably be easier to meet someplace downtown."

"Sure," I said, my brain racing to think of a suitable restaurant. One didn't take a classy lady like Mary Soderberg to a pizza joint. Not on the first date. "How about Danny's?"

She laughed. "You must be flush." Danny's was one of the most expensive restaurants in the Flats. "How about the Watershed? It's just as nice and you don't have to take out a second mortgage."

I was going to protest, not wanting to look like a piker, but I realized the logic of her position, and the kindness of it as well. "Watershed it is, then. Is seven-thirty okay?"

"It's fine," she said. "Do you remember what I look like?"

"Are you kidding?" I said.

CHAPTER SEVEN

When the speak about Cleveland's big comeback, from the edge of insolvency, from being a favorite target of stand-up comedians, it is most often to the Flats that people point, and with every justification. It had been the warehouse district in the early part of the century, situated as it is on a low-lying shelf of land dividing downtown Cleveland from the waters of the Cuyahoga River. After the river traffic slowed down and moved elsewhere most of the warehouses were abandoned to rot, rust, and rats. Then just a few years ago some enterprising folk decided to buy up the warehouses, gut and renovate them, and make the Flats *the* trendy place to go and see and be seen in the city. Suddenly the ghostly old warehouses were transformed into the most elegant and pricey restaurants and glittering night spots in northern Ohio, and it was a rare night indeed that the Flats was not jammed with upscale cars and fashionably dressed people of all ages, there for a great meal, a good time, or to meet each other and connect. Places never before heard of, like Danny's, Sammy's, DiPoo's, the River Rat, and the Watershed, were turning customers away on weekend nights, and during the warm weather even midweek was holiday time in the Flats. I didn't hang around down there very much, as I rarely had anyone to take to dinner and discos were just not my style.

I parked my car in a lot, paid the pimply attendant three bucks for the privilege, and walked down Old River Street, past the rust-colored facade of the old Rose Iron Works with its hundreds of small dirty windowpanes stretching for more than half a block, then under the eastern end of the Main Avenue Bridge, now officially named the Harold M. Burton Bridge but not called that by anyone in Cleveland—the way no New Yorker ever refers to Sixth Avenue as the Avenue of the Americas. The girders under the bridge are painted an improbably Day-Glo turquoise and seem to add to the funky, festive air that is part of the Flats' appeal. The night was cold and windy, more so here by the water. After all, it was only a few blocks from Lake Erie, where the wind whistles and fulminates malevolently with little regard for the residents of the city that had somehow grown up along its edge.

It was funny about Lake Erie, I'd always thought. In Chicago, Lake Michigan provides the city with its rhythm and pulse, and overlooking the water are the most desirable homes and apartments and some of the most famous of the city's attractions, like the Shedd Aquarium, the Museum of Natural History, and venerable old Soldier Field. People clog the Chicago beaches in the summertime and wisely avoid the shoreline and the Outer Drive during inclement weather. The lake is as much a part of the city as the Wrigley Building. In Cleveland, however, Lake Erie is just something wet that's up there north of town, and no one pays much attention to it. There are a few luxury condos on the lake over on the West Side, and Cleveland Municipal Stadium, where each year the Browns battle icy winds and freezing rain, is just a Hail Mary pass away from the water, but otherwise poor Lake Erie is pretty much ignored by most Clevelanders. The Cuyahoga River, which is drained by the lake, got pretty much the same treatment until the emergence of the Flats as Cleveland's wine, dine, and dance center.

The exterior of the Watershed hasn't changed much since its previous incarnation as a warehouse except for a champagne-colored paint job and a discreet awning. The interior is something else, however. The exposed overhead steam and water pipes are painted maroon and blue. The floors gleam with their waxed hardwood finish, and the fixtures are all shiny brass. At the front end of the restaurant is a staircase, the wood clean and new-looking and unpainted, leading up to a loft where every night at nine a jazz trio performs. I'd always wished I could have been a fly on the wall to watch them struggle up those narrow stairs with a grand piano, but there it was at the edge of the loft. They had managed somehow. Most of us manage—somehow.

On the river side of the building the walls are all glass, offering a panorama of the water, the skeletal bridges, and the docks of Ohio City on the West Bank. Sliding doors open onto a deck, unused from late September to May, that looms over the water's edge. It was beside this glass wall that Mary Soderberg and I were seated, thanks to my slipping the young host ten dollars when I walked in the door. I'd felt like a jerk doing it. He probably made more money than I do.

Mary had arrived about two minutes after I did, looking like the queen of Ohio in a long black leather coat with a bright red scarf wrapped around her neck and trailing over one shoulder. Under it she had on a pearl gray jersey dress that loved her body almost as much as I did. She kissed my cheek lightly when I met her at the door, and how special that made me feel was absolutely startling.

She let me hold her chair for her when we sat down, and as I helped her out of her coat her blonde hair brushed the back of my hand. Her cheeks were red from the wind off the river, and she looked as good as anyone I'd ever seen. She even smelled good.

We ordered a blanc du blanc, clinked glasses, and sipped. I said, "Here's to you, Mary." I was lousy at toasts.

"Here's to you picking up clues," Mary said, "and I don't mean your detective work. I'm glad you called me. I was hoping you would. I hinted enough."

"Because of my laughing eyes?"

"Partly."

"Are you going to tell me the other parts?"

"Oh, I don't know. Curiosity had something to do with it, I suppose. After all, a private eye . . ."

I laughed. That expression always made me laugh. "I don't want you to get the wrong impression, Mary. I do mostly security work in the industrial field. A little insurance business once in a while. It's very rare that I get a private case like the one I'm on now. I'm not Sam Spade and I don't look through transoms and solve murders."

"No bottle of rotgut in the bottom desk drawer? No solo saxophone moaning through the neon night? No small-time crooks and big-time gamblers, or beautiful blondes coming into your office and making your spine go weak?"

"That's very good, Mary," I said. "But small-time crooks tend to stay away from cops, even ex-cops like me. I don't know any big-time gamblers, my musical instrument is the button-box accordeen, and I drink beer, not rotgut whiskey."

"And what about the beautiful blondes?"

"I only know one of those—and she didn't walk into my office, I walked into hers."

"You're a nice man," she said. "I guess that's the other reason I was hoping you'd call me. I meet a lot of fancy guys in my business. Admen, producers, broadcast executives, all three-piece-suit types who are so busy being impressed with themselves they don't have the time or the inclination to be impressed with me. You just seemed like a regular guy, the kind of guy I grew up with in Boston. And you're the first man I've met in years who doesn't have an Anglo-Saxon surname."

"In Cleveland, Mary, Jacovich practically *is* an Anglo-Saxon surname."

"Not in the crowd I run with. They all think Yugoslavia is right across the street from Katmandu."

"What brought you to Cleveland in the first place?"

"Being fed up with Boston. I grew up there, went to school there, and wanted to see something of the rest of the world before I died."

"And you picked Cleveland?"

"It picked me. I was a communications major at Boston College, and when I graduated I sent out a lot of résumés to New

York and L.A. and Chicago. No bites. Then I saw an ad in *Broadcasting*—that's a trade magazine—for a job here with Channel 12. I took it, was good at it, got promoted, and now I'm head of the sales department, and Cleveland is where I call home. My folks come to visit me every summer—when the Red Sox are in town to play the Indians—and I haven't been back there in . . . God, it must be four years."

"Miss it?"

"I suppose, every once in a while. But I cut my Boston ties and I'm not anxious to put them back together anymore. You know what Thomas Wolfe said about going home again."

"A boring and pretentious writer," I said.

"I don't know. I thought he was pretty good."

"What an ego! To think his own life was so fascinating we'd all be willing to wade through four long, overblown novels to find out about it."

"That's another thing I like about you."

"That I don't write autobiographical novels?"

"That you don't start every sentence with the word I."

"Maybe my life isn't as exciting as Thomas Wolfe's."

A barge, heading downriver, moved wraithlike past the windows of the Watershed, and we both stopped talking to watch its progress into the purple dark until its running lights were all we could see of it. Mary said, "You went to college, didn't you? You don't develop violent opinions about Thomas Wolfe in high school."

"Kent State," I admitted. "A BA in business, master's in psychology."

"I guess that means you must like what you do. You have enough education, enough fancy degrees, to do whatever you want, so you must be doing what you like to do." She looked at me over the rim of her wineglass. "And you have enough class not to want to stuff that education down everyone's throat. Most of the men in my business think a woman's going to be carried off on a wave of unbridled lust just because they flash their MBA at her."

"I think you've been running with the wrong crowd."

"You've got that right. That's why I liked you right away. You seem like a real person."

"Like Pinocchio. A real boy."

"Let's hear it for Pinocchio," she said.

"And for real boys everywhere."

We ordered our food. She chose a poached salmon with dill sauce. I ordered the pasta at $8.95, glad we hadn't gone to Danny's after all.

"See what I mean?" she said after the waiter ("Hi, my name's Kim and I'll be serving you this evening") had left.

"Basic. No crap, no pretensions. You're all right, Milan."

"Mary, do you mind if I ask you a personal question?"

"Are you sure you want to?"

"No, but eventually I'll have to. Why Richard Amber? It seems to me he's everything you dislike."

"You haven't met him, have you?"

I shook my head.

Mary said, "On the surface I suppose you're right. But there is something of the eager child in Richard, sort of the poor little rich kid. When you take a second look, past the expensive suits and the important clients and that mako shark wife, all he really wants is to be his own man. He wants to write. I don't mean to make it sound cornball, and for all I know he doesn't have any talent, but he really wants to try. He's just waiting for the time when he can be financially independent to do it."

"And you didn't want to wait with him?"

The corners of her mouth tightened. "I have my own dreams, Milan. Besides, it was a long time ago. It didn't mean much then and even less now. I make no apologies about Richard, not for starting it and not for ending it."

"You certainly don't owe me any apologies."

"I know that," she said. "But I like you a lot and I want you to have a good opinion of me."

"So far, so good," I said. "Look, let's not talk about Richard Amber anymore."

"It doesn't bother me."

"It bothers me," I told her. "A little."

She put her hand on mine. "Thanks for saying that, Milan. I'm glad it does—a little."

Our dinners came, and as much as she admired my down-to-earth order she insisted I taste her salmon. I had to admit it was pretty good.

"If I hang around with you long enough," I said, "am I going to start eating radicchio and arugula and venison in lingonberry sauce?"

"I'll shoot you if you do," she said. "But in the meantime you'll have to take me to a Slovenian restaurant sometime for gibanica."

I was stunned. "How in hell do you know about gibanica?"

"I never reveal my sources," she said.

We had dessert—some sort of wickedly sweet amaretto cheese-cake for me and a triple chocolate something-or-other for her that she made me taste. It made my teeth hurt. We had coffee, with many refills. We had brandies. And all of a sudden it was after midnight, and Kim the waiter was yawning pointedly, probably anxious to get across the street to the River Rat disco. Though the loft up front was crowded with drinkers, we were the only ones left in the dining room. I paid the bill and we went down the street to where she had left her car, right at the water's edge. The river was frozen solid at its banks, although out in midstream the current was running enough to accommodate the barges and scows. But almost at our feet it seemed that the water was standing still.

And then I kissed her good night, and everything seemed to be standing still. Her lips tasted fresh and sweet from dessert, her tongue was velvet, and even through our heavy winter coats her body seemed to mold perfectly to mine. It had been years and years since I'd kissed a woman that tall, and it felt more than good. It was to me as a Big Mac might be to a starving man. It felt . . . right. And a little scary.

When I got home the light on my answering machine was blinking some unwelcome news. Judith Amber's voice was on the tape saying, "Call me right away, no matter what time you get in. Urgent!"

I called her right away.

"Urgent?" I said.

"Best you get over here right now," she said with no preamble.

"Mrs. Amber, it's one o'clock in the—"

"Someone broke into the house while I was gone. The place is a disaster area."

They hadn't much bothered with the pristine living room. The few rather tasteful and very expensive prints had been taken from the wall, and some of the knickknacks were strewn about on the floor, but there didn't appear to be much permanent damage. The real vandalism was in Richard Amber's den.

It took me a moment to realize I'd never been in there before. I'd only seen it through the sliding glass door the night I'd come to the house to answer his summons for a bodyguard, but it saddened me to see the pleasant, masculine-looking room in such a shambles. Every drawer had been pulled from the walnut desk and emptied onto the floor, the cushions were off the leather sofa and ripped open as if by a knife, the club chair had been torn apart, the books from the built-in shelves had been rudely dumped, most of them face down and open with their pages bent and crumpled. The hunting prints from the walls were now on the floor, glass shattered and frames broken. A particularly beautiful oil painting of hunting dogs had been ripped from over the hearth and the canvas slit all along the frame and destroyed.

Judith Amber just leaned against the doorway, all in pink this evening, her hand nervously playing with a pearl necklace I knew must be genuine. Her face was the color of day-old snow, her eyes bloodshot, her mouth pinched and tight. She was a perfect portrait of a frightened rich lady.

I didn't say anything. I picked my way carefully through the piles of papers, pens, paper clips, and other debris from the desk drawers, stepping over the chunks of cotton wadding from the chair and the sofa. It was indeed a mess. I said, "When did this happen?"

"I don't know," Judith Amber said. "I got home at about twelve-thirty and it was like this."

The thick glass door was smashed near the lock as though someone had put a hard fist through it. The intruder had obviously gained entry that way. I said, "Was anything touched upstairs or anywhere else?"

"No. Just in here and what you saw in the living room."

I went out through the broken door and around to the front of the house. There were footprints in the snow, all right, but they had been very carefully smudged so there was no telling the size or gender of the intruder. Whoever it was had covered his tracks.

I went back inside. "What about the kitchen?" I said. "Let's take a look."

The kitchen was what you'd expect in a house this size and style, what the real estate people call a "country kitchen," with lots of old exposed brick, well-done tile work, and copper pans hanging above the counters. It had a largely unused look. Certainly no one had gone tearing through it. I checked the lock on the garage door, but it was pointless since I knew where the vandal had come in. I cracked open the garage door and saw a red Nissan 300 ZX and a gray Cadillac Sedan de Ville.

"Your car, Mrs. Amber?"

She nodded. "The Z. The Caddy's Richard's. Oh, that son of a bitch!"

"Who?"

"Richard."

"Why?"

"This is him. He did this. He was back here tonight."

"Why would he do that?"

"To spite me. He's a spiteful man. This was his way of trying to hurt me."

I went back into the kitchen and sat on a stool along a counter tiled to make it look like brick. "Are you saying you think your husband left here Wednesday night of his own accord?"

"Certainly."

"I've been working under the assumption that he was taken forcibly."

"That's what I thought, too. Until this."

"Has he ever done anything like this before?"

"He put his fist through the laundry-room door once. A long time ago."

"This doesn't seem like the work of an angry man."

"I'd like to know what you'd call it."

"I'd call it a search."

"For what? Money?"

"You'd know that better than I. Do you keep a lot of cash in the house?"

"No," she said. "Hardly ever. Never more than a couple of hundred dollars. There was no money here tonight at all."

"No negotiable securities or bearer bonds?"

"Anything like that I keep in a safe deposit box."

I noted her use of the personal pronoun. "Mrs. Amber, where were you tonight?"

She hesitated. "At a friend's."

"Did anyone know you were going to be there? That you weren't going to be home?"

"Only you, Mr. Jacovich."

"I think you'd better call the police."

Some of the color returned to her white face. "No police," she said firmly.

"There's been a break-in here, a robbery—"

"Nothing is missing that I know of."

"The police should still be notified, and told of your husband's disappearance."

"I said no police and I mean it. This is my home and Richard is my husband, and I'll deal with my affairs in the manner in which I see fit."

"Mrs. Amber, the police don't care if you're seeing another man—"

"May I remind you that you are working for me and being well-paid for your time? The least you could do is respect my wishes."

"A crime has been committed."

"Richard is the one who did this. That's why I don't want the police."

I just looked at her until she said, "Don't you believe me?"

"It's not important if I do or not. I won't insist you call the police, but I think you'd be foolish not to. It's very likely the person who busted in here tonight was not your husband, and it might have something to do with his absence." She began to speak but I rushed right over her protests. "Mr. Amber must have keys to the house—why would he break in? And if he wanted to spite you, he would have destroyed your room, not his own."

I paused for breath while she chewed delicately on a red-tipped fingernail. She said, "Have you found out anything?"

"Only that you lied to me when you said your husband was close to Jerry Stendall. They don't like one another at all, and I'm sure you know that. And although you didn't exactly lie, you were careful not to let me know that your uncle is Richard's main client."

She clambered up on the stool next to me. For a slim, small woman she had excellent legs.

"All right," she said, capitulating. "I didn't want you going in and grilling Jerry as though he were some kind of suspect. Richard is, after all, his employee, and I wouldn't jeopardize his job nor his rather tenuous relationship with Jerry. And as for my uncle—I didn't want you to make the mistake that Richard Amber is some kind of lightweight who's gotten to where he has because of nepotism. I assure you that just the opposite is true. He's a talented, creative man and Marbury-Stendall is damned lucky to have him." I'm not certain, but I believe she tossed her head defiantly at the end of that little speech.

I ran my hand across the top of the tile counter. It was squeaky clean. I said, "You have me puzzled, Mrs. Amber. Half the time you sound like you hate your husband's guts, and the other half you talk as if you're very much in love with him."

She looked down at her lap for a long while, and when she raised her head her eyes were shiny with tears. "How very astute of you, Mr. Jacovich," she said.

CHAPTER EIGHT

Weekends in Cleveland have a character all their own. In the winter, especially when football season is over, weekends are for browsing in art galleries and shops and museums or for getting together with friends for brunches or dinners and the warmth of companionship. I often used my winter Saturday mornings for major grocery shopping, restocking the larder and watching other people doing the same thing. I like the idea that the stores are more crowded. I rarely have much else to do on weekends, and it gives me something to look at besides the carrots and endive. But this particular Saturday was just another workday for me, and the market would have to wait.

I was sure that the Amber break-in was related to the missing man of the house, and that the breaker-and-enterer had been looking for something, but I had no idea what. I was unable to put the pieces together—it was that lack of an edge that was holding me up. There seemed to be no more reason for the break-in than for Amber's absence in the first place. And yet things don't happen for no reason, not in my experience nor, I believe, in anyone else's. It's the law of cause and effect.

I could come up with plenty of reasons why Richard Amber might want to get out of his situation. Trapped by financial considerations in a marriage he no longer wanted and mired in a job that was stifling him and his more creative urges, it would make a

certain amount of sense for him to finally take the steps necessary
to get out. But to simply drop out of sight was uncharacteristic
of a man who enjoyed the confidence of governors and robber
barons and captains of industry. And even had he chosen such
a radical solution, why would he call for a bodyguard before his
disappearance? Why would he propose marriage to his long-time
mistress and two hours later drop off the face of the earth? And
what was hidden in the Amber den that prompted the break-in
on Friday night?

I was also thinking about Mary Soderberg.

Lila and I had been divorced for some time, and she was going on with her life with a new man. Well, not really new, since
Joe Bradac had been around since high school days, never part of
the crowd but always there on the outskirts, a bit older than the
rest of us, quiet and solid and sort of dull. And now he was eating
at my table, and for all I know rutting in my bed, and I can't say
that it didn't eat away my insides when I thought about it. But
for all that, I couldn't help feeling a kind of wacky disloyalty to
Lila where Mary was concerned, a vague guilt. I hadn't been to
bed with many different women in my life, only a very few since
Lila, and there'd been no emotion with them, only expediency
and availability. But here I was, acting really silly about a woman
I'd just met, who'd been the lover of the man I was now trying
to find. A woman whose face kept intruding on my thoughts all
night and all morning. Uh-oh, Jacovich!

I pushed the three-by-five cards around on my desk for a while
longer trying to make order where there was none, and then went
across the street and bought some German rye and some bologna
and a six-pack of beer, and came back home and made lunch. I
sat down with it to watch a college basketball game I didn't give a
damn about. The day was gray, cold, and oppressive, so I kept the
curtains drawn and the lamps on to deceive myself into coziness
and cheer. It didn't work.

At one-thirty I showered and donned a button-down white
shirt and maroon tie and the double-breasted blue blazer and
gray slacks I'd worn to dinner the night before. Walter Deming's

cautionary word about the Gun's dress code still rankled, and everything in me wanted to go wearing my old Kent State sweatsuit, but I needed his cooperation badly enough to allow his intimidation. Then I drove out to the Valley Gun Club.

The Chagrin River Valley is beautiful any time of year, but I prefer it in winter. The rolling hills and the naked birch and dogwood trees whitened by fresh snow, the gentle slopes dipping down to the ice-encrusted river, and the serenity and stillness make the valley not only a favorite getaway of mine, but attract a good bit of the big Cleveland-area money as well. The homes are all set well back from the road on lots that are, by law, at least three acres, most often larger, and almost everywhere you look recalls a Currier and Ives Christmas print. It also seems a uniquely American place; winter woods in Austria or Switzerland might be just as lovely, but I'm sure they have a different feel. European. The Chagrin River is an American kind of river, the sort on which everyone wishes they had spent their childhood. It's an elegant place to be, never more so than in the snow, and despite the nature of my visit I was glad to have the occasion to see it in its winter clothes.

The Gun Club building, an ordinary sprawling one-story in contrast with the two-level houses all around it, fronted right at the curb. There were several cars parked out front, so I had to walk some distance through the snow once I found a space. I missed the comfort of my Totes, but I'd been so psyched by Walter Deming's damned dress code that I'd decided to let my feet get wet.

My reception committee was a man dressed similarly to me, blue over gray, and I had to admit he looked better than I in his crisp blue blazer with the club emblem shining on the breast pocket, a gold crest with lions and dragons on a purple and red escutcheon. "How may I help you?" he patronized. "I'm the club steward." He was no doubt wondering why I hadn't used the tradesmen's entrance, if there was one.

"I'm here to see Mr. Walter Deming," I said. "My name is Jacovich."

"Kindly wait here," he said, and disappeared through a small archway. I got the impression that the only other people whose names ended in *ich* to cross these portals had been delivering party ice.

I warmed my heels rather than cooled them, having sunk into plush carpet almost to my shoe tops. The foyer was done in warm rich woods and the light sconces on the wall were all candelabra-shaped, with bulbs like flames that gave off a burnished, cozy light. Hunting prints were the decor, not surprisingly, and over the archway through which the steward had made his exit was the club's crest again, this time in brass and pewter. Opened on a stand to the right of the door was the club's register, and I noticed several famous names inscribed there, to which I was about to add my own when the steward returned and instructed me to sign in please. Just like the mystery guest on *What's My Line?*

"Mr. Deming is in the taproom," he said, and led me down a corridor replete with bronze and gold and silver plaques commemorating all sorts of good works and noble achievements, and officer-emeritus photographs browning with age. It had the air of a place that took itself much too seriously, like a medical convention or an earnest conclave of Housewives Against Pornography. The steward himself moved as if he'd had an iron rod surgically implanted from tailbone to skull.

Walter Deming was in the corner of the dimly illuminated taproom. He wore a cashmere sports jacket in a milky tan, a yellow shirt, and a woolen tie into which a gold stickpin had been carefully implanted. His hair was brush-cut almost to the scalp showing healthily pink beneath, and his face glowed with an outdoorsy flush. He was drinking Scotch neat from a brandy snifter. He neither rose nor offered a handshake, but waved me into the chair opposite him, hand-pegged wood with wraparound arms and a seat sculpted to fit the soft buttocks of the wealthy. It was the most uncomfortable chair ever to assault my behind, and I hoped the meeting would not drag out. I didn't know how long my butt could hold out.

"So, Jacovich," he said. "You're working for my niece."

It made me smile. Such an obvious ploy to establish who's the billionaire and who's the bum. I was going to enjoy this.

"I have to tell you I think this whole business is just a lot of crap. Richard decided to hightail it out of here for a few days to let things cool off, and the inconsiderate son of a bitch didn't bother telling anyone where he was going. Made me drag all the way out to his office for nothing on Thursday, too."

"Let what things cool off, Mr. Deming?"

He blew air out through his lips, a kind of genteel Bronx cheer. "We all have problems. Some cope better than others. Some people talk to their wives or psychiatrists or clergymen, and some just hang around till they have a stroke or a cardiac arrest or develop a bleeding ulcer. Maybe Richard takes off. I think he'll turn up in a day or so and Judith will have paid you a lot of money for nothing. I think you think so, too, and are taking advantage because she can afford it."

I had no doubt that before his famous characterization of all businessmen as sons of bitches the late President Kennedy had at one time dealt with Walter Deming.

"I hope you're right, Mr. Deming. But on the off-chance that you aren't, I trust you'll cooperate with me."

"I'm seeing you now, am I not? All right," he said, martyred in the manner of a teenager who's been told to pick up his room. "What can I do for you?"

"First off, you might offer me a drink."

He blinked his eyes like a toad on a lily pad. Offering me a sociable drink was a brand-new thought. When the waiter arrived, summoned by Deming's raised finger, I ordered a Rémy Martin, and I used the French pronunciation. I thought it affected even as I did it, but I wanted him to know I wasn't some Bohunk from the firebox at one of his mills. I'm ashamed at how important it was to me.

When I had my drink I said, "You mentioned things cooling down for Richard. I ask you again to be more specific."

"I told you—"

"I know you did, but it wasn't good enough. Mr. Deming, Richard Amber's life may be in danger while we sit here playing one-up with each other. Are you going to help me or not?"

He was not used to being spoken to that way and didn't know how to handle it. He harrumphed around a bit, had a good stiff belt of his drink, and said, "Well, exactly what—"

"To begin with, what needed cooling down?"

He pouted. "Well, I guess it's no state secret that their marriage is not the stuff dreams are made of. Maybe he and Judith had a fight."

"Maybe," I said, "but she probably would have told me that. It was more likely something else."

"One of his tramps, possibly?"

"He was just seeing one woman that I know about, and there wasn't any trouble with her."

"Hmmm."

"Business, then. Richard Amber only works on two accounts, Mr. Deming—yours and the governor's. Since there is no campaign this year, that leaves Deming Steel."

"If you want to ask me what I know about Richard Amber, go ahead, Jacovich. But my business is none of yours."

"As it relates to Amber it's very much mine. Unless you have something to hide."

He bristled. "You have a smart mouth."

"I take that as a compliment. I know your company is not in a healthy mode right now. If I ran a firm such as yours and I needed to cut back, probably advertising would be the first area I'd examine. And that would affect Amber very much, as well as John Marbury and his nephew. Am I correct?"

"You're impertinent," he said without hostility. I believed that by being as aggressive and unpleasant as he, I was earning a grudging respect. "Well, then. My company's troubles are not a secret to anyone who reads the business pages. We've been negotiating with Washington for some time now. It's not just Deming Steel—it's the whole industry. Construction is down, the Japs are sabotaging the automobile business, and the scrap merchants are doing the rest. I'm trying very hard not to go belly up, Jacovich, and if that means cutting some corners here and there, by God I'm willing to do it."

"And I suppose Mr. Amber was aware of this?"

"He's no dummy."

"Was that by any chance what the meeting was to be about Thursday morning?"

"It was on my agenda, yes. I'd told Richard it was soon to be belt-tightening time and we would have to make adjustments."

"Excuse me, but don't you have a contract with Marbury-Stendall?"

"Certainly, man, but the contract hasn't been drawn that's loophole-proof. In my case they'd be damn fools to fight me on it. I've been their major account for four years, and when things get better I will be again."

"Provided they're reasonable."

"Let me tell you something about advertising people, Jacovich. They're always reasonable. Even a whore says no sometimes, but an ad man is always amenable to the client's wishes. That's really why we pay them. It isn't the copywriters and the artists and the media buyers. It's the bullshit. We pay them to bullshit us and kowtow to us and tell us what we want to hear, and they do it gladly. It's their raison d'être."

He took an expensive Cuban cigar out of his pocket, along with one of those cute little cigar tools, and expertly poked a hole in the tapered end of the cigar. Then he licked it all over and took a gold lighter from his pocket with which he carefully passed a flame up and down the length of the rolled tobacco, turning the cigar so that all the leaves would be thoroughly warmed. Finally he stuck it in his mouth, put the fire to the end, and puffed until his head almost disappeared in a wreath of blue smoke. The ritual of the cigar as practiced by serious smokers amused me almost as much as the ceremony accompanying the opening of a wine bottle.

"But that won't explain Richard's disappearance," he said between smoky lip-smacks. "He knows I'll take care of him."

"How's that?"

He examined the cigar as if it were a foreign object. "I pay a public relations expert some seventy thousand a year at Deming Steel in addition to my ad budget. I'd replace that man with Richard until things got better for the company. Richard's a damn bright man, and he's also family, if only by marriage. And I take care of my own."

"Richard knew this?"

"Not the specifics. But when we've talked about current conditions I've told him repeatedly not to worry. No matter what happens with Marbury, I'd see Richard didn't suffer."

"How would he feel about being tossed a bone?"

"A bone? Goddammit, man, seventy thousand per year is no bone! Lots of men would give their soul for seventy a year." He peered at me. "Wouldn't you?"

"My soul is worth considerably more than that, Mr. Deming, but that's neither here nor there. You suppose he might have taken off to think it over?"

"Very possibly, which is what I meant when I said he might want to let things cool down."

That theory didn't explain last night's break-in, but if Judith hadn't seen fit to mention it to her uncle, I wasn't going to.

Deming said, "Were I you, I'd check out that summer place in Indiana. God knows they don't use it much. Foolish indulgence."

I finished my drink and stood up. "Thank you, Mr. Deming. I hope I can call on you again if I need any further assistance."

And before he could answer I leaned forward, took his hand in mine, and shook it. It seemed to unnerve him; he wasn't used to shaking hands with the hired help.

As I left the taproom the steward appeared as if by conjuring and led me back through the passageway to the foyer, where he wordlessly opened the door and sent me out into the cold. I suppose he wanted to ensure that I didn't steal any of the pictures of past presidents.

I trudged through the slush underfoot to where I'd left my car. The sun had disappeared behind the hill early, as it does in the valley in winter, and the air had chilled considerably for lack of its warming rays. There were drawbacks to the best of things, and an early sundown was the price the wealthy paid to live in the beautiful Chagrin River Valley.

I had my keys out of my pocket when I noticed that my two left tires, the ones exposed to the roadway, were flat. I bent down to examine them, noting they had been slashed with a sharp blade, and the bending saved my life, because a rifle cracked from the copse of dogwood across the river and a bullet whizzed past my ear, sounding very much like one of Hitler's buzz bombs. It smacked into the stand of birch behind me, taking a fearsome bite out of one of the trees.

I hit the ground hard, face first, jarring every bone, and crawled like a baby around to the other side of the car, where I was more or less protected from the angle of fire. My mouth tasted like cotton batting, and in spite of the cold, pockets of sweat immediately formed under my arms. I couldn't do much but keep my head down, lying there in the wet slush and the mud, feeling as vulnerable as hell. At least in Vietnam sniper fire was something we came to expect. It was a bit of a shock in suburban Ohio. After a minute I lifted myself up carefully to my knees and opened the passenger door, dived into the glove compartment, and got out my .38. It wasn't much of a match against a rifle, but it was better than my bare hands. Way up in the woods, over the sound of the mournful wind in the trees, I heard the slamming of a car door, and I waited a good thirty seconds after that before I gingerly stood up and looked around. Nothing visible disturbed the sylvan tranquility of the twilight.

I ran around the side of the car, crossed the road, charged through the trees to a little footbridge that spanned the river, the bare branches whipping at my face, and went pounding across in a kind of infantry crouch, my .38 at the ready with the safety off. It was a rather stupid thing to do, I suppose, because I was outgunned, but I figured if my unknown assailant was still there he would have taken another shot. I headed down the road on the other side of the Chagrin until I was parallel with my car. Then I stopped. There were footprints in the snow leading down the embankment and back up again, but it looked as if the sniper had been wearing rubber Totes—I guess there was no dress code for assassins in the woods—so it was impossible to tell the shoe size. I scrambled down the incline, taking care not to obliterate the existing tracks. There the prints got muddied, as though someone had been standing in the snow for a long time, waiting. Waiting to kill me. Jesus Christ!

Through the trees I could see across the water to the entrance of the Gun. I also had a clear view of my car, listing sadly to one side on its two left rims. In the snow and mud at my feet was an ejected rifle shell, a .30-.30. Probably a deer rifle. I put on my glove and picked it up and put it in my pocket. Then I climbed back up the embankment to the tarmac road.

The snow clearance in the valley was excellent, so there was no chance of picking up any tire tracks. Too many cars had been along here since the last snow for any sort of meaningful identification, so after a cursory look around I didn't bother.

My right pants leg was ripped at the knee, and I could feel that I had torn the flesh, but I was certain I'd survive a skinned knee. I was damned lucky to get off that easily. A shiver went through me that had nothing to do with the air temperature.

I dogtrotted back over the footbridge, but it wasn't until I got through the door to the club that I put my gun in my pocket. The steward was not overjoyed at my reappearance. Not only was I not a member, but my pants and car coat were covered with mud and dirty snow, in clear violation of the dress code.

"I need a telephone," I said, and when he hesitated I almost snapped his head off. "Someone just tried to shoot me, and I'm calling the police!"

"Oh," he said. "Oh, my goodness!"

CHAPTER NINE

Deputy Police Chief Ethan Kemp of the Chagrin River Valley P.D. was a mere stripling of about twenty-eight, but in those few years he'd managed to pack a great deal of muscle onto his six-foot-five frame. From the way he squinted and the peculiar swagger of his walk I suspected he'd been christened after John Wayne's character in *The Searchers* and had spent his whole life living up to it. I didn't remember Wayne chewing gum, however.

Chief Kemp got out of his black-and-white, came over to my grievously crippled car, and looked at it the way he might regard a dead cow blocking the highway. He questioned me about the shot, and then we walked together into the woods behind the Gun Club, where he examined the bullet gouge in the tree. Calling out to his companion in the car to search for the spent bullet, he turned and sighted across the river, to where I'd told him the gunman had waited.

"Amateur," he said with contempt. "A pro would've taken the top of your head off." He took the spent shell from me and held it in the palm of his mittened hand like a Mexican jumping bean. "Deer rifle. You put your prints on it?"

"I used to be a uniform with the Cleveland P.D. I'm smarter than that."

He continued staring at the shell while absorbing what I'd told him. Then he nodded his head and walked back to the roadway and along the tarmac toward the club entrance. I was unsure whether to follow him until he turned and looked at me. "C'mon," he coaxed.

The steward was on the verge of a severe case of the vapors as Kemp, wearing a red and black checked lumber jacket and a Stetson, walked through the door, directly into the taproom, followed by a dirty, muddy, bleeding Slovenian. The club members present had naturally been filled in on the day's excitement and were all crowded into a corner, murmuring through their bristly white mustaches and casting ill-disguised glances at us. Apparently we were a new species for them. Things like sniper attacks don't happen at the Gun, and we were resented for bringing shame and scandal down upon their heads, even though no one yet knew of the shooting except the people in this room. And the trigger man, of course, but he'd be unlikely to gossip.

"Wanna tell me about it?" Kemp drawled, and then he turned and called over to the bartender, "Can we have a couple o' brewskis over here?" As the man scrabbled around beneath the bar to find some beer while we occupied a vacant table, I noted the merry glint in Kemp's eye and realized he was enjoying himself. He said, "I never drink on duty, but hell, beer ain't drinkin.'"

We were served Heineken in Pilsner glasses. Kemp held his glass up to the dim light and looked through it as if checking the color, then took a quaff. When he brought the glass down he had a mustache of foam, which he wiped off with his sleeve. "It makes 'em nuts when I come in here," he said, and chuckled, shaking his huge head. "Brewskis."

I showed him a copy of my license. He said, "How long were you a cop?"

"Four years. Army M.P. before that."

"I spent my time on a big-city force," he said. "Indianapolis. Too much bullshit and too much politics. This is better." He slid my license back to me. "I'm listening."

"You know it all, Chief. I came out here at the invitation of one of the members. We talked, maybe about fifteen minutes, and then I went outside. I was just getting into my car when I noticed the tires, and then someone mistook me for a whitetail and took a shot at me."

"Now who'd wanna do that?" he said, his accent corn-belt.

"If I knew, I'd tell you."

He took another gulp of beer and expelled an "Aaahhh!" of satisfaction. "Would you?" he said. "You wouldn't go after him yourself like you was Wyatt Earp, would you, Mr. Jacovich?" With the hard *J*.

"I would have," I admitted, "but it's too late for that now. I won't. I wouldn't know where to look."

"You here on business at the Gun, or is this a social visit?"

"I don't socialize in these circles, Chief."

"Who did you come here to see?"

"I'm not sure I should divulge that information."

"Is he your client?"

The bastard had me. "No, so I suppose I'll have to tell you."

He smiled, nodded. The country-rube pose was just that, a pose. Ethan Kemp was scalpel-sharp.

I said, "Walter Deming."

He lifted his eyebrows a bit, but waited for me to go on. "I'm on a missing-persons case, and Mr. Deming is acquainted with the party."

"With the party."

"Yes."

"The missing party."

"Right."

"And is the missing party your client, then?"

"No."

"Good. Then you can tell me who that is."

I squirmed, a butterfly on a pin. "His name is Richard Amber. He lives in Pepper Pike."

"And what is his connection with Mr. Deming?"

I said, "Amber is in advertising. Walter Deming is his client."

Kemp shifted his bulk around in his chair and looked over his shoulder at the cluster of middle-aged men off in the corner. "Is there a Mr. Deming here?" he called with a studied casualness.

Walter Deming emerged from the knot of Gun Clubbers and came over to the table and introduced himself.

Kemp said, "Did you ask this man to come here today?"

"I did."

"Did you tell anyone else he was expected?"

"No. Why should I? Well, the club steward, of course. I told him when I arrived that Mr. Jacovich would be here at around three."

"Did you tell anyone *you* were coming here today, Mr. Deming?"

Deming said with some heat, "I generally spend Saturday afternoons here. Is there some law against that?"

"No, sir," said Kemp, "and I thank you for your cooperation."

He hadn't stood up, nor invited Deming to sit. It was a strange role reversal for Deming, one that made him uneasy. Finding himself for all intents and purposes dismissed, he walked shakily back to his peer group, all of whom averted their eyes as he joined them. Kemp turned back to me.

"That leaves you, Mr. Jacovich. Who knew you were coming to the Gun today?"

"No one," I said.

"Sure? You sure you didn't brag on your friends that you'd been invited to this tony establishment?"

"Oh, cut the hayseed bullshit, Chief. I'm a pro, just like you."

He scratched the corner of his mouth. "'S right, you are. Sorry. So what do you think? Someone mistook you for an out-of-season deer?"

"I imagine that I was followed here."

He nodded again, sagely. "That's what I imagine, too. Seems to me a professional"—and he italicized the word—"would have spotted a tail."

"Wasn't looking for one. I'm on a missing-persons squeal here, not a criminal case."

"It's criminal now," he said. "Taking potshots at people with .30-.30s, that's a criminal matter. You think the missing husband is on to you and wants to stay missing for a while?"

"Enough to kill me?"

"Stranger things have happened," Kemp said, talking to a spot some three feet above my head. "When I was on the force in Indianapolis I pulled all the shit details. Vice. Narcotics. Special weapons and tactics. Ooh, it got ugly, I'll tell you. So when this job opened up I couldn't wait to get out." He was speaking slowly, maddeningly so. "I come here, I ticket speeders, I see to it the landed gentry don't drive themselves into the river when they've had too many brewskis, I kick asses of their pimply kids when they smoke pot behind the gym at school. Every once in a while I mop up a fight in one of the local shot-and-a-beer bars. It's a quiet life, Jacovich. Not a bad life for a cop." He finally looked at me. "You know where I'm heading now, don't you?"

"You're up to the part where you're going to tell me you don't like shootings in your valley, right?"

He grinned that squinty-eyed John Wayne grin. "That's right. That's exactly right, I don't. People start shooting and then things get ugly again. They get complicated. I like things simple."

"Are you telling me to get out of your town by sundown?"

He laughed and looked at his watch. "It's a little late for sundown," he said. "But I am saying I don't want private cops poking around here without letting me know first. Your missing person lives in Pepper Pike, you stay in Pepper Pike. You don't come out to the valley anymore without checking it out with me first, so I can keep you safe. Wouldn't do to have a visitor from Cleveland get shot in my valley. I'm just looking out for your ass. Now is that fair, or what?"

"Sure it's fair," I said, "because it's your town, Chief."

"Yeah," he breathed. "It is. Are you a member of auto club?"

"Yes, I am."

"Well, then, best you call them and have them do something about those tires, so I don't have to write you up for illegal overnight parking. And after they do, I'm hoping we don't have to see each other anymore."

"As I said, I was invited here."

"I was once invited to go jump in the lake, but I didn't. Next time you do your talking on your own turf. Or else check with me first. That's only bein' courtesy. And it stands to reason if you're courtesy to me, I'm gonna be courtesy right back to you. Is that 'kay?"

He stood up and stretched. I stood up, too, feeling small next to him. There aren't many people who make me feel like a little guy. He said, "In the meantime I'll ask around up and down that road back there if anyone saw a car. And if they did—and if I find out whose car it was—and if that someone isn't from this valley—I'll give you a call."

"That's damned nice of you, Chief."

"Well, sure. If people are going to go 'round shooting deer rifles at you, I think you ought to know who they are."

It was after eight when I finally got home. I was dog-tired, dirty, hungry, and pretty shaken up, to say nothing of being out the price of two new tires. I took a quick shower, put on my robe, and plopped down in front of the TV, a couch potato, to think about how my day had been. After such a great Friday evening with Mary, my weekend had gone downhill like an Austrian on skis.

It wasn't the first time I'd been shot at, even from ambush. It had been an almost weekly occurrence in the Mekong Delta. It had also happened once in Garfield Heights when I was a police rookie checking out an armed robbery in progress, and once a few years later in an alley about two blocks from Terminal Tower when I'd been working vice and chasing down a particularly obnoxious pimp. But being a target isn't something you ever get used to, no matter how often it happens. I opened a beer but my throat was closed from tension and I could barely swallow.

It was one of those Saturday nights when there's nothing to watch on TV. A soccer game revealed that Kai Haaskivi of the Cleveland Force had already scored three goals and it wasn't even halftime. *Saturday Night Live* was preempted for wrestling. One of those Saturdays when the bars are empty because everyone has paired up early and gone home. One that lasts about sixty hours because you have nothing going for you to look forward to on Sunday. When cops lurk behind every bush and billboard, ticket books at the ready. When you stop at a light and check out the driver of the car next to you in hopes it'll be someone beautiful and lonely like you—only it turns out to be a fat guy smoking a cheap cigar who's checking you out for the same reason.

When I finally went to bed I didn't get to sleep for a long time. I was thinking what would have happened if I hadn't bent down at just that moment to look at my tires. I kept hearing that bullet roaring past my ear, feeling the air disturbance it created against my cheek. I'd have given a month's pay to know who fired it.

And why.

Morning came early on Sunday. I made some coffee and toast and read the paper, and when it got to be ten o'clock I called Mrs. Amber and told her what had happened to me out at her uncle's club.

"I don't see what that could have to do with Richard," she said, but her voice betrayed her worry. Women like Mrs. Amber didn't understand about people shooting guns at other people. It wasn't part of her scene. She lived in a world where injury was inflicted by innuendo, not by rifle fire.

"I don't either," I answered, "but I'm sure as hell going to find out. This has become a personal matter. Give me directions to your cabin in Wawassee."

"Richard wouldn't be there," she said definitely.

"He was there four years ago when he walked out after a fight with Jerry Stendall."

I heard a sharp intake of breath. "That was in the summertime. He wouldn't go there now. It's a long drive, and usually the roads are snowed in all winter."

"Give me the directions anyway," I said. "I feel like a Sunday drive."

She did, and I wrote them all down. It would take me the better part of five hours to get there.

I threw a clean shirt, a pair of jeans, and some fresh under-wear and socks into a gym bag that said CLEVELAND INDIANS on it, along with my spare toothbrush, some paste, and a hairbrush. I wasn't planning on staying overnight, but I like to be ready for contingencies. I dressed for warmth and comfort in a pair of chinos, a flannel shirt, some heavy-soled work boots, and an Irish tweed cap to keep my head warm. I usually skipped headgear, but today I felt like it. I took a couple of tapes to play in the car for when I hit those rural areas where there is no radio reception except for country music and the Sunday religious programs. Then I secured my apartment and went downstairs to my car. It was sunny and cold.

I unlocked the door and tossed the gym bag into the back seat and was just about to slide under the wheel when two men got out of a car that was parked illegally in someone else's parking space. They were big men, swarthy-looking, and both were wearing zippered jackets with collars of fake fur. They appeared to be in their twenties, and each had about a quart of oil in his hair. I know punks when I see them. One of them was wearing mirrored sunglasses, which might be okay in Hollywood, but anyone who wore sunglasses in Cleveland in the middle of February just had to be pretty much of an asshole.

"Are you Milan Jacovich?" the other one said, screwing up both names.

I corrected him.

"You mind coming with us?" he said. "We have a friend would like to talk to you."

"I was on my way somewhere."

"Yeah. Well, this friend would like to see you a lot."

"Are you police?" I said, knowing the answer but stalling for time.

The question seemed to amuse them. The one with the sunglasses cackled a high-pitched laugh that went with his acne. "No, man," the other one said, "we're not the police."

"Well, tell your friend to call and make an appointment tomor-row. Like I told you, I'm on my way out."

"This'll only take a little while."

"Not today," I said.

"Today," he said. He unzipped his jacket partway and showed me the butt of a pistol under his arm.

"*Not* today," I said. I unbuttoned my own coat and showed him that I was carrying, too.

That's when the one with the sunglasses hit me over the head with something hard. It was a glancing blow, not powerful enough to put me down but adequate for inducing instant dizziness. I shot out a stiff right and caught him in the mouth, but there wasn't much steam behind the punch, and although it staggered him, he kept his feet. I turned to see the other one pointing his .38 at my chest. My own gun was still in my armpit. I put my hands up at about chest level while Sunglasses spit blood out of his busted lip and relieved me of my weapon.

"Today," the other punk said. "Now."

I felt an egg forming on my forehead as they marched me over to their car, a four-door Olds 98. The one with the gun opened the back door and motioned me in, and when I stooped over to enter Sunglasses punched me wickedly in the kidney and I sprawled forward on the seat. He jumped in on top of me and then something crashed into the back of my neck. The pain shot through my head like pulsating jolts of electroshock, and as hard as I tried I just couldn't seem to keep my eyes focused.

Pretty soon I stopped trying and went to sleep.

CHAPTER TEN

I t was more of a light doze than a deep loss of consciousness, because I was aware of things like motion, bumps, and potholes in the street, and the smell of Aqua Velva from the punk in the sunglasses, who sat in the backseat with me. The problem was that I could neither open my eyes, sit up, nor remember my name or those of my children. I just lay there and enjoyed the motion as if it were one of the "baby" rides at an amusement park. Nothing was expected of me, and that was a good thing because I had little to offer at the moment.

Then the ride ended, as all rides must, and I was pulled roughly into an upright position and slapped in the face until I got my eyes open. Focusing them was another story. I persevered, and when the fuzz blew off the edges of my vision I saw we were in a parking lot off a fairly busy thoroughfare. When I was dragged out of the car and down the incline to the street, I recognized it as Mayfield Road, specifically that section of the street just above University Circle and Severance Hall known as Little Italy. All up and down Mayfield were Italian bakeries and delicatessens, espresso shops, and some of the city's best Italian restaurants. A lot of cars lined the street, mainly because it was Sunday morning and the faithful had turned out for Mass at nearby Holy Rosary. The residents of Little Italy were not all Italian, though most were. But they were all white, and it was well known throughout the city they intended it to stay that way.

Next to the now-defunct Mayfield Theatre was a door discreetly marked FIRENZE SOCIAL CLUB—MEMBERS ONLY, and it was through that door I was roughly propelled before I could protest I was not a member. We went up a flight of stairs, uncarpeted and smelling from years of marinara sauce and tobacco, and the punk who had the gun took out a key and opened the door at the top of the stairs, stepped aside, and watched as Sunglasses shoved me through into what looked like a large club room. Several round tables suitable for card playing were distributed randomly about, and there were a few wooden booths against one wall. There was also a small service bar, behind which was a well-stocked wine rack and an espresso machine shining gold and rococo in the morning sunlight that streamed through the room's single high window.

The punk with the gun pointed to a chair at one of the round tables and said, "Sit there." Since I was not yet able to stand without a feeling of vertigo I gratefully accepted the invitation. Sunglasses disappeared through a door, and his buddy stood off to one side, waiting. A good soldier.

The five minutes or so I sat were agonizing, as I felt the moments of my life ticking away, never to be recovered. Finally Sunglasses returned with two men. One was a few years younger than I, tall, slim, darkly handsome, with a mustache. He wore black wool slacks, expensive Italian shoes with tassels, and a beautiful white cable-knit sweater with some sort of abstract modern design in red and yellow. He had a cup of coffee in his hand and seemed a pleasant enough fellow. He was followed by an older, shorter man, almost painfully skinny, with a dark suit and tie, and a face that was a grid of deep lines and creases. His eyes were brown and bright and earnest, and the corners of his mouth were pulled down into a permanent grimace, showing nicotine-stained teeth. I recognized him from news photographs, and the recognition gave me small comfort. He was Giancarlo D'Allessandro, and he ran Little Italy. In fact, when it came to illicit gambling, prostitution, and narcotics, he pretty much ran northern Ohio. They stood looking at me for a moment, taking in my swelling forehead and my rumpled clothing. Then D'Allessandro sat down opposite me and looked up at the two punks.

"Assholes!" he said without much malice. His voice was like a buzz saw. "You think with your muscles. Go away."

The punk with the gun started to say something and then switched to his edit mode as he glanced at the man in the sweater. He and Sunglasses went away as ordered, with not a word of protest.

"Are you hurt, Mr. Jacovich?" D'Allessandro curled his upper lip back over his teeth when he spoke.

I fingered my forehead. "No, I'm not, Mr. D'Allessandro, but thanks for asking."

The old man beamed that I had recognized him. "This is my associate, Mr. Gaimari."

I looked up at the younger man, who smiled at me. Victor Gaimari, I knew, was D'Allessandro's lieutenant and anointed successor, and I remembered reading somewhere that they were vaguely related by blood. Gaimari was the respectable one in the organization, head of a downtown brokerage house and, if memory served, a graduate of Ohio State. He was something of a playboy, managing to show up at society functions where D'Allessandro would never be invited, and always with a beautiful woman on his arm. It was also said that in the recent years of D'Allessandro's ill health, Gaimari called most of the shots. Yet he stood while the older man sat. These people were big on showing respect.

Gaimari said, "I'm sorry John and Joey got a little too enthusiastic. They're young."

"It's tough to get good help these days, isn't it?" I said.

"Can I get you something, Mr. Jacovich? A coffee?"

"No, thanks. I would like to know why I'm here and why I was roughed up, though."

D'Allessandro took a cigarette from a silver case, and Gaimari lighted it for him with a Dunhill lighter. The old man took a big drag, and began coughing in phlegmy, wracking spasms. When he finally stopped, he patted his chest. "Damn things are killing me," he said, speaking with only the barest hint of an Italian accent. He had been in this country for fifty years. He remembered his manners and excused himself, extending the cigarette case to me. I took one, and Gaimari lighted mine as well.

"The boys were told to be polite," D'Allessandro said. "They'll suffer for it, and you have my sincerest apologies. We'll try to make this as brief as possible so you can get on with your day. It's a beautiful day, isn't it? Too nice to be cooped up in here."

"I agree with you," I said.

"Well, to the business at hand. We are very interested in getting in touch with someone you know. We were hoping you can help us out."

I waited.

"A man named Richard Amber."

I sucked in some air and waited some more.

"We hear you've been making inquiries around."

"How did that happen to come to your attention, Mr. D'Allessandro?"

Gaimari said pleasantly, "That's not important."

"What's important," the old man continued, "is that we'd very much like to talk to Mr. Amber."

"So would I."

"Eh?"

"So would I like to talk to him. I've been looking for him the past four days, but so far no luck."

"No ideas, even?"

"If I had any, I'd have acted on them by now."

Victor Gaimari asked, "Where were you off to when John and Joey met you this morning?"

"It's Sunday," I said. "I was going for a drive in the country."

"You're a religious man?" D'Allessandro said. "You don't work on a Sunday?"

I laughed, and D'Allessandro laughed easily with me, except that his laugh became another paroxysm of coughing and wheezing. He covered his mouth politely and turned his head away until he was through. Then he turned back to me with tearing eyes. "Goddammit," he said, and stubbed out his cigarette.

"Most of the people I'd want to talk to aren't reachable on Sundays, so I thought I'd take the day off. Even detectives need to play sometimes."

"And who would those people be?" Gaimari said.

I thought a long while before I answered. "I'm not really at liberty to say."

"Mr. Jacovich," the old man croaked, "please be advised we aren't crapping around. I know about your professional ethics and your legal rights, and I assure you they don't mean a fart in the wind here."

"I know that, sir," I said. "I've been talking to Mr. Amber's friends and business associates, and I'm sure you know their names as well as I do."

He nodded and did here's-the-church-and-here's-the-steeple with his fingers. Gaimari went behind the bar and began fooling with the espresso machine. There was a great hiss of steam, and in a moment he was back with a tiny cup and saucer, which he placed before his patron. D'Allessandro sipped daintily, looked up at Gaimari, and nodded his acceptance. Then he said to me, "It's a harsh world, Mr. Jacovich. We all have expenses, bills to pay. It's taken as an article of faith that people will pay those bills on time so the creditors can go on functioning efficiently. Mr. Amber, unfortunately, does not pay his bills promptly. We can only extend credit so far."

I protested, "I don't even know Amber personally. I certainly can't be held responsible for his debts."

Gaimari said, "We're not suggesting you are."

"It is, however, a substantial sum of money, and we intend to see it made good," D'Allessandro warned.

"How substantial?"

The mafioso shrugged as if to say it was not important, but Gaimari told me, "You remember the Browns-Denver game?"

One could not have lived in Cleveland and been unaware of the Browns' Central Division Championship that year. The whole city had united in the common cause of rooting the Dogs home. Stores and bars had been festooned with orange and brown balloons, bumper stickers, and buttons seemed to bloom overnight, and conservative-looking secretaries had carried pompons to indicate their support. Posters of Cleveland's Bernie Kosar were everywhere, and some witty bartenders had even displayed images of Denver quarterback John Elway hung upside down over their back bars. Unfortunately the game had gone into overtime, and a Denver field goal had dashed Cleveland's hopes of a Super Bowl trophy.

"Mr. Amber had the Browns and two," Gaimari said. "That wasn't quite good enough."

"I remember."

"That one little point cost Mr. Amber some thirty thousand dollars."

I whistled. "What's the vigorish?"

"Standard," the old man said easily. "Ten percent. Per week." He pronounced *per* as if it were spelled "puh."

Math was not my strong point, but the calculation was easy enough to do in my head. The game had been played five weeks before. "That's another fifteen grand."

"There comes a point," Gaimari said, "when even interest accrued becomes unwieldy on the books. We're anxious to get this cleared up."

"It's unwieldy, all right—but I don't see how I can help you."

D'Allessandro said, "You're a businessman. I'm a businessman. Maybe we can do some business together. If you were to locate Mr. Amber for us, and let us know of his whereabouts at least twenty-four hours before informing your client, we could see our way clear of awarding a finder's fee of, say, ten puh cent. I'm sure that is superior to the figure offered you by your client."

"Yes. But it would hardly be ethical."

The old man waved his hands in front of his face with annoyance. "Ethics have to take hind tit to practicalities, Jacovich. You surely see the folly of alienating this organization?"

"That would be foolish," I agreed.

"In addition, you'll be the richer for it in terms of goodwill. We occasionally have need of a person with your talents, and we could throw some rather lucrative contracts your way."

I stubbed out my cigarette carefully, making sure every last ember was squashed. "Sir, you're a careful man. I'm sure you realize with whom you're dealing here. I used to be with the police. You must know that."

He nodded.

"I don't mean to be rude, but I wouldn't be interested in any contracts from you. It's not my style."

He sighed. "Indeed a pity. But the offer of a finder's fee still goes. You seem like a smart man. A smart man don't piss away forty-five hundred dollars for doing what he was going to do anyway." He stood up as quickly as an arthritic man in his seventies could stand. "There's no reason two businessmen with a mutual respect can't work together for a common interest. Mr. Gaimari will expect a progress report from you each evening."

Gaimari took his wallet from his hip and handed me a business card: Gaimari and Associates Brokerage, with a downtown address and phone number. "I'm usually there until six," he said.

"It's been a pleasure talking with you, Mr. Jacovich. I like you. You don't get mad easy. The offer to work for us still stands if you change your mind," Mr. D'Allessandro said.

I rose, too. "I'd like my property returned," I told him.

"Yes," he said. He leaned on the back of the chair with both hands, his weight whitening his knuckles. "An impressive weapon, the Magnum. Indispensable for a Sunday drive in the country. Good day." He turned slowly and disappeared through the inner door.

Gaimari said, "John will return it to you when he gets you back home." Like a gracious host he led me to the door and down the stairs. "Are you a betting man, Milan? You like to bet money on the games?"

"Rarely," I said. "I'm a lottery player."

"Uh-huh. Well, anytime you'd like to get a few dollars down, we'd be glad to handle your action. Mr. D'Allessandro likes you."

"You could tell?"

"Oh, yes. You were very polite and respectful. A bit unusual for someone in your line of work. That's why we'd trust you to do some work for us."

"Well, as I said, I don't think that will happen. And I'm sure you'll understand that on the rare occasions when I do put a bet down, I do it with a Slovenian bookmaker."

He threw back his head and laughed. "That's very good. Fair enough. You're a frank and honest man."

"Now you be frank and honest with me," I said. "Someone took a shot at me yesterday and came too close for me to joke about it. Was it one of your people?"

He actually looked concerned. "Milan, I don't know anything about that. Tell me what happened."

"Just that. At the time I had no reason to think about your organization, but now—"

"We had nothing to do with it, really. Believe me, Milan, if we wanted you hurt we wouldn't be standing here talking now, would we?" And standing we were, as we had reached the parking lot where the two punks were waiting for us by the Oldsmobile. Sunglasses's busted lip was crusted over and puffy. Gaimari said, "We want to do business with you. We like our business partners healthy." He turned to the two punks. "Take Mr. Jacovich home and then come right back here. *Right* back. And treat him with all the courtesy you'd extend to Mr. D'Allessandro's grandmother. You understand?"

"Yes, Mr. Gaimari," Sunglasses mumbled. I couldn't see his eyes, but I'll bet they were shooting daggers at me. To be humiliated in front of a stranger was something these people don't take to very well. I wondered whether all this shit about respect and honor came before or after *The Godfather* movies.

Gaimari shook my hand warmly and smiled. He acted like he was either desperate to make new friends or was running for office. "Thanks for coming by," he said, as ludicrous then as it is in hindsight. "No hard feelings, I hope."

"I only have hard feelings when I can do something about them," I said. "Thanks for your courtesy." I felt trapped in a Victorian comedy of manners.

The punks both sat in front this time, leaving me to the backseat. The one with the gun drove and Sunglasses rode shotgun.

The drive took barely ten minutes and was carried out in silence; we didn't have much to talk about. They deposited me exactly where they'd found me, next to my car.

I got out and stood by the front door. "I want my piece back," I said.

Sunglasses opened his door and got out, taking my gun from his jacket pocket and handing it to me. I took it with my left hand and slipped it into my own coat pocket, and with my right I gathered up a fistful of shirt and jacket and slammed him back against the open door of the car. It must have hurt his back. I know it knocked the wind out of him, because he said something that sounded like "Guhhh!" as he expelled most of his air.

"If you ever put your hands on me again I'll rip out your throat," I said. "You understand me, snot-rag?"

So much for being polite and respectful.

He didn't say anything, maybe because he couldn't find the breath for a conversation. His skin went pale beneath the olive tan and his lips all but disappeared. I held him there a few seconds, noting that his friend had made no move to help him, and then I let go and slowly, deliberately, and with a show of more unconcern than I felt, walked to the entrance of my building. I knew there would be no retaliation because they'd had their orders, and knowing that, I suppose what I did was a cheap shot. But I don't like getting roughed up by punks. They watched me until I had gone into the building, and then I heard the car door slam and some rubber burning as they careened out of the lot.

My adrenaline was pumping when I got into my apartment. Even though it was barely past noon, I needed a drink, and a beer was not going to cut it. I got out my bottle of slivovitz and poured myself a healthy portion in a coffee cup, which I downed in two fast swallows. I was angry, feeling intimidated and put-upon, and I had no intention of cooperating with Giancarlo D'Allessandro. But only a dummy would deliberately incur his displeasure. I figured I'd worry about that when the time came.

I also couldn't help wondering how D'Allessandro had found out I was involved with looking for Richard Amber. It was obvious someone had told him, but I couldn't imagine who. It certainly hadn't come from my friends Ed Stahl or Rudy Dolsak, and although there had been times in the past when Marko Meglich hadn't been too fussy about where his perks came from, I doubted he'd ever let himself get boxed into a position where he was D'Allessandro's ear in the police department. He was too smart for that. So that left all the people I'd spoken to since I'd gotten on the case, the folks at Marbury-Stendall, Walter Deming, Karen Wilde, and Mary Soderberg. I didn't want to think it was Mary, for personal reasons. I didn't want to think it was any of them, because if so, things were going on regarding Richard Amber that went far beyond anything I'd been able to uncover, and I didn't like operating in the dark.

It was too late to start on my drive to Wawassee, especially since I was feeling more than a little shaky. An attempt had been made on my life, and I'd been mistreated by organized crime. I needed a little friendly feedback. I dialed my former phone number. It rang twice and then a male voice answered.

"Hello, Joe," I said.

"Oh. Oh, hello, Milan, how are you?" Joe Bradac said. He sounded embarrassed about answering Lila's phone.

"Pretty good. You?"

"Can't complain." There was a pause through which you could have driven a convoy of Peterbilts. Then he said, "The guys aren't here, Milan, they went to a birthday party Milan Jr.'s friend Richie—turning thirteen today. Well, tomorrow, really, his birthday's tomorrow, but they're having the party today. Uh . . . did you want to talk to Lila?"

"That's okay. I really called up to talk to the boys, see if they wanted to do something. I'll check back another time."

There was another awkward pause. I always hate it when I'm on the phone with someone who doesn't talk back; it makes me feel as if I should have prepared a monologue. Finally I said, "Well, take it easy, Joe."

"Yeah. You, too, Milan." He sounded relieved I was hanging up.

I poured myself another slivovitz, a stiff one. I drank it more slowly than the last, but it still hit my stomach like battery acid. Some friendly feedback, I thought. I wondered if Joe had just arrived there at Lila's house—my house—or if he'd spent the night. As if I didn't have enough to think about. I didn't seem to be able to let go of my feelings for my former wife, or for that matter my former house and former phone number. Perhaps I'd been sitting around brooding for too long, pondering what went wrong and how. I somehow couldn't accept that a person I'd spent more than half my life with had simply grown away from me, not quickly or for any particular reason, but just in the way that happens between two people who really care about each other but perhaps not enough, or maybe it was that caring had become a habit. I was sure that if I were bleeding to death I could call Lila and she'd be there in a second to take care of me, but that as soon as my wounds healed she'd be off again, back to Joe Bradac or back to wherever she'd gone when she simply faded out of the marriage.

I hadn't snapped back into the mainstream the way she had. I'd become something of a recluse, with no social life to speak of and no love life at all. It wasn't what most healthy, nearly-middle-aged people did in the world of the eighties, but it had been an unconscious choice for me, born out of not caring enough to do it differently. I looked at my surroundings, my apartment that was not so much masculine, or a reflection of myself, as it was a place to eat and sleep and brush my teeth, and realized that within these walls I had simply been marking time until I decided to start living again. I'd done well financially in the past year or so, and had several clients to whom I supplied security systems, and several others, mostly insurance companies, for whom I investigated claims; there were three or four lawyers around town, mostly Slovenian and Serbian, who used me whenever the services of a private investigator were required. I knew a lot of people, but there were few, beyond Ed Stahl and Rudy Dolsak, whom I saw with any regularity, and even they were just drinking pals or guys I went to ballgames with. I'd distanced myself from the old neighborhood except for an occasional foray to Vuk's, and I'd done nothing about replacing old relationships with new ones. I was in a pretty bad way, and I didn't have many places to go for succor.

So I made a mistake. I phoned Mary Soderberg. You couldn't call it a major mistake, since she wasn't home and there was no harm done. But it got my imagination going about where she might be, what she might be doing, and with whom, and in my present state of mind that had to be classified as a mistake of sorts. I didn't even leave a message on her machine because I didn't want to risk her not returning my call. Oh, I was in a great place, right in the oncoming path of the attack of the giant paranoids. It was nothing that a squeeze from some loving arms wouldn't cure, but I have had better days. Better Sundays, even, and Sundays are always a pain in the ass.

I switched on the television, but other than a few religious programs, a videotaped replay of yesterday's ski meet in Aspen, Colorado, and a terrible stinker with Paul Newman that no one ever remembered when they rated him one of the major stars of the last fifty years; there was nothing much to watch, and after three complete tours around the dial, as if somehow switching off Channel 12 and then switching it right back on again would magically transform the Reverend Robert Schuller into a basketball game, I cut the set off and sat watching a videotape replay of my own thoughts on the VCR inside my head.

I had to start taking better care of myself. Oh, I fed the body and got an adequate amount of sleep, and every few days I'd get energetic and knock off a set of push-ups on the floor beside my bed. But for a long time now I had been neglecting that part of a man's life that keeps his head healthy. The result was now this shaky and lonely Sunday with nowhere to turn.

Back in college when I'd been a hotshot football player there had been lots of people, the hangers-on, the groupies and jock-fuckers and car-sucks, who'd wanted to get close and be my friend and bask in the reflected glory of a winning season, but I'd had no time or use for them then; I'd had Lila and that was enough. Later, in Vietnam, I'd kept my distance from the rest of my unit, since most of them were high school dropouts and stoners and we had little in common besides a uniform and an often unseen enemy. And in the Cleveland Police Department I had avoided the traps so many young cops step into, drinking, punk-bashing, illicit sex with the hookers in exchange for not running them downtown, the genteel graft. I had Lila and then the boys, and I didn't need anything else.

Now there was no more football for me, the war was a dim memory, and most of the guys in my rookie class at the police academy were wearing their bellies over their belts these days and thinking about their pensions, and Lila was gone and the boys were being driven to birthday parties by Joe Bradac, who may or may not have climbed out of their mother's bed to make the trip. Yesterday someone had shot a deer rifle at me and today two Mafia punks had thumped me around and their boss, the *capo di tutti capi*, had threatened me very politely, and there wasn't a single soul in all of Cleveland who gave a shit.

Not true. Not quite true. There was a single soul. And after I'd thought about it awhile I picked up the telephone and dialed her number.

"Auntie Branka," I said when she answered. "It's your nephew. Milan."

"Milan?" she said in her cracked old voice, and I heard the delighted surprise. "You don't call me for a month! Vatsa matter? You die or sometink?"

CHAPTER ELEVEN

Euclid is a suburb up in the northeastern corner of Greater Cleveland, just west of the borderline separating Cuyahoga and Lake counties. The Conrail tracks run right through the middle of town, although neither side of the tracks is particularly fashionable, and the nearby lake sends gusts of subpolar winds racketing across the low-lying frame houses that have been there since the early part of the century. A lot of Slavic families live there and have done so for generations. My Uncle Anton and Aunt Branka moved to Cleveland from Ljubljana just before the outbreak of the Second World War and lived in the same house until Anton died a few years back, probably from acute boredom after working for Standard Oil of Ohio for forty-one years. Branka had seen no reason to move, and now lived in the three-bedroom lathe and wood house alone, cooking gigantic meals each night for her children, nieces and nephews, cousins, and the unacknowledged sisterhood of black-clad Slovenian widows of Euclid. There was always something on the stove at Branka's.

As I came up onto the porch the acrid smell of smoke from the chimney blended in the icy air with the aromas of the kitchen, and my nose told me that tonight there would be cevapcici, a sausagelike mixture of ground lamb, pork, and veal, served lovingly on pita bread and accompanied by sarma, a kind of soft cabbage that was as ubiquitous at a Slovenian table as french fries at Mc-

Donald's. The smells took me back to a quieter era, a less-complicated time of my life, and I thought that as tough as it might be to go through childhood and adolescence, those years were much simpler for everyone compared to adulthood and the real world. A major problem back then was sneaking into the movies without paying, or how to surreptitiously slip your sarma to the dog so you wouldn't have to eat it.

I rang the doorbell. It was the kind you twist, set in the middle of the heavy oaken door with a fine thin film of rust powdering the spot where ten thousand thumbs had left their oily imprints. It had probably been in the door since Anton and Branka moved in.

The old lady greeted me at the door with a wet and bristly kiss on the mouth, holding my face between her two rough hands, her ankle-length dusty black dress swishing as she moved. Fifty years in Ohio had not changed her customs a whit. Not for her the church socials at St. Vitus's to find a well-to-do Slovenian man who'd recently lost a wife; Branka would wear her widow's weeds forever.

"Milan," she said and peered into my face as if my eyes could divine the future.

"*Tetka*," I said. The frail little body felt good in my arms, the brittle old bones echoing a thousand remembered hugs.

She stepped back to take another good look at me. "Ach, so skinny you are, Milan. Why you don't eat no more?"

I shrugged helplessly. To my aunt, anyone was skinny who didn't look like Sydney Greenstreet, and it was useless to protest. I was actually putting on more weight than I cared to, from too many beers and not enough exercise, but you could never convince her of that.

"Come," she said. "Give coat, then you'll eat."

She hung my coat on the tree in the hallway and took me through the living room I remembered so well, warm and dark and somehow mysterious and awesome with the crucified Christ over the mantel looking down on the TV set with the bent rabbit ears that I had never seen turned off except at Anton's wake. Currently playing was an old black-and-white show that I thought I recalled as an *Alfred Hitchcock Presents*. It wouldn't surprise me to discover Aunt Branka's TV didn't pick up any programs that were made after 1958. I wondered if I had come too late for *Mister Ed*.

The kitchen looked to be of similar vintage. The old wooden table had a worn oilcloth covering with faded blue tulips on a dotted white background, and the sturdy wooden chairs had been fashioned and hand-pegged by Anton Jacovich himself, with some help from his sons, my cousins Dragan and Loy. Dragan had died in the Tet offensive, and Loy, short for Aloysius, a graduate of Case Western Reserve University, was a dentist in nearby Garfield Heights and the quintessential Yuppie, with a BMW, a Cuisinart, and a VCR to record shows received on a wall-size television set. He and his sister Helen, who lived on the West Side in Parma with her blue-collar husband, visited their mother not nearly enough, and so Branka was doubly happy to see me, only son of her husband's brother.

"Kvass," she said in the manner of one just discovering a cancer cure. She took down a smoky-looking jug from the pantry shelf and brought it to the table with a jelly glass, and poured me a healthy slug of homemade wine, derived from rye flour and probably purchased illicitly from old Mr. Slak, who had been operating a still in his basement down the street for longer than memory stretched. The kvass tasted like kerosene, but I drank it and it warmed me when it hit bottom, just as Branka's kitchen, her very presence, seemed to help me ward off the chill of my world. There was a copy of *Ameriska Domovina*, the Slovenian newspaper, neatly folded on the kitchen table.

I hadn't seen my aunt since Christmas—Twelfth Night—and I felt guilty at having ignored her for so many weeks. I made a solemn self-promise to be a better nephew in the future. I grinned up at her and she sat down at the table, feet apart, hands on her hams, staring at me. I'd always thought of it as her Vince Lombardi pose.

"So, Milan. How you are?"

"I'm fine, *Tetka*, fine."

"You liar. I see. I see how you are."

My smile didn't fool her.

"Still you cry over the wife, yes? Milan, no good to be sad for so long. Go out, find yourself new woman. Lots of new women." This coming from someone who, to my knowledge, had only known one man in seventy-odd years.

"Easier said than done."

"Eh?"

I laughed. "Not so easy."

She leaned over and took a fold of my cheek between her thumb and forefinger and squeezed until my eyes teared. "Go on! Nice-looking boy." She got up and went to the stove to begin dishing up my dinner. "Next week," she ordered, "you come again. My Helen and her man come, too."

"Next Sunday?"

"Sure." She put the plate down in front of me like a hash-house waitress, with a thud, then settled back onto her chair. "Aren't you going to eat?"

She waved her hand in front of her face as if the subject was too inconsequential to even discuss.

"You aren't sick, are you, *Tetka*?"

"Who, me? Never sick. Just not hungry."

"Okay," I said. I started eating. The cevapcici was delicious, as always. Like Julia Child with a souffle, Branka made cevapcici without thinking about it. The sarma was not so delicious. I had never liked it as a child, liked it less as an adult. But for a Slovenian to get through his life without experiencing sarma was as unlikely as a Jewish kid's avoidance of chicken soup or a Chicano youngster's ignorance of refried beans. It was something I had borne stoically all my life. Each bite I took was washed down with the kvass.

Branka watched me eat. Quick as a cat, she leaned over and put her hand on the knot on my forehead, prodding at it so it began hurting again. "This?"

"It's nothing. I bumped it on a cabinet."

"Someone hit you," she corrected. Her tone conveyed her assurance that she was right.

"It's nothing."

"It's something if a man hits you. Who?"

It was my turn to wave away a question.

"You mixed in with bad men?"

"That's my job," I said.

"Milan, you not police no more. Why you don't quit, get nice safe job?"

"What's the fun in that?"

"Ach, fun! You a big man now, forget fun." She crossed her arms on her skinny chest, each hand grasping the opposite bicep, fixing me with a hawklike regard. "What you do now?"

I said around a mouthful of cabbage that threatened to trigger my gag reflex, "A man disappeared. His wife wants me to find him."

She nodded, but she wasn't finished. "Who this man?"

"He's in advertising."

"The wife, she's pretty, yes?"

"I suppose."

"Yes?"

"Yes, she's pretty."

Branka shook her head. "No good. No man runs from pretty woman. He's dead, Milan."

"*Tetka*," I chided, but the skin on my back crawled with the feet of hairy creeping spiders. "What a thing to say!"

"No man runs from pretty woman," she repeated. The jerky nod of her head finalized it and made it truth for all time to come. After a moment she said, "So who hit you?"

"Some other men want to find him, too. We had a disagreement."

"Why they want him?"

"He owes them some money."

"Lot of money?"

I nodded yes, and she shook her head again. "No, the man dead, Milan."

Her doom-saying didn't make me feel all that terrific. Not only was it an unsettling thought, but it had crossed my mind yesterday while I lay in the roadside slush at the Gun.

When I left my aunt's house I looked carefully around before getting into my car. I hadn't forgotten the sound of the bullet singing past my ear in the woods yesterday, and though I had come to Euclid in a roundabout way to discourage pursuit I was taking no chances. My gun was in the car, as I hadn't wanted to wear it in to dinner; Branka worried about me enough as it was. But after the events of the past few days I was fairly worried about myself.

And something my aunt said was nibbling at me. She was sure Richard Amber was dead, and though I had no concrete evidence to back it up, I tended to agree with her. There was no logic to his disappearance, none that I could see. If he'd planned it, he never would have called me on Wednesday evening. If he'd voluntarily stepped out of the picture, it had to have been a dazzlingly quick decision. What had prompted him to change his mind so quickly? If he had. And if he hadn't—what happened to him?

I slipped my .38 out of the locked glove box and into my pocket as I started the car. I drove around several blocks of blue-collar homes and taverns, mean dwellings that had been proudly maintained and painted for fifty years but now were victims of the years' attrition, but I couldn't spot a tail. It was Sunday night and there was little automobile traffic in Euclid, most residents having buttoned up earlier to watch the hundred and fifth rerun of a Dirty Harry film on the tube, so if anyone had been following me I probably would have noticed. Finally I hopped on the freeway and drove home. When I berthed my car in its assigned space I took the gun from my pocket and flipped off the safety before going upstairs.

I unlocked my apartment door, standing to one side of the doorframe, and made a violent spinning entrance like Starsky and Hutch. I felt like a horse's patoot. The place was empty and smelled from stale tobacco smoke. Opening the parlor window was no help; it chilled the air in the apartment so that I had to sleep under an extra blanket.

In the morning I made my daily phone call to Judith Amber.

"I assume there have been no more break-ins or you would have called me."

"No, it's been quiet. What do you have to report?"

"I'm not sure. Mrs. Amber, are you aware that your husband has been gambling rather heavily?"

The silence on the other end was louder than any protest. "Where did you hear that?"

"I heard it," I said. "Did you?"

"Oh." And that little word was so offhand it could only have been carefully calculated. "I know he gambles sometimes."

"Often?"

"I don't know. It's not the sort of thing a man like Richard discusses with his wife."

"Have any of his gambling . . . associates contacted you in the last five days?"

"Why would they do that?"

"I'm asking you."

"I don't know anything about it, and I don't see where this is getting us. I'm paying you to find Richard, not to poke into my private life."

I chewed on the eraser of the pencil I was holding. It had been a bad habit of mine since childhood, biting erasers off pencils. Most kids stop doing it when they're nine, but I never had. It made me a lot more wary of making mistakes. "No one is poking into your private life, Mrs. Amber. I was asking about your husband's gambling. That's all."

She sighed. "I'm sorry. It's been a very difficult time for me."

"Look," I said, "I'm not going to be reachable today, but I think you ought to have someone in to watch the house in case there's another break-in, if the prowler didn't find what he was looking for. If you still won't call the police, I can have someone out there."

She said slowly, "It's been taken care of."

"Oh? By whom?"

"Don't push me, Mr. Jacovich. I'm just about out of patience. I've arranged privately for someone to watch the house and to watch me, and that's all you need to know."

"I could help you a lot better if you weren't so damned secretive with me."

"It has nothing to do with Richard, or with you. If you wish to withdraw I'll be happy to settle your bill right now."

"Are you firing me? Because if you are, you should know that I intend to keep on looking for your husband until I find him, whether I'm on the payroll or not."

"Why would you do that?"

"I have personal reasons, now," I said. I didn't want to tell her about my encounter with Giancarlo D'Allessandro. Not yet.

"Well," she said in the way people have of saying "Well" when they really don't have anything to add to it. "I don't see what personal reasons you could possibly have."

"I don't want *you* poking into *my* private life, either, Mrs. Amber. I'll talk to you tomorrow." And I hung up before she could respond. I was just able to switch on the answering machine before the phone rang again, and I let the tape get it. I didn't want to talk to Judith Amber anymore.

I was all set to leave, then decided I had one more call to make.

"Mary, it's Milan Jacovich."

"Milan, how nice to hear from you. Did you have a good weekend?"

I had a hard time choking down the laughter. I said, "I tried to call you yesterday but you weren't home," and I hoped it didn't sound like "*J'accuse!*"

"I went with a girlfriend to the art museum for the French Impressionist exhibit. Have you seen it?"

"No."

"Oh, it's breathtaking. You should go."

"I'd like to go with you if you could stand to see it again."

"I'd love to. But I probably can't get away till next Saturday."

"That's a date," I said. "I'd like to see you before then, but I'm not sure when I can get free. This case—"

"Oh, Richard," she said, sobering. "No word yet?"

Her concern for Richard Amber bothered me, but I had to tell myself it was natural, and also had to remind myself their affair was long over. "No, but I'm working on it."

"I hope he's all right. He's a nice man, no matter what you think."

"Why would I think otherwise?"

"I'd like to believe it had something to do with me."

"Mary, you're way ahead of me," I said.

"Not yet, but I'm catching up. Milan, I'm really glad you called."

"Me, too," I said. "I'll see you Saturday."

"Or before, I hope. Depending. I won't make any plans this week anyway. Just in case."

"You'd do that for me?"

"Aren't you worth it, Milan?"

I smiled for the first time since Friday night, for the second time in more than a year. "Yes," I said. "Yes, dammit, I am!"

When I double-locked my apartment door and went down to my car I was feeling better than I had in some time, so good that I didn't even keep my fingers wrapped around my gun. It was in the shoulder holster where it belonged.

The blues call it Stormy Monday, and this one was well-named. An icy, almost invisible snow was not so much falling as blowing horizontally, beating a tattoo on the windshield, melting when it hit the freeway and leaving a wet and treacherous slick on the dark pavement as it rushed along beneath my wheels. I switched on the radio and listened to Top 40 rock for a while, then the signal faded and I tossed in one of my tapes. Neil Diamond. "A Solitary Man." Sure.

I headed due west on the Shocknessy Ohio Turnpike, through Elyria and curving down around the natural shoreline of Lake

Erie, then nicking the southern tip of Toledo and driving in an al-most unbending line toward the Indiana border. After Toledo the snow let up as I distanced myself from the water, and though it was a relief not to have to squint through the whiteness, it made a boring drive that much more boring. For all I knew I was off on a long and dreary fool's errand, but it was one I had to try. If I couldn't find any clues to Amber's whereabouts in Cleveland, maybe there was something in Wawassee that might give me a hint.

I stopped over the state line and had lunch in a little place off the highway. I've always found when traveling across America that the best food is served in little mom-and-pop diners on the side roads. The various corporations that run the big roadside chains tend more toward plastic booths and plastic food, and after Aunt Branka's home cooking I wasn't going to settle for a tasteless cheeseburger. I had an excellent fried steak with a crisp salad, home fries, and scrambled eggs, and the coffee was better than I might have hoped for in a place called Marie and Bill's.

The waitress, a perky little fifty-year-old wearing a brown uniform and one of those cardboard caps with wings on it like a novice nun's, glanced out the window at my car's license plates, noting I was from Ohio.

"Did that guy with the winning lottery ticket show up yet?"

"Not that I know of."

"Nine million biggies. That's more than I make in a week, for God's sake."

"If you're hinting for a nine-million-buck tip you've got the wrong guy."

"Huh! Story of my life. Where you headed? Shy?" That's what people who didn't live there called Chicago. People who did live there tended to start fistfights when auslanders called their hometown "Shy."

"No. Little place called Wawassee."

"Never heard of it. Then again, they prolly never heard of York neither. That's where y'are right now, York, Indiana. You a sales-man?"

"No."

She beamed. "Didn't think so," she said, picking up my water glass and dabbing at a wet circle on the counter. "You don't look like a salesman."

"Oh? What does a salesman look like?"

"You know," she said, flicking her wet rag at me flirtatiously. "You don't have the gift of gab. A salesman's got to smile a lot and tell jokes or else he don't make any money. One product is just like another; people don't buy the product, they buy the man."

"And the jokes."

"Right, the jokes. You know, I hear some terrific jokes on this job, from the salesmen passing through."

"I'll bet you do."

"Here's one I heard from a guy out of Shy, I think. What do you call a bull that's masturbating?"

I had to admit I didn't know.

"Beef strokin'-off," she said. She laughed so hard at the joke she never noticed that I didn't. She wiped her eyes and said, "Oh, Lord!" and then looked at me. "That's kind of a restaurant joke."

"It was very amusing," I said. "Are you Marie?"

"Naw. Marie's about seventy years old. I'm Ruthie. We got apple pie today; it's delicious. Made just this morning."

"No, thanks," I said, patting my stomach. I took the photo of Richard Amber from my jacket pocket. "You didn't happen to see this man come through here the last few days, did you?"

She put on her glasses, which were hanging around her neck on a ribbon, and looked at the photo. "Isn't that the governor of Ohio?"

"No, the other one."

"Nope. Don't look familiar, and I'm here twelve, sometimes fourteen hours a day."

"It was just a long shot."

"I knew you weren't no salesman. You're a cop."

"Yes," I said. I didn't feel like explaining.

"Well, I wish you good luck," she said. "Feel free if you want to use the facilities. They're out back."

I left her a two-dollar tip. It wasn't quite the nine million she was hoping for, but it was the most I could justify on my expense account.

The topography changes almost at the state line. Indiana, while a beautiful state, lacks the rolling, pastoral hills and stands of birch and dogwood that characterize the Ohio countryside, but makes up for it with some really interesting farmhouses that must have been there during Teddy Roosevelt's presidency, each one beautiful in its own individual way, painted in reds and greens and blues. It was almost four o'clock when I turned off the Indiana Turnpike and headed for the tiny dot on the map that was Wawassee. It wasn't hard to find because there was absolutely nothing else around it—no towns, rivers, red-line highways, or operative rail lines. There were a lot of trees, scrub pine and oak, and the remains of an old resort hotel from the early thirties, once painted an improbable pink that had faded into the color of a white handkerchief that no one had quite been able to clean of bloodstains. The walls were now crumbling like a proud Etruscan ruin, victimized by the ruthless and relentless onslaught of Indiana winters. The hotel perched on the edge of a lake across which a major league outfielder could have heaved a ball on one bounce. Jutting out into the water for about sixty feet was a sad, rickety pier that had probably been used for speedboat rides during the resort's heyday in the thirties and forties. From the looks of things nothing had been repaired since then. There is something desolate about a place that once rang with the laughter of children and the splashing and shouting of vacationers having a good time, now deserted and gone to seed.

I sat in my car by the hotel and the lake, smoking a cigarette. A thick layer of ice covered the water, a dirty gray as the sky darkened. I put out my smoke and drove around the bend of the lake until I found the roadway—not much more than a path the width of my car—that Judith Amber had described to me. There was a small cabin at the side of the road with wispy smoke snaking from the stone chimney, so I stopped the car and idled, waiting for someone to come out.

The old man who emerged from the cabin was dressed in a bright blue parka with the hood up, concealing all of his head but the middle of his wizened face. His skin looked like a mirror that had been punctured in the center, the hole being his near-tooth-less mouth, and the cracks spreading fanlike across the rest of his features the wrinkles that came from a lot of years of squint-ing into the wind. He was wearing bright-yellow woolen mittens, and corduroy pants stuffed inelegantly into worn mountaineer-ing boots, a bit odd since the closest facsimile of a mountain was four hundred miles away.

"Afternoon," he said, coming around to the driver's side of the car. I rolled down my window. "Are you lost?" It came out "losht" from lack of teeth.

"That depends," I said. "I'm looking for the Amber cabin."

"Oh, yeah. You keep going up this road about half a mile, you'll see a stone house, 'bout half again as big as this one. That'd be her. Ain't nobody there now, though."

"Have you seen Mr. Amber recently?"

"Lordy, no, not for a couple months. He don't come here much in the bad weather; not much point in it. No one comes around here in the winter." He said that last wistfully.

"Mind if I drive up and have a look around?"

"Don't matter to me, I ain't the caretaker. But you stop by here on your way out. I'll brew y'a cup of coffee for the road. I don't get many visitors."

"That sounds good," I said. I put the car in gear and bumped and jostled over the road in the direction he'd pointed. I passed another wooden cabin on the way and finally reached the Am-ber place. It was more like two miles than half a mile, but why quibble with the old-timer?

It was a pretty cottage, faced with flagstone over a rich hard-wood frame. I parked and got out, noting there were no footprints in the snow around the cabin. The wind coming up from the wa-ter was growing colder by the minute, and I flipped up the col-lar of my car coat and pulled my tweed cap a little lower around my ears. I walked through the snow to the door and tried it, but, not surprisingly, it was locked. A raffia mat on the doorstep said WELCOME. I went around to the side of the house and looked in the window. There were filmy net curtains across the glass and behind them, opened, were a set of heavier drapes to block out light and cold. There was another window on the other side of the cabin, and the light filtering through the net was enough to let me see what the inside was like.

It was ordinary, filled with inexpensive furniture—sofa, easy chair, queen-size bed with a spread of native American design over it. A colonial-style dinette table with four chairs over in the kitchen area, which had a two-burner gas range, a waist-high refrigerator, and the usual plumbing. All the walls were pine-paneled. A few magazines and paperback books were spread across the dining table and on the small nightstand next to the bed. Off in the corner was a door I assumed led to the bathroom. A small stone fireplace took up most of the back wall.

I went around to the rear of the cabin, where a high, small window provided the bathroom's only ventilation. I tried to open it but it was locked, as was the window on the other side near the kitchen. Peering through that, I could see there were plastic picnic-type dishes in the drainer on the counter, and coffee mugs and silverware. There were also two upside-down wineglasses.

About twenty yards behind the cabin was a thigh-high cinder block wall enclosing a trash dump. I trudged through the ankle-deep snow, the wind cutting through my clothing as if it weren't there. There had been a burning recently, the smell of toasted garbage still strong, and I was able to make out some steak bones and some charred foil trays that once held frozen TV dinners. There seemed to be two of everything. There were also four empty wine bottles, one of which had a still-intact label showing it to be a '79 California Zinfandel, and an Absolut vodka empty. I kicked around in the trash hoping to find I wasn't sure what. Everything paper had been incinerated, and the effluvium of burnt and rotted fruit assaulted my nose.

I took out a cigarette, cupping my hands around the match flame and taking three tries to light it, and walked around to the front of the house again. Then the inspiration hit me. I looked under the welcome mat and came up a winner. A little silver key.

I followed the mat's advice and made myself welcome.

The books on the table were a Stuart Kaminsky mystery, a copy of *Iacocca*, a book on aerobics, a *Cosmopolitan*, and a *Business Week*. There was also a Cleveland newspaper dated two Fridays ago.

I checked the larder. Nothing remarkable—a half-filled jar of instant Yuban, a few cans of baked beans, some sugar substitute in little blue packets, and a collection of those one-helping boxes of dry cereal they used to serve on railroad dining cars. The refrigerator yielded about as much information—a few bottles of Perrier and a six-pack of Diet Pepsi with two cans missing from their plastic rings. I vaguely remembered seeing those cans, empty, in the trash heap. I noticed a plastic salt and pepper set on the table and a neatly folded dish towel.

The bathroom was so tiny I could hardly fit in it. It appeared to have been constructed after the cabin was completed, a rather strange oversight. It contained a stand-up shower stall covered by a blue plastic curtain that had that awful wet-plastic smell to it, a commode, and a small basin. The soap in the dish in the shower was half used up. From the smell and color of it I believe it was Irish Spring, as if anyone would possibly care. A four-pack of toilet paper was on the floor next to the john with one roll gone and one on the holder screwed onto the knotty pine wall. When I total up the boring afternoons I've spent in my life, this one will be in the highlight film.

I went back into the main room and looked around some more but nothing unusual caught my eye. There were ashes in the fireplace, but I couldn't make much out of that. There were supposed to be ashes in a fireplace. One thing did strike me, and that was the odor in the room. It was expensive perfume, too expensive for me to identify the brand. I didn't much hang around women who wore perfume that dear.

I went to the bed and threw back the coverlet, revealing a blue electric blanket and dark blue sheets with blue flowered pillow slips. On the bottom sheet was a dried whitish stain that I scratched with my fingernail. It was familiar. When we were kids and had nocturnal emissions we called those telltale stains on the linen "pecker tracks." It was dried semen. Someone had obviously spent a terrific weekend here on the shores of Lake Wawassee.

I poked around the cabin looking for a scrap of paper or something else that might surrender some information. I knew someone had been here recently, someone with strong, expensive perfume, but I doubted it was Richard Amber's scent that permeated the room and the sheets. I had smelled that scent before. In the Amber house in Pepper Pike. I quietly let myself out, locked the door, and replaced the key under the mat. Then I drove back to the old man's cabin near the main road.

"C'mon in," he said as I got out of my car. "Java's on." I couldn't remember the last time anyone had called coffee "java" and was rather charmed by it. I wiped my feet before entering.

The cabin wasn't as fancy as the Ambers' but it was warm and homey, and the fire was crackling merrily. The furniture was old, well-made and sturdy and strictly for utility, with faded slipcovers that bespoke a woman's taste and sensibility. Over the mantel was a shotgun, oiled and sleek-looking and obviously not there for decoration.

The old man extended a gnarled hand that felt like a goat-skin purse. "Amos Sperry," he said. "Glad to meet you."

"Milan Jacovich."

"Polack?"

"Slovenian."

He frowned. "Where in hell is that?"

"Yugoslavia."

"Oh. Yeah." He'd obviously never heard of Slovenia. "Take off your hat and coat and stay awhile." He went and poured two mugs of coffee. "Want a little something in this to make it interesting?"

"Sure. Why not? But go a bit easy with it—I've got to drive."

He added a dollop of inexpensive bourbon to each mug and handed me one. I sat on the sofa and he at a chair at the dining table.

"So you're a friend of those Ambers."

"Yes," I said, not wanting to go into it. "I was hoping Mr. Amber would be here."

"Nope. He don't come around much in the cold weather. Matter of fact, he don't come much at all. I only seen him once last summer. She comes around more than he does—the missus." His blue eyes twinkled as he first inhaled the aroma of the doctored coffee, then drank some.

"When was the last time she came around?"

"Must of been—well, last weekend, I think, or the weekend before. She was here three days."

"Alone ?"

He looked at me. "You're police, ain't you?"

I took a sip of my coffee. The bourbon was young and strong and cut right through the coffee taste. "This is good," I said. "I used to be with the police. Not anymore."

"I could tell," he chortled, delighted with himself for guessing right. "Big man like you."

"Lots of big men aren't cops."

"Maybe so, but you just got that look on you. Is Amber in some kind of trouble?"

"I don't think so," I said. "I just want to talk to him." Sperry bobbed his head like a feeding bird. "Well, he ain't been around here."

"When Mrs. Amber was here the last time—was she alone?"

He suddenly looked worried. "Look here now, Milan. I'm not much for tales out of school. I mind my business. Living up here that's just about all I got to do."

"I promise what you tell me will be confidential."

"Well," he said. "Well, then." He got up and wandered to the window and looked out at the twilight gathering in the woods. "Wouldn't make much sense for a pretty woman like that to come to a cabin in the woods for three days or so by herself, would it?"

"No, it wouldn't."

"Well, then." He leaned his left hand against the wall and drank from the mug in his right hand. "No, she had some fancy guy with her, looked to me like some pimp."

"You didn't happen to get his name, did you?"

"Shoot," he said with a guttural chuckle, "she didn't bring him around to introduce me. She's pretty standoffish at the best of times. The mister, he always been friendly and polite to me, but I don't think she's said squat to me since I know her. Thinks she's better'n everyone on account of being rich and all. Never had much use for people like that. A man's who he is with two dollars in his pocket or two thousand, is the way I figure it."

"You're right, there."

"Damn tootin' I am. Damn society woman, cattin' around with other men like some whore in a tavern, and she don't have the common decency to even say hello."

"Well, some people are like that," I said.

"I know it. I run into that kind all of my life. Used to be the handyman over to the hotel before it shut down, and I met a lot of them rich people. Some of 'em was real folks, but most of them weren't worth the powder it'd take to blow 'em to hell."

"Now, this man Mrs. Amber was up here with—?"

"Yeah. She's been up here with a few different ones over the years. This one been here three or four times in the last six months with her. Fancy man, looks like that movie actor Cesar Romero. When he was younger, o'course, much younger. They come up here on a Friday afternoon with a load of grosheries and they hardly come out of the cabin for three days. I leave it to your imaginings what they was doin'."

"Did Mr. Amber ever come up here with another woman?"

He scratched his chin, and the stubble made the sound of one of those guiros in a bossa nova band. "Long time ago," he said, "and only once. Maybe two years ago, or thereabouts."

I nodded. The heat from the fireplace felt wonderful. I took another pull from the mug.

"I don't suppose," Amos Sperry said, "that you'd like to clue me in on what's going on here?"

"I can't."

"Figured as much. Ah, well. Where you from, Milan? Cleveland, like the Ambers? God, I ain't been there in years. Didn't used to be much of a city."

"It wasn't," I said, "but it's changed a lot. It's a good place to live."

"Nah, too many bodies. Cities are full of people that are either dirt-poor or dirt-rich, with nobody in between. That's why I like it out here. Country people don't take no notice of what kind of car you drive or the fancy labels on your clothes. And they don't take no welfare, neither. They make their own way. You oughta get out of that city, Milan. You a married man?"

"Not anymore."

"Well, then." He took down a pipe from the mantel and began stuffing it with long-leaf tobacco. The pipe looked as if it were fifty years old.

"You have a telephone here, Mr. Sperry?"

"Amos," he corrected. "Got nobody to call. But they's one at the package goods store if I really need it."

I handed him my card. "If Mr. Amber shows up here within the next few days I wish you'd call me. Collect."

He looked at the card for a moment. "You're a private cop now? That don't sound like it'd be much fun."

"Sometimes it's not," I said, "and sometimes I get to meet nice folks like you."

He beamed. "I'd like it if you stuck around here for dinner. Got me a couple of nice ducks in the freezer—could thaw 'em out in a jiffy."

"I'd like that, too, Amos, but I'm afraid I have to get back. I do thank you for the invitation, though. And the information."

"Shoot," he said. "I guess I'm just a gossipy old fart. But it was nice talkin' to someone who's not a damn dummy. You ever go duck hunting, Milan? You like to shoot?"

"Sometimes."

"Well, then. Anytime you get the urge, you come on over here. Stay a few days, you can bunk on the couch. Duck season's a few months off, but you come on over. I'm a pretty good cook—have to be, living alone like this. We'll have us a nice couple days."

"I think that would be nice, Amos."

"I know it. And in the meanwhile, if Mr. Amber shows up here I'll drive down the road and call you."

"Great." I stood and shook his callused hand again. "I enjoyed meeting you."

"Same here, Milan. You drive careful now."

I did. I got back to Cleveland at about ten o'clock. There was a light snow falling, melting as soon as it hit the street. I was down and depressed. It had been a long drive, and I felt as though I'd wasted the day. The only thing I'd found out was that Judith Amber was sleeping with a guy who looked like Cesar Romero, and that didn't seem very important in locating her husband. I also felt I was doing my job badly. And I wasn't used to that.

CHAPTER TWELVE

The day dawned unseasonably warm, the thermometer flirting with the fifty-degree mark and the sun making a weak, pale effort to shine through the overcast. The light hardly penetrated into my parlor as I sat and shuffled some more cards around on my desk. It was as if I were attempting to play out a game of Patience suddenly gone awry.

Richard Amber had called his current inamorata, Karen Wilde, at shortly before eight o'clock on Wednesday evening, a time that was particularly inappropriate to her since she was moments from going onstage, and asked for her hand in marriage, which must mean that he was suddenly and unexpectedly considering divorce from the woman whose money and influence had placed him in his present high position and were keeping him there. At nine o'clock he'd called me to act as a bodyguard and suggested I bring my gun. By ten o'clock he had disappeared, his car still safely garaged, and hadn't been heard from since by anyone who knew him. His career situation was shaky, but there was a job promise of sorts from his wife's uncle, Walter Deming, one that certainly would be withdrawn were he to obtain that divorce. He was indebted to Giancarlo D'Allessandro to the tune of forty-five G's, and D'Allessandro wanted me to find him, which either meant that D'Allessandro truly didn't know where he was or that he did and was using me as a cover. That second possibility was unlikely. Men like D'Allessandro and Gaimari may have been many disagreeable things in many ways, but they were rarely devious. If they had done violence to Amber, it would have been in a dramatic and public way as an object lesson to anyone else foolish enough to try leaving the Firenze Social Club holding a large, empty bag.

In the meantime, Amber's wife, though anxious enough for his return to hire me, was carrying on a torrid affair in town and at their summer cabin with a Cesar Romero look-alike. His employers, Marbury and Stendall, were sweating bullets because the loss of Amber meant the loss of their largest account, but that account seemed to be in jeopardy in any event. Amber's girlfriend had no intention of marrying him, his already married secretary was pining away with unrequited passion, the two men he'd brought with him from his own agency figured their jobs depended upon his, and his former girlfriend, who I was hoping would be my future one, hadn't seen him for months. Someone had trashed his den looking for something, someone wanted him to stay missing badly enough to make an attempt on my life, and my Auntie Branka thought he was dead.

I'd found no edge to frame the puzzle yet, and I couldn't see any that had accidentally fallen out of the box.

Unless the burglar hadn't found what he was looking for and I could find it instead.

I called Judith Amber as soon as it got to be a decent hour, like 8:30 A.M. It apparently was not decent enough as she sounded fuzzy and cranky with interrupted sleep.

"Are you going to be home today, Mrs. Amber?"

"No," she said, "I was going out at about ten-thirty for the whole day. Why?"

"I'd like to come over and search your house."

"What on earth for?"

I explained it to her.

"I'm not happy about that at all," she said. "I don't like the idea of strangers poking around in my private things."

"I'm not a pervert, Mrs. Amber. But if you like, *you* can search your lingerie drawer and tell me if you find anything of interest in it."

She didn't speak.

"Look, I'm sure whoever broke in Friday night was looking for something specific. There's no way of telling whether or not they found it, but if it's still there maybe I can locate it, and if I do it might give us a clue as to why your husband is gone. I can't believe the two incidents are unrelated."

"All right." She said it grudgingly. Unhappily. Meanly. "Get here by ten-thirty and I'll let you in. How long will you be?"

"I don't know. As long as it takes. I promise I'll be more careful than your other visitor."

"You'd better be," she said darkly.

She wasn't in a much better mood when I arrived there at ten-fifteen, although she looked great in a pastel pink pantsuit with an almost-white pink scarf around her neck. "Please try to put everything back where you found it," she said as if talking to the exterminator.

"Yes, ma'am. Anything to report regarding your underwear?"

"I don't find you the least humorous, Mr. Jacovich."

"I'm glad, because I wasn't trying to be."

"That's good," she said.

"Fine," I said.

"Fine with me," she said.

And then we both started to laugh. Her laughter turned into a half-groan as she pushed her soft blonde hair back from her forehead. "Aaah, God, but this is awkward! My husband missing, some nut breaking into my home, and a private detective looking through my panties."

"Why don't you just relax, Mrs. Amber? I'm not going to steal the family silver or do anything furtive and obscene with your underpants. I'm trying to help you."

"I know," she said. "And I suppose my thousand dollars has run out."

"Just about."

She wrote me another check, this time for two thousand. "Let me know when you use this up."

"Do you want a written report from me? I'll be glad to put everything that I've done in writing."

She shook her head. "I'd rather you spend your time doing

what you do best. Interrogating suspects is what you do best, isn't it?"

Funny thing about that. Most private investigators are not good interrogators because they lack the powers of persuasion the police have built in. A private ticket can't threaten to run you downtown or have the fire inspector come out and condemn your wiring; he can't thunder at you with the majesty of the law, invoking the U.S. Constitution, the Pledge of Allegiance, or various numbered articles from the city and state penal codes. He can't even force you to talk to him at all. So a private detective usually has to kill a witness with kindness, use psychology and depend on flattery and cajolery, appeal to the subject's better side or baser side, whichever applied. I was a good interrogator because that particular art is given many hours of training time at the police academy, and, as opposed to the classes in marching and close-order drill and shining your shoes and belt buckle, I had paid attention. I'd never had anyone flatly refuse to talk to me, either in or out of uniform, and I don't think it's because of my size. I seem to have the knack of getting people to open up and commit themselves.

I decided to try it now. "Mrs. Amber, had you and your husband recently discussed the possibility of divorce?"

The blue eyes almost disappeared behind hooded lids, and her teeth showed a bit too much when she answered, giving her the appearance of a beautiful but deadly cobra. "Every couple talks about divorce from time to time. It's one of the constants of most marriages."

"Recently? Within a week before he disappeared?"

"I told you, ours was a marriage of convenience. Neither of us were terribly anxious to get out of it because we were perfectly content and had total freedom functioning within it."

"You're still not answering my question."

"That's funny, I thought I had. No, we have not talked of divorce for several months. Anything else?"

"Yes. Do you have a safe deposit box?"

"Two of them."

"In both your name and your husband's?"

"That's right."

"Will you do something for me? Will you go and look in both of them today?"

She glanced at her watch as if going to two banks would seriously disrupt her busy schedule. "If you say so," she said. "What am I supposed to be looking for?"

"Anything you didn't know was in there. Anything your husband might have put in without your knowledge."

"Can you give me a hint?"

"If I could I'd know a lot more than I do now."

"Very well," she said. Not too many people can say "Very well" and not sound like the queen of England. Judith almost pulled it off. She went to the hall closet and shrugged herself effortlessly into a raccoon coat that must have cost eight thousand dollars, then took her car keys from the table near the front door. "Oh, Mr. Jacovich, if the phone should ring while you're here—don't pick it up. The machine will get it."

And, in a flurry of pink and raccoon fur and blonde hair, she was out the door into the halfhearted sunshine. I sat down on the living room sofa for a moment and thought about her exit line. She was quite the lady for preserving her privacy, and that made me curious. She'd already admitted her extramarital involvement, so her not wanting me to answer the phone could only mean it was somehow important for her not to reveal *who* her boyfriend was, which led me to the inescapable conclusion that it was someone I knew, or at least knew about. Jerry Stendall's name popped into my head simply because I knew of the bad blood between him and Amber. Perhaps Judith was the reason.

Then again, Jerry Stendall, with his bald spot and his nerve tics, was nobody's idea of Cesar Romero.

I elected not to look in Amber's den, at least not until later. Whoever had broken in Friday had done a good job of tossing in there. I wondered if the burglar had known what to look for. It would have made things a hell of a lot easier for me if I was searching for a checkbook or an address book or an insurance policy or an elephant. As it was, I'd have to poke into every nook and cranny of this large house and see what I could see.

I began with the kitchen, opening every cupboard and cabinet, moving pots and pans around and shuffling canned goods and cereal boxes and packages of rice and croutons, even looking in the coffee tin, the flour canister, the large economy-size box of Tide. It was times like these when I missed the support the police force offered, the team of experts and forensics guys who would come in and do this part of the job. I did discover a veritable treasure trove of vitamin bottles on one shelf of the kitchen, everything from kelp to garlic tablets, which I suppose helped to prevent sea monsters and vampires. One of the Ambers was a health nut, and I had the feeling it was Richard. She looked too pale and drawn to take that good care of her health. Self-indulgence in her case probably took the form of weekly facials and pedicures and hot oil packs for her wispy blonde hair.

I looked in the refrigerator. People often hide valuables in there because of the incongruity, not knowing it's one of the first places a burglar will look. I didn't have much luck, though; there were no emeralds frozen into the ice cube trays because the Ambers had an automatic icemaker, and the milk cartons and mayonnaise jars held what they were supposed to. I looked in the vegetable crisper and the butter safe, but the only thing I deduced was that the Ambers didn't eat in very often. Their refrigerator's contents belonged in a swinging bachelor pad.

Next I tried the garage, even searching around inside Amber's Cadillac. There were shelves against the wall, holding paint cans and lawn food and semirusted garden tools, but there was a thin layer of dust over everything that told me nothing had been moved in here for a long time. It was just as well. Garages are mostly cold, impersonal places, repositories for the detritus of lives, the old carton the waffle iron came in, the black-and-white TV that no longer worked, the out-of-date newspapers and books and fifteen-year-old clothing you'll never wear again but haven't the heart to throw away. There is a melancholia in all that junk, as if the passing of time, quick enough as it is, is marked only by a child's discarded Hot Wheels or a cardigan sweater with a hole at the elbow.

There was little of that sort of thing in the Ambers' garage. Mostly it was a stark, gloomy enclosure that smelled of dust and motor oil and the long-ago droppings of a mouse who'd wandered too far east from University Heights.

The living room was next, and there were damned few places to look. I moved all the cushions from the furniture, looked in and under all the drawers, even took down the prints from the walls and checked their frames and backings, even though the burglar had done all that before. I'm not much into psychics and astrologers and people who read the bumps on your head, but I do get feelings sometimes, and what I felt about this room is that I had spent more time in it on my three trips to this house than anyone else had in years. It was a showpiece, all color-coordinated and pristine, just as Judith Amber herself was a showpiece. Both were used rarely and only on special occasions. The room contained no vibrations, no echoes, almost as though it had no past.

I went through the den to the outside. The sun was still out, sort of, and the snow wasn't quite melting yet, but it was thinking about it. I smoked a cigarette out there, and it tasted hotter in the cool air than it would have inside. I decided halfway through that I didn't want to finish it, but I looked around and couldn't find a receptacle, so I field-stripped it. Besides learning to shoot straight, field-stripping a cigarette was the most useful thing I'd picked up in the army. Oh, I knew how to frag villages and look for land mines, but there was little call for those skills in modern Cleveland. The sniper out at the Gun on Saturday had been the first such attack on my person in many years, and all my military training hadn't helped me much. It was instinct that had put me face down in the slush, pure survival instinct.

I went back into the den and slid the door shut. The broken glass had been repaired, and it looked like the lock had been changed. I worried about Fair Judith here by herself, but she had told me there was no cause for alarm, and it wasn't my job to worry anyway.

A kind of rumpus room lay off the den, containing a drafting table, a student desk, a day bed, a personal computer, and a stack of old magazines and reference books. It lacked the austerity of Amber's more formal den, but I thought if I wanted to write, create, or even think about things quietly I would prefer this room to the wood-paneled stiffness of the other. The room hadn't been "decorated"; it just was. Obviously Judith had put little into the makeup of this room. I went through the magazines, dictionaries, the thesaurus, shaking them to see if any-thing interesting fell out, but the only thing I netted was a subscription card to *Time* that offered a free 35-mm camera with each twenty-seven-week commitment. I turned down the coverlet on the day bed, but nothing so interesting as the sheets in the cabin was revealed to me. I even looked in the pillow slips. I went through the closet, finding nothing unusual but a *Playboy* from 1981, and I wondered why Amber had kept this particular issue. I thumbed through it, more than half expecting to see Karen Wilde or Mary Soderberg in the centerfold, but Miss October was a pneumatic brunette named Cindy who liked men who didn't play games, linguini with clam sauce, walking on the beach, and John Travolta, and whose favorite books were *Valley of the Dolls* and *Nine Coaches Waiting*. What do you suppose Cindy is doing these days, pushing thirty and frantically smearing Moondrops on every little laugh line?

I headed up the stairs, noticing one of them creaked. Maybe it was just my weight—I couldn't imagine either Amber making noise on the staircase. On the second-floor landing I stood still to get my bearings. There seemed to be three bedrooms up there, and a guest bath, a linen closet, and another storage closet that contained a vertical ladder leading to the attic. I decided to try the master suite first.

It was a big room, almost as large as my whole apartment. The bed was king-sized, the dressers as well, all done in tasteful blond wood, and there was a mirror that must have stretched six feet across and four feet high, making it impossible to go anywhere in the room without seeing your own reflection. The sliding doors of the closets were also mirrored, and off the bedroom was a dressing room large enough to accommodate six guests for a sit-down dinner. All the closets and the clothes racks in the dressing room were full of Judith Amber's finery—dresses, suits, blouses, sweaters, coats, jackets, sportswear, evening gowns, cocktail dresses, jodhpurs, skirts, designer jeans with someone else's name stitched on the ass—raiment for every occasion. There was no sign of a man living anywhere near this room. None of Amber's effects were in sight.

I very quickly fumbled through the hanging clothing, feeling in the pockets in case Amber had tried to hide something he wanted his wife to find. Then I went through the drawers, including Judith's lingerie drawer. There was nothing there to interest me—I'm rather indifferent to ladies' underwear unless the lady happens to be in it. I also looked in her jewelry box, which contained only inexpensive costume pieces. I figured that sometime this morning she'd be pawing through the real stuff in one or both of her safe deposit boxes. Smart people don't leave expensive jewelry on top of their dresser as an invitation to burglars; I imagined Judith Amber had been wealthy long enough to know that. There were no cute little secret compartments in the jewelry box either; as a matter of fact, it was a cheap one, the kind you get at discount import stores or Chinese curio shops.

After I determined that there was nothing else worth looking at in the master bedroom I moved down the hall to another room. It was a guest room, about half the size of the master suite, although plenty big enough for the king-sized bed and dresser, a rocking chair, and one of those multishelved entertainment systems that held a TV, a stereo, and a VCR. In checking the spacious closets I finally discovered where Richard Amber kept his clothes. In the dresser were his socks, underwear, handkerchiefs, and some rather expensive camera equipment. Interesting. The Ambers had separate bedrooms. I wondered if either of them ever made the long walk down the hallway to the other's bed, or if this were truly a marriage in name only.

In the nightstand I found a couple of paperbacks of the pornographic variety, well-thumbed. Poor Richard Amber, lying alone in the guest room reading dirty books while his ice princess wife lay on the other side of the wall. She might have been a thousand miles away. Which came first, Richard's infidelities or his wife's? And did it matter? People who play, play. They don't always need a reason. Again I felt along the underside of the drawers to see if anything might be hidden there, but got only several fingertips full of dust for my troubles.

I sighed, frustrated, and pulled the curtains aside to glance out the window. At least looking at the rare February sunshine might cheer me up, I figured. And through the window I saw something that, while it didn't exactly make me cheery, certainly got my attention. Parked about 150 yards down the street, on the opposite side, was a dark-colored four-door Olds 98 that I recognized. There was someone sitting in the driver's seat. I couldn't see him from that distance, but I had a pretty good idea who it was.

I went downstairs and let myself out through the den door. I was fortunate that very few homes in Cleveland are protected by fences—they're a lot more friendly in Ohio than, say, in California—and that I was able to make my way behind the four houses just to the north of the Ambers'. Pepper Pike was, indeed, a high-rent district. Two of the places were even grander than the one I'd just left, and had large outdoor swimming pools, drained for the winter. Apparently no one was home in any of the four, because two of them had dogs, fortunately locked inside, and they set up quite a ruckus. When I got where I wanted to go my pants legs were soaked from the soft, wet snow, my shoes squished when I walked, and I had left a set of footprints from the Ambers' house across four other backyards that even Stevie Wonder could follow.

When I got to the north side of the fourth house I circled around, padding down a utility sidewalk that ran along the side of the house to the front. I peeked out. I had gauged it right—I was now about twenty yards past the Olds 98. I crossed the street very slowly and started up behind the car, hoping the driver wasn't looking in his rear-view mirror. But then why would he be—he was supposed to be watching the front of the Amber house, where my station wagon was parked in full view.

I got up almost even with the car and saw that the driver was my old friend Sunglasses. He was still wearing the shades, and had the window open and his elbow out, eager as the rest of us for the first warm day in several months. It would cost him. I jerked open the car door with my left hand and he almost fell out, but I caught him, dragged him off the seat, and slammed him down on the street. He reached toward his belt but I kicked his hand away and then stood on it while he squirmed. I leaned down and removed what he'd been looking for, his .38 automatic, which I had seen, and felt, before. I slung it across the street, and when he tried to sit up I backhanded him hard across the face, and if it hurt my knuckles as badly as it did, I can imagine what it did to his mouth. His lip, already puffed and cut from when I'd hit him on Sunday, started to bleed again.

"I thought I told you to stay out of my face," I said.

"What the fuck you think you're—"

I slapped him again, this time forehanded. It stung him more but probably didn't do as much damage, although he did put his head down on the street and think better of trying to get back up. The impact knocked his sunglasses off, and he squinted against the light. He had little piggy hazel eyes, set too close together. If my eyes looked like that I'd wear sunglasses, too. I was standing on his right hand with my left foot and now I knelt on his chest, not gently, with my right knee too near his throat for him to get feisty.

"What are you following me for?" I said.

He choked out, "I'm not following you."

"You always come out to Pepper Pike to take your coffee breaks, right?"

He didn't answer. I thought about hitting him again until he did, but it wasn't my style. I also realized we were rolling around the middle of the street in a fashionable neighborhood on a sunny afternoon, and very likely to be seen. I hauled him onto his feet and slung him into the backseat of the car like a pile of clothes for the dry cleaners, and then followed him in while he was still off balance and twisted his arm up behind his back.

"Talk to me, sweetness."

"I got nothin' to say to you," he said. I did give his arm a little twist—I'm not as saintly as all that. He squealed; he wasn't very tough without his gun and his glasses.

"Try again," I said.

"I didn't even know you was here!"

"Then what's the deal?"

"No deal."

Another twist, another yelp. That's the way it was going to go until I heard what I wanted to hear. I told him so. "You're gonna be able to scratch your ankle without bending your knees."

"Hey, ease up, pal. I'm tellin' you this's got nothing to do with you."

"What's it got to do with, then?"

"I'm just doin' a favor."

"For who?" I said. He started to thrash around, and I was having trouble hanging onto him. He was pretty strong for a punk, and he seemed to draw a lot of his strength from the obscenities he was snarling under his breath. We wrestled around a bit and he finally managed to roll over on his back, though his arm and mine were pinned underneath him. He tried to knee me in the groin, missed, but managed to really bruise my thigh, and I hit him in the jaw to make him stop. He did it again. I did it again, a bit too hard. He went out, blood running from his mouth. He had bitten his tongue.

I sat up, pulling my arm out from under him, and pried his mouth open to see how badly he'd injured himself. It wasn't much worse than when you bite your tongue while trying to eat a tough steak, just a little ragged edge, and it wasn't bleeding much so there was no danger of him choking on his own blood. I rolled him over on his stomach with his head turned to the side, just to be sure.

I backed out of the car, tucked his feet in carefully, and closed both doors. Then I looked around. Our little rough-and-tumble had apparently gone unobserved here on a busy street in Pepper Pike, but I figured I'd better not stick around to make sure. I went and picked his gun up from where it had landed on somebody's front lawn, then went back to the Amber house, through the den door, which I locked behind me, and scrawled a note to Mrs. Amber on the back of a business card. I left it by the front door on the table.

I was beginning to see a vague pattern forming; nothing I could really put my finger on, and nothing that had one of those straight edges I'd been looking for, but somewhere in an obscure corner of the picture I thought I saw some pieces falling together. I drove down to City Hall—it took me about forty-five minutes.

"Mr. Jacovich," said the lady behind the counter in the Records Room. "Haven't seen you for a while—how've you been?"

"Just fine, Renee," I said. "How's that grandson of yours?"

"Growing like a weed," she said. "Wait." She went to her desk, got her wallet from her purse, and brought it to me open, displaying a picture of a fat one-year-old with black hair like Moe of the Three Stooges. Could have been worse—he could've had hair like Larry. I made all the admiring noises I was supposed to and then got to work.

Renee and I knew each other so well because in the course of my work I spent a lot of hours in the Records Room. It's no trick to be a private investigator most of the time. Public records are open to anyone—just drop in to the right place in City Hall and read all about it. Everyone is on record somewhere. They don't have to be a known criminal or a registered sex offender. They just have to have been born, gotten married, taken out a driver's license or bought a car, owned a house or applied for a civil service job. It's one of the less glamorous parts of my profession, but one that many uniformed cops ignore, and this time it proved valuable to me.

I looked up North Coast Developers, the real estate company in which Judith Amber had twenty percent of the stock. According to the records North Coast Developers, a Cleveland-based company that also did business in Lake and Geauga counties, was a subsidiary of the Boot Corporation, which was listed as an investment banking concern. North Coast Limited was wholly owned by a company called Clearing House Partners, a firm that specialized in finding or supplying venture capital for the building and real estate trades. And when I looked up Clearing House Partners, I found there were two of them. The majority share, fifty-five percent, was owned by one Giancarlo D'Allessandro of University Heights. Apparently the shape of Italy had given the Boot Corporation its name. The minority share was in the name of Victor Anthony Gaimari. And Victor Gaimari not only was the man who gave Sunglasses his orders—but there was no denying, if you stretched it a bit, a certain resemblance to Cesar Romero.

CHAPTER THIRTEEN

A law was made a distant moon ago here in Cleveland that within the city limits no building could be constructed that exceeded the height of the Terminal Tower, a former railroad terminal built practically on the bank of the Cuyahoga that was destined to dominate the skyline of the city in perpetuity, as secure in its preeminence as Mount Everest. The powers-that-be, having ensured an icon that would forever say "Cleveland" to the world, now saw fit to bathe their pet skyscraper in floodlights from dusk till dawn, a beacon to anyone on the North Coast who might have too much to drink of an evening but is thus assured of at least being able to find downtown no matter where he is. So the lighting of Terminal Tower is more than a civic ego trip, it is a public service.

According to the card Victor Gaimari had given me, his offices were on the eleventh floor, high enough to escape most of the traffic noises down on Superior Avenue but not quite lofty enough to take advantage of the more spectacular views that denizens of the upper stories were privy to. A nice, modest-yet classy office for a respectable commodities broker. And the woman at the reception desk fit the image as well: a very pretty gray-eyed brunette in her very late thirties who looked as though she probably juggled her job with the raising of two nice apple-pie teenaged kids and being supportive of her husband, a member of some local realtor's Two-

Million-Dollar-a-Year Club. She seemed ever so happy to see me and buzzed right through to Mr. Gaimari, who said he'd see me right away. I'd had a feeling he would.

"Milan, you've been a busy boy," Gaimari said when I walked into his office. It wasn't quite as fancy as I'd expected, although the suit Gaimari was wearing would have cost me a week's salary. He stood up and shook my hand, but there wasn't that much warmth in his big brown eyes. "I thought we said you were going to call me every evening. Yesterday I didn't hear from you. And then today I understand you were very rough with one of my people."

"Victor," I said, "you've been a busy boy yourself. Why didn't you tell me you were having an affair with Judith Amber?"

He looked hurt as he sat back down behind his desk, indicating a chair for me. "Milan, your job was to find Richard, wasn't it? Not to poke into other people's—"

"Damm it, Victor, I'm getting pretty sick of people telling me to stay out of their private lives! A man is missing, maybe even dead, and all anyone else can think of is their reputations!"

"That's right," he said, leaning forward, and whatever friendliness he'd affected earlier fell away. "There are plenty of reputations at stake here, and as far as I'm concerned they're all a hell of a lot more important than Richard Amber's."

"Did you kill him? Or have him killed?"

"Don't be an ass! Of course I didn't. Why would I?"

"To clear the way for you and Judith."

He laughed nastily. "Grow up, Milan. The way is as clear for Judith and me as we want it to be. We're together quite enough, thank you, and we have a wonderful time. She's not going to marry me even if she's free."

"Why not?"

"Oh, come now! You and I both know who and what I am, and we both know that Judith and her family have connections that reach clear to Columbus and beyond. She's much better off being married to Richard, especially since he doesn't particularly care what she does or with whom."

"Does he know about you?"

"He knows there's someone. I'm not sure if he knows it's me. I don't think his gambling habits have anything to do with Judith, though. He bets with a gentleman in Shaker Heights who decided he couldn't handle that kind of action and laid it off on us, as per our business arrangement. And I've never been so mad at someone that I'd want to have him . . . taken care of when it would cost me forty-five thousand dollars. You're not even warm on this one, Milan."

I chewed on the calloused skin on the side of my thumbnail. I didn't have a pencil eraser handy.

Gaimari said, "How did you find out about me and Judith?"

"That was easy. She as much as admitted to me she was seeing someone, but was almost paranoid about not letting me know who. From the beginning she's been adamant about not involving the police in this business, even after her place was burgled. She told me she'd arranged to have the house guarded, and then I see your punk parked across the street this afternoon. It all fell together, especially since someone saw you and gave me your description."

His dark eyebrows came together in a frown. "Who?"

"I doubt if you could get me to tell you that under any circumstances," I said.

"Don't be too sure of that, Milan."

"Count on it, Victor. Especially if that punk with the sunglasses is the best muscle you've got."

"Oh, I think we might surprise you," he said. "But it isn't important. What's important now is finding Richard and getting this whole thing cleared up."

"You can help me in that by keeping your goons caged."

"You were pretty rough on Joey."

"I didn't even start."

"You know, Milan, I thought you were a smart man, but you aren't acting like one. I shouldn't have to spell things out for you."

"Go ahead, Vic old pal, spell them out."

"We asked for your cooperation in finding Richard Amber. We usually don't like asking twice. And we don't like our people getting hurt."

"Your people better stay out of my way."

"Damn you, you don't tell me!" He slammed the flat of his hand on the desk. "You do as you're told."

"Vic, you have the wrong guy here. Nobody talks that way to me." I stood up and started for the door.

"Get wise, Jacovich. We know you're a family man—"

Whatever he was going to say died aborning. I turned back to him quickly, reached across his desk, dragged him out of his chair over the desktop, and slammed him against the wall. When he bounced off I hit him in the nose. His head snapped back, and he went down like a dead bird. He lay there on the floor looking up at me, blood pouring out of his nose and soaking his dark mustache. He didn't look frightened, he hadn't lost full consciousness. He was just stunned; no one had ever used him this badly in his life. Well, it was about time.

"You just said the secret word, Victor. If anyone even looks cockeyed at my family, your wake is going to be standing room only."

I stormed out the door, past the nice-lady secretary who had evidently heard the banging and crashing and was wide-eyed and frightened like a rabbit caught in the headlights of an onrushing car. It was entirely possible that she really believed Victor Gaimari was only a stockbroker, and I'm afraid I might have shaken her up a bit.

I was shaken, too. I've been threatened before. It comes with the job, along with the fast food and coffee from cardboard cups that you can taste for hours afterward, the late nights and early mornings, the long and boring stakeouts and tails, the afternoons spent bent over dusty ledger books in the Hall of Records, the punks and the chiselers and the small-time crooks and the big-time con artists, the ribbon clerks and the robber barons. But when someone threatens my family I become a different animal altogether, one with stripes and teeth and claws. I think Gaimari knew it. He'd get his revenge somehow—it was a matter of honor, and I suppose I knew that even before I hit him—but he'd leave my family alone. I'd see to it.

I drove back out to Pepper Pike. The Olds 98 was gone, but there were lights on in the house. I parked in the driveway and rang the doorbell.

Judith Amber was wearing the outfit she'd left the house in several hours before. She had a drink in her hand. "I didn't expect to see you," she said. "Working late, aren't you?"

"Could we stow the small talk, Mrs. Amber?" I pushed by her into the house and stood in the living room. I was still hyperventilating, and she looked a little frightened as she shut the door behind her and followed me.

"It's the cocktail hour," she said, holding her drink up to show me. "Join me?"

"This isn't a social visit," I said. "I just saw Victor Gaimari."

The glass in her hand began to shake and the ice cubes played "Sleigh Ride" until she put the drink down on an end table. No coaster, either—that was going to leave a nasty ring on the expensive wood, which gave me a certain satisfaction I wasn't proud of.

"I'm through playing games with you," I said. "I don't give a damn who you're sleeping with. I'm not a priest. But I wonder if you're aware that your husband is in to your boyfriend for forty-five thousand dollars and counting?"

"What?" Either she was the one that belonged onstage at the Playhouse or she truly hadn't known.

"He had two of his trained oxen pick me up Sunday and drag me into Little Italy to tell me that when I found your husband I'd better tell him first."

"Why . . . didn't you tell me?"

"You hired me to find your husband, not to give you a running diary of how I spend my day. I put it together when I found the punk watching your house this afternoon, but I did some checking just to make sure. I know all about North Coast Developers, Mrs. Amber, and I'm here to ask you to fill in the chinks for me."

"I don't know what—"

"Bullshit!" I said. "Here we have a lady from one of the richest families in Ohio, whose husband is in a sensitive job where he gets to hobnob with governors, and not only is she literally in bed with the number two man in the state's biggest organized-crime family, but she's in business with him as well. Now I think you'd better explain that."

"How do you explain being attracted to someone—"

"I told you I don't care about that. Tell me about North Coast."

"It's just a good investment."

"So is General Motors, lady. Come on, you'll have to do better than that."

She looked at me for a long while, then picked up her drink and finished it. "I really need another one of these," she said, "and I don't want to drink it alone. Please have one with me."

"All right." I didn't even know what she was drinking.

She left the room for a moment and then came back with two identical drinks in old-fashioned glasses. When I tasted mine it seemed to be vodka on the rocks with a twist of lime. When Judith Amber drank she didn't fool around. She sat down in her thronelike chair, I sank into the overstuffed sofa, and we looked at each other for a long moment. I raised one eyebrow. I didn't want to browbeat this lady—she was obviously in all sorts of pain and confusion. But I wasn't going to leave until I knew what was going on. I was tired of stumbling around in the dark; it was like trying to pitch a baseball game while wearing a paper bag over your head.

"I've made no secret of the fact that my marriage is—how can I delicately put this—an unusual one, Mr. Jacovich. It didn't start out that way."

"It never does."

She smiled sadly. "No. All the love, honor, and cherish business—people usually really mean that. At the time. We both did.

There were people who said that Richard married me for my money, but I never believed that. I never wanted to."

"For the record, Mrs. Amber, you're an extremely beautiful woman, and I'm sure men would line up around the block to marry you."

"You're very gallant. Anyway, we got married. Richard was a struggling ad exec with a small agency downtown, making about thirty-five thousand a year and lucky to be getting it. He was good at what he did, but the agency was just too insignificant to attract any important clients. I talked to my uncle about it, but he flatly refused to move his account from Chapman and Winslow, where he'd been doing business for years. Well, in my family we have a tradition of helping your own—so I decided to put up the money to allow Richard to open his own agency."

I remembered Walter Deming telling me that he always took care of his family.

"I set things up so that Richard could hire a whole staff of creative and media people to service the Deming Steel account and nothing else for a whole year. After that, if they proved to my uncle they could handle his business, they could expand, go after new accounts."

"Now, is this the period when Richard hired Charlie Dodge and Jeff Monaghan and Rhoda Young?"

"Yes," she said. "Charlie and Jeff were the first two he'd thought of—Jeff for his youth and talent, Charlie for his knowledge and experience in doing commercials."

"Okay."

"They did very well that first year, and when the time came Amber Advertising expanded, got more clients, started making some real money, began making its presence felt in this state. Then George Kinnick decided to run for governor. I had known George for years—I'd even dated his roommate in law school. So I called him and asked him to let Richard make a presentation to handle his campaign. He did, Richard got the account, George got elected, and the rest is history."

"I don't see the problem so far."

"The problem is that my husband is an extremely proud man, Mr. Jacovich. After a time it really started to get to him that none of this could have happened without my money, my uncle, my contacts. It started to affect our marriage in an adverse way. Richard began drinking a lot. Not what you'd call an alcohol problem, but it seems he always had a drink in his hand, from lunchtime on. We quarreled a lot. Our . . . physical relationship dwindled to practically nothing. He began not coming home evenings, not calling." She took a gulp of her drink to fortify herself. "Finally I found out he was having an affair."

"With whom?" I said.

"It's not important. There have been so many of them since. I believe the first one's name was Joanne, and she was twenty-two years old. Anyway, there it was."

"Did you confront him with it?"

"Of course, several times. There were such ugly scenes at night, one would think we were rehearsing for a very unpleasant play. It did no good."

"Did you think about divorce?"

"Naturally. But as much as Richard hated it that I was responsible for his success, he also knew that without me it would all go away—the agency, the Deming account, the governor's office. And as much as I hated what he was doing, I was not about to open myself up to the scandal of that kind of divorce. The papers would have had a field day, and I would never have been able to show my face in this state again."

I shook my head. "Could it have been that important?"

She smiled without humor. "Mr. Jacovich, you've never been rich and socially prominent. Lucky you! It's like a school of sharks—let one of their own show a sign of weakness, and they'll turn on them and tear them to pieces."

"Sounds like a pretty sorry way to live," I said.

"It is—but some of us have no choice."

"Everyone has choices, Mrs. Amber."

She regarded me coolly. "You're a pretty moralistic son of a bitch sometimes, aren't you?"

I suppose I am, but it didn't take away the sting of her saying it. I said, "I'm sorry. Go ahead."

"Anyway, I do have my pride. I was neglected and rejected, so I did what anyone would do. I got back at Richard in kind."

"You had an affair?"

"You might not understand, because probably in your world one doesn't fool around with a friend's wife or husband. But in our circles bed-hopping is fairly common. Yes, I had an affair—but I soon discovered the man I had chosen was just like Richard—rather languid, uninvolved, almost distant. After that anytime I had an affair it was with someone outside our social circles. A man I met at the health club. A bartender. Even one of the Cleveland Browns—and he wasn't Caucasian, either." She added wryly, "He's since been traded."

"Did your husband know?"

"He knew. Oh, he didn't know any names or faces, but he knew I was seeing other men. It didn't seem to bother him, or stop him from his own extracurricular fun. But on the surface, we were the beautiful Ambers. We attended all the right social functions together, belonged to the right country clubs—we played the game. It was dreary and tiresome and sad, but we played it."

"What happened when Marbury and Stendall bought up his agency?"

"He thought he was going to retire and write books. But I wanted him to keep working, so he took the job with Marbury."

"Why didn't you want him to retire?"

She stared into her drink, watching the ice cubes swirl. "The only hold I had on him was his career. If he gave it up, I'd have nothing. So when John Marbury made him the offer to buy Amber Advertising, I demanded that Richard repay the loan I'd made to him to get Amber Ad started in the first place."

"It was a loan?"

"As I've said, Mr. Jacovich, I don't like relinquishing control—in anything."

"All right. Now tell me about Victor Gaimari."

"I met Victor because I had some money that I wanted to invest in a sheltered area. A mutual friend introduced us. We went to lunch to talk investments, and there was a tremendous physical attraction immediately. I was . . . between entanglements at the time, and Richard had just become involved with his little actress friend, so I thought to myself, Why not? It wasn't until later that I learned who Victor was and who his . . . friends were."

"And yet you stayed? And you even invested in North Coast Developers?"

"That was my grand strategy. You see, Mr. Jacovich, when all is said and done, I love Richard very much. And about a year ago—just about the time he met Karen—I sensed I was going to lose him. Really lose him. I believe he reached a point where the money and the connections didn't matter to him. He just wanted out. So I had to find a way to stop him."

"I don't understand," I said. "What did this have to do with North Coast Developers?"

"If he had made any attempt to leave me—to leave me and to leave Marbury-Stendall and start his own agency again—I'd have made that investment very public."

I nodded, understanding. I wished I didn't. What respectable firm would want to do business with an ad executive whose wife had made major investments in a business owned and operated by the Mafia? Judith was quite a piece of work.

"I don't quite understand, Mrs. Amber. You sound like a very unhappy lady. Why in the hell would you want to keep him from leaving anyway?"

"I know it's hard for anyone to understand, Mr. Jacovich. But Richard is the only man in my life that I have ever truly loved. And now, after all I've gone through to keep him where he didn't want to be, Richard has disappeared anyway, and here I am." She drained her drink like a longshoreman, and I suddenly had the need to do the same.

On my drive home I reflected on the whole institution of marriage and whether it was all worth it. God, the games people play with each other! I'm not sure how people like my parents managed to stay married for thirty-four years. Did they scheme and plot, manipulate one another, lie and cheat and set traps? Back then people got married to stay married, but when they did, were they happy? Or was it something they each accepted as their lot, another hard facet of a hard life? In the old country marriages were arranged, often without the two parties even meeting until the wedding day, and there was no talk of loving and cherishing, no deluding oneself that there was anything meaningful or romantic. It was a fact: people were supposed to get married, work hard, have babies, and die. Maybe it's easier that way, maybe it's better when the love comes later, after you've put in the thirty years. In every marriage I know about the partners are more like combatants, savaging each other at every opportunity until finally there is nothing left but the hard shells of two people who've been emptied, scooped out like the meat in a lobster tail. And Richard and Judith Amber were about the worst examples I could think of, sleeping with other partners, hatching Machiavellian designs, unable to stay in the marriage and unable to let go, bound by ties of money, status, family pressures, habit, and somewhere deep down under all the crap, by love that had all but forgotten how to be. And now he was gone, and she was torn up inside, her feelings ricocheting between wanting him to return so she could throw her arms around him and start over and wanting him to never be heard from again.

I was sick and sad from this whole Richard Amber situation, and frustrated as well. I'd thought when I made the connection between Judith and Victor Gaimari that things would come clear, but it just muddied the waters further. And it had also made me take a hard and unflinching look at what my own marriage had become, and I didn't like that either.

It was eight o'clock or so when I got back home, and I was hoping there would be something diverting on television so I could fall asleep watching it. But I got some extra help falling asleep when I unlocked my door, walked into my apartment, and something that felt like a leather sap hit me behind the ear and put me flat on my face.

The blow hadn't been hard enough to put me out. I guess all

the years of getting hit in the head playing football had toughened me. I rolled over and looked up into the faces of Sunglasses, his buddy from Sunday morning, and another man, a bit older and even bigger than I was. Sunglasses wasn't wearing his shades, and the delight in his eyes was apparent. The big man I'd never seen before leaned down and relieved me of my gun, and then he said, "Jacovich? Mr. Gaimari thinks you need to be taught a lesson."

And so saying, they proceeded to teach me one.

CHAPTER FOURTEEN

Waking up in the morning was my first big mistake. An error in judgment, you might say. When every square inch of the body hurts, as much as mine did, waking up can definitely be called a bad move. When I opened my eyes, the question was whether I really wanted to or whether it wasn't a lot more comfortable just to stay asleep and not have to deal with the pain. I staggered to the bathroom and looked in the mirror, and that was my second mistake. Gaimari's boys had done a job. Both my eyes were swollen almost shut and at the moment were a vivid purplish-pink, promising to be black-and-blue tomorrow. There was another egg on my forehead to go with the one they'd put there Sunday, and angry purple welts blossomed along my jawline to add to my colorful appearance. My lower lip was puffed out bigger than Maurice Chevalier's, and a sharp ache in my right upper canine told me the tooth was a lot looser than it had been yesterday. My ribs pained me when I moved, my stomach muscles cried out for relief, and there was a dull ache in my left kidney. I was a mess, although to their credit, the boys from Little Italy had not broken any bones nor drawn any blood. Maybe those were their orders. When I think of what might have been done to me had it been Giancarlo D'Allessandro's nose I'd punched instead of Victor's, I have to thank whoever watches over me that Gaimari was a modern, educated, civilized man. Anyway, I'd taken my beating and now it was over, the slate was cleaned as far as Gaimari was concerned, and I could go back to my business. As long as I behaved myself.

I gulped down three Advils and boiled some water for tea—I didn't think my stomach could handle coffee on this particular morning. I didn't feel any worse than I had the morning after the big game with Indiana State back in college during which I had been roundly thumped, but I didn't feel any better, either. It was one of the things, I suppose, that comes with the job. Maybe Amos Sperry was right—being a private detective wasn't much fun. But I'm too old to play football anymore, and not pretty enough to be a model—especially this morning. My hands are too big and clumsy for brain surgery, and computers puzzle the hell out of me. No line of endeavor seems to suit me as well as the one I am currently in, and if it means waking up with aches and pains once in a while, or going to sleep with nightmares—well, everything is a trade-off.

I brewed my tea and used it to wash down a couple of slices of toast. I had to smile, or as much as my damaged mouth would allow me to, remembering that my mother had always fixed me tea and toast when I'd been sick as a child. Upset stomach, strep throat, chicken pox, it didn't matter—tea and toast were the ticket back to health. I wondered if they would help heal the effects of a mob-administered beating. The tea felt pretty good going down, and I sensed my strength returning with every sip, but of course it was probably my imagination. Next I'd be gulping down cans of spinach.

By the time I'd showered—steaming hot water for the bruises and then icy cold to wake up the rest of me—I felt almost human again. I struggled into a pair of chinos and a plaid shirt, and while still in my stocking feet I heard the phone ring, and I raced to get it before the machine clicked on and lied to someone that I wasn't home.

"Mr. Jacovich?" a feminine voice said, and it sounded vaguely familiar.

"Yes?"

"Would you hold for Mr. Gaimari?"

"What?" But she had gone, and I was in the limbo of being on hold. They even had some Barry Manilow music to keep me from getting too bored while I waited. After a moment I heard Gaimari's voice.

"Milan, it's Victor," he said. Like we were old buddies. Like we were golfing partners. Like I had him handle my stock deals for me. My dear friend Victor. Who'd sent three goons to my home to administer a beating.

"Are you all right?" he said with what sounded like sincere concern.

"How quaint of you to ask."

"Look, Milan, we both lost our tempers yesterday. I shouldn't have said what I said about your family, and you shouldn't have hit me."

"How about you shouldn't have sent your wrecking crew over here?"

I heard him chuckle. "I'm *really* sorry about that. But if I allow you to come in here and punch me in the nose, pretty soon everybody's going to do it, and then I'm really in difficulty. I can't run an organization like mine unless I have everyone's respect. You understand that, don't you, Milan?"

Respect again. Sometimes I think there is more face-saving in the higher echelons of the mob than in feudal Japan. And now he was calling up to apologize!

"I hope you're okay," Gaimari was saying. "I left very explicit instructions you weren't to be seriously harmed. But you had to be taught a lesson."

"I know," I said. "I got your message."

"Milan, there's no sense in our being enemies. I like you, and Mr. D'Allessandro likes you. I think we can work together."

"Look, Gaimari," I said. "I really appreciate your having me beaten up so gently. And you seem like a very pleasant guy—your concern for my physical well-being this morning touches me more than I can say. But be advised—I don't like your kind, I don't like the things you do or the way you do them. I'm working for Judith Amber, and that's all. Any information you want, you get from her the way you get other things from her."

I heard him suck in a dismayed breath. What I'd said wasn't very gentlemanly. "And if you think you're going to send your boys around to teach me another lesson, better tell them to come shooting, because I intend to take a few of them down with me."

And I slammed the receiver down, a childish thing to do. My whole final speech had been childish, I guess, but I wasn't feeling in the mood to do the whole "with-the-deepest-respect" charade that Gaimari and D'Allessandro and the rest of the vicious clowns in their organization affected, probably to fool themselves into thinking they weren't all punks and hoodlums and scummy blights on the landscape. I also knew my threat was a pointless and hollow one; Gaimari had paid me back for my defiance and my punch in the nose and it was over between us. If I hadn't learned my lesson this time, the next session would be no mild punching around and it would end up in the river.

One thing had come out of all of it, however. I was pretty convinced that whatever the reason for Richard Amber's disappearance, it had nothing to do with the boys at the Firenze Social Club. Judith Amber's story about her marriage, her involvement with Gaimari, and the North Coast Developers situation was just too silly and convoluted not to be the truth. It still left me with the problem of finding out what was.

I made some more tea and collected the morning *Plain Dealer* from the hallway where the deliveryman always managed to leave it several yards from my front door so that I often had to make a long walk down the hall clad only in a bathrobe. The front page told of a record warm spell for this date in February, shattering the previous mark of fifty-three degrees set in 1925; a committee from the Rock and Roll Hall of Fame was in Cleveland to select a site for the construction of a building; the Cavaliers dropped another one on the road; and after a whole week, no one had yet come forward with the winning ticket for last Wednesday's nine-million-dollar lottery drawing. Just a typical day in Cleveland and the world.

The phone rang again, and I hoped it wasn't Victor Gaimari wanting to go through another excruciatingly polite ritual of telling me he was going to have me hit. I toyed with having the machine collect the call, but decided against it. It might have been someone I loved.

That hope was quickly dashed.

"Mr. Jacovich, this is Chief Ethan Kemp. You remember me?"

"How could I forget you, Chief? You were there for one of my festival days."

"I wonder if you could come on out here to the valley for a bit?"

"I suppose so," I said. "When?"

"As fast as your little legs can carry you. I think we've located your Richard Amber."

I quickly gulped down the dregs of my tea. "Where?"

"In the river."

Ethan Kemp and I stood on the bank of the Chagrin River, about a mile downstream from the Valley Gun Club. The snow had melted, turning the banks to wet, sucking mud that was creeping up over the soles of our shoes. Kemp's entire staff was there, as well as the Ohio State Police, an ambulance, a reporter and photographer from the *Plain Dealer*, and camera crews from most of the area's TV stations. Four men wearing rubber suits and hip boots had waded into the icy water to retrieve the body, which was wedged between two rocks about twelve feet out into the middle of the river. The victim, or what was left of him, had been wearing a pair of casual slacks and a shirt and sweater when he went into the water. He was barefoot.

Kemp sourly took a cigarette when I offered it, but lit it himself with a wooden match taken from a box he'd picked up at a local restaurant in Chagrin Falls. He shook his head. "Why couldn't he have turned up in Pepper Pike, where he belongs?" he said. "Damn, I'm not set up for this."

"How did you find him?"

"Couple of ice fishermen decided to get an early jump this morning. This warm weather we've been having the past couple of days melted the ice and got the river running again. They were standing right here when all of a sudden this body comes floating downstream big as you please and hangs up on the rocks. Enough to turn you into a golfer."

"What makes you think it's Amber?" I said.

"I was hoping I could get an ID from you."

"I've never met the man," I said. "But I've seen his photograph. I'll do what I can."

The four policemen had managed to get the body out from between the two rocks and were bringing their grisly burden back to shore. Two ambulance attendants had readied a stretcher down at the river's edge and were waiting patiently. I looked away. I didn't have the stomach for things like this.

Kemp glanced at my face. "You moonlighting as Marvelous Marvin Hagler's sparring partner these days?"

"Something like that."

"I s'pose you'll tell me about it? I s'pose you have a lot you want to tell me?"

"I s'pose I don't have much choice."

He grinned wryly. "That's exactly right," he said. "You come on back to my office, I'll buy you a cuppa coffee."

Kemp's office—in a nondescript building about twenty-five years old—looked as if it should house a friendly neighborhood real estate agent, with fluorescent lighting, venetian blinds on the windows, and a neat and orderly metal desk. The coffee came from a Hamilton Beach drip coffee maker that also told the time, and he served it in ceramic mugs that said WINE, DINE, ENJOY, FROLIC, PARTY, LOVE, LAUGH, PLAY . . . I DID IT ALL IN CLEVELAND.

I needed the coffee. Kemp had made me look at the corpse's face before they put it in the meat wagon. From what I could tell, it was certainly Richard Amber, although the face was bruised and distorted.

"I think, Mr. Jacovich, that it's time for you to tell me everything that you know. If you'd like to have an attorney present, that's your right."

"Wait a minute," I said. "Am I under arrest?"

Kemp laughed. "You aren't even under suspicion. But four days ago you come out to my valley looking for Richard Amber, and someone takes a shot at you. This morning your Richard Amber turns up taking a February swim in the river, also in my valley. Now the way I add that up is that you know a lot of things that I don't, and I just hate it when people get ahead of me like that. I want to catch up. Unless you have something to hide."

"I have nothing to hide," I said, "and I don't need an attorney. At least I don't think I do. But I can't compromise my client under any circumstances. How about if I give you my word that I won't withhold anything from you that might have any bearing on who killed Richard Amber?"

"Your word, eh? Well, that certainly is impressive, Mr. Jacovich. I assume you have the expertise to know what has a bearing and what hasn't?"

"No offense, Chief, but I've probably handled more of these things than you have."

"That's right," he said. "I forgot your extensive credentials in the field. Okay, then. Why don't you give me everything you think I ought to be told? Then we'll see."

I took a breath and went back to the beginning, Amber's phone call a week earlier, which had started the whole business. I went through the list of people I had spoken to, with a few omissions. I didn't mention Giancarlo D'Allessandro or Victor Gaimari, because then I would have had to get into Judith Amber's personal involvement and her financial dealings with North Coast Developers, and since she was my client I didn't feel I could in good conscience do that. And I didn't say anything about Mary Soderberg.

Kemp scratched his long jaw during the recitation, nodding, grunting, squinting, squirting air through the cracks between his teeth in sporadic little rapid-fire bursts, lapping at his coffee. Half the time he looked as though he wasn't paying the slightest attention, but I was certain he was absorbing every word. When I finally finished he didn't say anything for a long while, but I was sure he was compartmentalizing all the information in his mind.

"You got anything to do today, Mr. Jacovich?"

"How do you mean?"

"Well, you think you could hang around here awhile until the coroner comes up with something?"

"That'll take a few hours. I could come back," I said. "I think it's my job to break the news to my client."

"I see where you might feel like that," he said. He looked at his watch. "It's eleven o'clock. You be back here by two this afternoon and we'll talk a little bit more."

"All right," I said. I felt lousy, and not from the bruised ribs or sore jaw, either. I felt lousy for Richard Amber and for all the people who had loved him for whatever their reasons. I felt lousy for myself, too, because maybe if I had gotten to his house a little quicker last Wednesday night he wouldn't be lying on a slab in the M.E.'s office with his skin blue-white and his body opened like a mail sack and strangers poking around inside him like necromancers looking for auguries of the future in the entrails of a chicken. There were so many reasons to feel lousy it made me tired just listing them all. The main one, of course, was that a man was dead, and he had probably died for nothing, for a stupid reason, and when someone dies for nothing a piece of all of us goes into the box with him. And then we lie awake nights and a loathsome little creature called Fear beats at our midnight window with its fuzzy wings, and we wonder who's going to be next and hope it isn't us. That's enough to make any citizen feel lousy.

When I told Judith Amber her husband had been found dead, she didn't cry. She just went into the kitchen and sat down on a stool and stared at the designer copper cookware and her lips got very tight as though she were suppressing something terrible like a primal scream or hysterical laughter or a temper tantrum that would have smashed every piece of crockery in the house, and then she put her face in her hands and stayed motionless for a long while, and I didn't know what to say or what to do so I just sat there drinking coffee. I couldn't leave, but staying didn't seem to be doing much good, either.

"So it's finally over, then?"

"Mrs. Amber, I'm so sorry."

"Everybody's going to be sorry," she said. "All the people at his office, and all the friends at the Advertising Club, and all his women past and present, and the mayor and the governor and the president of the United States, for all I know. Everyone's going to be sorry, and sorry doesn't mean shit because it doesn't bring Richard back and it doesn't change anything, and what is real and what is written in the history book is that we spent most of our lives together playing dirty tricks on each other, and I feel empty and lost and ashamed of myself and I find myself hating Richard a lot, too, and one isn't supposed to feel that way about the dear departed, is one? So I guess I'm the sorriest of all, and sorrier for myself than for anything. And I'm not proud of that."

She aired out a lot more dirty linen while I sat there. She was really into a self-pity mode. The fact that the man to whom she had promised till death do us part was in the morgue wearing a tag on his toe didn't seem to be bothering her all that much, but she was certainly feeling sorry for herself, sorry and guilty. She finally told me she wanted to be alone, and she wrote out a very generous check I hadn't earned and insisted that I take it, and then she said she'd be in touch sometime to get a full report, and sent me packing so she could be alone and perhaps unbend enough in solitude so she could at last cry for her husband.

I looked in the phone book to find that Karen Wilde lived in University Heights, and went over there and broke the news to her, and she didn't cry, either. Richard Amber's death seemed to produce numb reactions in the women in his life.

"Oh God, that stinks," she said. "That really sucks."

"I'm sorry," I told her. "There's just no easy way to say something like that."

She manifested her grief by running around the apartment busily, dusting, emptying ashtrays, straightening piles of magazines and scripts, and lighting a cigarette in a very theatrical manner, the way she did everything else.

"I'm not sure what I'm supposed to do here," she said. "I mean, I'm not the widow, am I? I can't make the arrangements." Her voice caught, like June Allyson's in *The Stratton Story*. "I can't even go to the funeral, can I?"

She went to the kitchen cupboard and took down a bottle of vodka, poured some neat in a glass, and downed it. She didn't offer me any, and though I wasn't a vodka drinker, the idea of having one was kind of appealing at that moment.

"Karen," I said, "we'll find out what happened. Believe me."

She shook her head. "It's not my place to worry about it, is it? I mean, I'm just the girlfriend. The mistress. The twice-a-week trick. It's not like I was going to marry him or anything. Oh, god-dammit, why does everything I touch turn to shit?" She didn't expect an answer, and poured herself another drink to keep me from having to give her one. "I suppose you're wondering if I'm going to call in sick tonight. I'm not. I'm a trouper. The show must go on and all that. I'm just wondering how I'm going to be able to say my line in the show about things that happen between a man and woman in the dark that make everything else seem unimportant. But I'll manage. That's what we show folk do."

"You're being a bit rough on yourself, Karen."

"I'm always rough on myself. That's why I go out with married men. So that I can get dumped in the end, one way or the other. He wants to patch it up with wifey. He can't take the guilt any-more. Or one day he just quits calling. Or floats down the river. That way I can use the pain in my work. You ever hear of Stan-islavsky? Method acting? Brando and Lee Strasberg and that whole crowd? Well, I learned well. And look at all the pain I'll have to draw on tonight. I wonder if there's any way of alerting the critics?"

She finally started to cry, and I didn't want to be there to watch her do it, but what bothered me the most is that I didn't know if she was really crying for Richard Amber and what might have been, or if she was putting on the performance of her life.

I got back to Ethan Kemp's office in the valley just before two o'clock, and interrupted his lunch. He was a brown-bagger and was eating what appeared to be a roast beef sandwich with horse-radish on a French roll. Several peeled carrot sticks and celery stalks were encased in plastic wrap and a bottle of natural-flavored soda was half-empty on his desk.

"Had lunch yet?" he said. "There's half a sandwich here."

"No, thanks."

"Don't be bashful. My wife made it. She always makes too much food for my lunch. I have to give most of it away damn near every day." He held out the other half of the sandwich. "Go ahead."

It did look good, and I realized I couldn't run all day on a few pieces of toast washed down with tea. I took it from him and was glad—it was an excellent sandwich, and the beef was lean and medium rare the way I like it.

"My compliments to the chef," I said.

"I'll tell her. She's a hell of a cook. Indiana girl. She makes jewelry in her spare time, and she's got a lot of that, on account of we don't have any kids. You married?"

I explained my marital status to him.

"It must be a big adjustment being single again after all those married years. Hell, it was a big change for me going the other way. But then if I was still single I'd be eating Big Macs for lunch every day—I'd get fat, I'd get an ulcer, and that would make me pretty mean around the office. And there's nothing worse than a mean man with a gold badge, don't you agree?"

I figured he was trying to tell me something, but I was too achy from my previous night's visitors and upset over Amber's death to play games with him. I just finished the half sandwich and waited until he was ready.

He very neatly cleared away the remnants of his lunch and brushed the errant salt and crumbs off the desk top into his palm and dumped the whole thing into a wastepaper basket, then put on a pair of glasses that made him look like a San Francisco intellectual in cowboy drag and scanned a report in a folder in front of him.

"It says here in the coroner's preliminary report that the cause of death was a massive coronary." He looked up over his glasses at me. "That surprise you?"

"Nothing surprises me," I said.

"Well, that's good." He went back to perusing the report. "Because there's some things in here that were a revelation to me, I'll tell you."

"When did he die?"

He looked over his glasses again, then back at the report. "Hard to say since the body's been in freezing water for some time. But, ah, pending further tests, it says, the doc's best guess is several days."

"How many is several?"

"Several," he said heavily, "is several. That's more than two and less than fourteen thousand two hundred and eighty-one. It's several. Give the doctor time—we only fished the guy out of the drink this morning."

"Patience was never my strong point," I said.

"All right then. Now, the things that really got me to prick up my ears—our friend Mr. Amber did not go gently into that good night." He grinned at me. "That's that poet Dylan Thomas."

"I know."

"No, not gently at all. The coroner found bruises on his face and abdomen that were put there before he died—in other words, they didn't come from being bounced around in the water. What does that tell you?"

"That someone hit him in the face and abdomen before he died."

"That's exactly right," Kemp said. "And they did something else, too. You have any idea why he might have been barefoot when he went into the river?"

Several rude and sarcastic responses suggested themselves to me before I simply shook my head.

"Well, it was because someone went to all the trouble of burning the bottoms of his feet with a lighted cigarette. Several times." He glanced up. "That's eleven times. And there are raw marks around his wrists as though his hands had been tied tightly together. Do those facts suggest anything to you?"

"The current regime in El Salvador?"

"Don't make light of this, Mr. Jacovich, it's not funny. Richard Amber was tortured, and I suspect that his heart gave out before his will did. Now why, in twentieth-century America, would someone do that to another human being?"

"Probably because he wanted to find something out that the human being knew and wouldn't tell him."

"That's exactly right. Now, what do you suppose that was?"

"When the Amber home was broken into last Friday night the burglar was looking for something. I suppose he tried to get Amber to tell him where it was."

"You have any notion as to what that something might have been?"

"None, Chief," I said. "If I did it would have made my work a lot easier."

"Now, Mr. Jacovich, let me understand this. Amber called you on Wednesday night last, and said he wanted a bodyguard?"

"That's right."

"And you and he had never met before?"

"That's right. He got my name from the phone book and called Lieutenant Meglich at the Cleveland P.D. for a reference. Then he called me. You can check that with Meglich."

"And an hour later he had disappeared?"

"Right."

Kemp laced his fingers behind his head. "Let me make a hypothetical here, just for grins. What if—and I'm not saying this is so—what if the person who called you on Wednesday night was not really Richard Amber, but someone who was just saying he was Richard Amber? Might that explain some things?"

With my tongue I worried a piece of roast beef that had gotten stuck between my teeth. "It would only explain his quick disappearance," I said. "But it wouldn't much explain why someone would do it."

He mulled that over a bit, then nodded. "The interesting thing about this job is those inexplicable things. Is that the right word?"

"You know damn well it is," I said.

"Oh, that's right, my country bumpkin act doesn't work with you. Sorry." He gave me a wry smile. "Well, I guess we have our work cut out for us here."

It was my turn to smile. "What you mean we, white man?"

"Well," Kemp said, "the way I have it figured is that you and I can both bring some things to the party that might help each other out."

"I'm off the case."

"No, not exactly," he said in that laconic way of his that was so studied. "The way I see it, you're going to help me crack this one. Because if you don't, I'm going to make it really tough for you to practice your trade anywhere east of downtown. I'm going to call an inquiry because you came out here looking for a murdered man and got involved in a shooting, and in general I'm going to be up your butt for a long time to come. Now in order to avoid that you can surely give me a few days of your time, can't you?" He delivered the threat the way he might have announced a basketball score between two teams he didn't particularly care about.

I thought about the several responses I could have made, and the one that sprang to the fore was punching him in the nose, but I had already gotten into trouble for being too free with my fists and I wasn't anxious to run afoul of this Ethan Kemp. He acted like a shit-kicker and looked like a movie cowboy but I had the feeling he was a good cop, and tougher than hell, to boot.

Besides, I had no intention of abandoning the Richard Amber case. Mrs. Amber had given me a generous severance check, and I'd been through too much to let this one fall through the cracks. So I figured I might as well cooperate with the law—one never knows when a friend with a badge is going to be valuable. And there was no percentage at all in making an enemy of that badge.

I said, "What did you have in mind, Chief?" and made it sound as much like my own idea as I could.

Kemp said, "I think it's my job to run around making official inquiries, investigating the crime scene, et cetera. What I'd like you to do, Mr. Jacovich, if you will, is to try and find out, if you can, what it was that prowler was hoping to find in Mr. Amber's home, because if we find out what that was we'll know why Amber was killed."

"And if we know why, we know who."

He smiled. "That's exactly right," he said.

CHAPTER FIFTEEN

John Marbury was saying, "We're all absolutely prostrate over this. Prostrate! My God, Richard was like a son to me." His hand over his eyes in a show of grief, he sat in his ornate office, one more suited to a Beverly Hills attorney, with its dark paneling and wall sconces. Jerry Stendall stood nearby, wearing a dark gray suit, a somber expression, and a round Band-Aid on the side of his face to cover a shaving nick. He kept nodding at whatever his uncle said so I would know the older man's sentiments were shared by the nephew.

As might be imagined, everyone at Marbury-Stendall Advertising was pretty shaken up by the death of Richard Amber. Murder is something that just doesn't touch most people's lives, and when it does, no matter how remotely, it makes them stop and think, and double-lock their doors at night, and look over their shoulders as they walk the dark streets, and always sit in public places making sure they face the door. It makes them question things heretofore taken for granted: the safety of the streets and the sanctity of their homes, the trust of their friends and loved ones, the security of their jobs and families and routines. The Constitution only works when everyone obeys the rules, and murderers don't play by those rules. They operate under a peculiar and secret set of their own devising, and when people don't know the rules they tend to get nervous. With good reason, too.

"Who does things like that?" Marbury was saying. "What kind of a monster would do such a thing to a wonderful guy like Richard? Jesus, it doesn't add up."

"It adds up to someone, Mr. Marbury," I pointed out. "Is there anything you could possibly tell me that could shed some light on it?"

"My God, I wouldn't know where to begin. I mean, this is incomprehensible to me."

"There's no one in the advertising business who hated Amber?" I said. "No enemies?"

"We're talking civilized people here, Jacovich," Marbury said. "College graduates, family men, people who have the respect of the community. I mean, ad guys don't do things like that!"

It amused me that he was able to categorically remove an entire group of people from suspicion of murder by reason of occupation. I suppose in John Marbury's well-ordered world murders were committed by drug dealers and people whose names ended in vowels or maybe even in *ich*, and certainly by those whose skin was darker than his. But WASPs and MBAs who made salaries in the six-figure range never did anything shadier than bet a few dollars on a football game. It was Marbury's kind of thinking, the peculiar blindness the very rich sometimes develop, that was responsible for many of our society's ills, but I was not about to tell him that.

"Let's talk about the office for a minute."

"Mr. Jacovich," Jerry Stendall said, "I think we've been over that. I find even the suggestion that someone in this office is capable of such a disgusting thing offensive."

"Murder is offensive, Mr. Stendall," I said. "Even more offensive is deliberately putting our heads in the sand and not finding out who did it. Remember, when your head is buried in the sand, your ass is up in the air."

Marbury put up a hand. "Now, stop it, you two. No one's going to get anywhere with us fighting among ourselves. I assure you, Mr. Jacovich, this agency is at your disposal and that of the police, until this is solved." He put his head down onto his hand again, shading his eyes from the overhead fluorescents. "This is a new one on me," he said.

"If you really want to help, Mr. Marbury, I'd like to talk to you alone for a few minutes." Stendall opened his mouth to protest, but I said, "And then I'd like to talk to you, Mr. Stendall."

"I have nothing to add to what I've already told you."

"Jerry, for Christ's sake, stop flexing your muscles and do what Mr. Jacovich asks you," Marbury barked, and the color fled from Stendall's face as if it had been poured out of a glass pitcher.

"I'll be in my office," he said, and stalked out.

Marbury looked after him, and the expression on his face was part disgust and part panic that came from someplace I didn't know anything about. "Jerry's great farting around with figures on a piece of paper and making them come out the way he wants. When it comes to people . . ." He shook his head. "Jerry's under the impression that this agency needs him."

"I don't understand, Mr. Marbury. You hired him. You appointed him to the presidency."

Marbury waved a hand. "I'm not a kid anymore, Jacovich. I've worked most of my adult life to build up this agency to where it is. Unfortunately I have no sons to pass all this on to. My only blood relative just walked out of the office. He's a putz, I grant you. But better him than some stranger."

Everyone takes care of their own, I thought. Giancarlo D'Allessandro, Walter Deming, John Marbury. It was not a comforting thought for me that I had no one of my own. My marriage was broken like Humpty-Dumpty, my kids were becoming more and more distanced from me all the time, and the chances were they'd have a new dad pretty soon. Who was going to take care of Milan Jacovich? My Aunt Branka was the only name that came to mind.

"Mr. Marbury, it's pretty common knowledge that Richard Amber was holding the Deming account together with spit and chewing gum. What are you going to do now that he's gone?"

He regarded me as someone who'd just committed an inexcusable lapse in taste. "I don't see where that will help you find Richard's killer."

"I'm sure you don't. I don't, either. But then again it might help. Would you mind answering it?"

He rocked back in his chair. "You're so damned polite, Jacovich. I never talked to such a polite cop. You'd make a good account executive."

"Are you offering me a job?"

He shrugged. "I've got to replace Richard pretty quickly. And that's an answer to your question, I guess."

"Well, I'm flattered if that was a serious offer, Mr. Marbury, but I don't think it's my field. Who are you thinking of?"

"I don't know. Maybe give Jeff Monaghan a try—if he'd shave off that damn beard and look like a real person. Jeff could certainly handle the creative end of it. There are a few other people here in town that might be possibilities—maybe someone in Chicago. But Jeff has been with the agency and knows the account. Jesus, I don't know. Richard Amber is dead, let's not dance on his grave just yet."

"And what about the Deming account?"

"Keeping it, you mean?" He sighed, the weight of the world bearing down on his seventy-year-old shoulders. "Whatever it takes. Cutting the agency commission, maybe. Even waiving the commission. Getting down on my hands and knees and begging to kiss Walter Deming's ass or whatever else he might want me to kiss. Maybe making a deal with Judith—"

"I don't understand."

"Judith's relationship with her uncle is what kept Richard in the ballgame, and kept this agency in it by extension. If we can make some sort of arrangement with Judith, perhaps Walter will see fit to leave the account where it is."

"What sort of arrangement?"

He shrugged. "A percentage, an ownership position—something along those lines."

I ran a hand through my thinning hair. "Why would you do that for her and not for Richard?"

He smiled at my naïveté. "Richard needed this agency as much as we needed him. He was very good at what he did for us, but

he wasn't that terrific at the whole enchilada. He was very creative and a great customer's man, but he lacked the toughness
you need to survive in the ad game. He couldn't go out and steal
business away from other agencies without getting a galloping
case of the guilts."

"And you have no such hang-ups?"

He answered with iron filings in his voice. "I've got callouses
on my feet from forty years of kicking ass. This is no business for
wimps and pussies. It's too damned competitive, there's too many
vultures out there waiting to pick the flesh off your bones. You
either get tough or you get out, and all the creativity in the world
isn't worth a pair of stainless steel testicles." He fumbled around
for his coffee cup, but when he finally picked it up the coffee was
evidently cold because he put it right back down again. "Judith
isn't in the business, and she doesn't need 'a job.' She'll want more
concrete reasons for staying in." He turned his hands palms up-
ward. "You've got to be realistic, you've got to give some to get
some. That's the way you do business."

As I walked down the corridor toward Stendall's office I
couldn't help but reflect how much of a child I always felt after
talking to one of these high-powered executive types. Maybe I was
just an innocent wandering around in a wild-animal preserve,
but somewhere along the line I never got the same dose of ethics
as they did, or maybe I got too many doses of the other kind. I
always thought the American Way was to work hard, do your own
thing, honor God and country, raise your kids not to knock over
gas stations and convenience stores, and after it was all over retire to Florida and live out your golden years. No one ever told me
about making deals with widows or kissing someone's behind on
your hands and knees. But the single-minded pursuit of a buck
seemed to have replaced the old-fashioned Protestant work ethic,
and the one who dies with the most toys wins. It was no wonder I
wasn't rich, and I suppose it was at about that moment I realized
I probably never would be.

Rhoda Young came up behind me and touched my sleeve. I
smiled down at her. She was wearing a black suit and had been

crying. Hard. She was taking this murder business bigger than anyone. She'd always known that Richard Amber would be nothing more than her fantasy, but now someone had taken the fantasy away, and she was left with a handful of dry dust and no memories at all. Dreams make the biggest crash when they go down in flames.

"Can I see you?" she whispered.

"Sure, Rhoda."

"Not here." She was looking nervously around like a mob stoolie at a Columbus Day parade. "Meet me downstairs in the parking lot. Around the side where no one can see us out the window. Five minutes."

And she was off down the hall with that brisk walk all secretaries eventually develop almost unconsciously—designed to make the boss think she was busy, to make the other women in the office envy her confident job security, to make the men in the office notice her without promising anything except that she might be walking back this way again before the day was over. Just another urban survival technique.

I went to the reception area and asked the woman behind the desk where the restroom was, just for a cover. She gave me the directions, and I went out into the corridor, around a bend, and down the stairway to the first floor. I put on my gloves and went outside. Rhoda Young was waiting for me.

"I'm sorry about Mr. Amber," I said.

"Look," she said, "we don't have a lot of time. I just wanted you to know a few things."

"Shoot."

"Mr. Stendall likes to give people the impression that he and Mr. Amber were great friends," she said. "But they weren't. Stendall was so jealous of him he couldn't even see straight. And Mr. Amber didn't have much respect for him, either. The fact is that last Wednesday—Mr. Amber's last day here . . ." She stopped to compose herself, her pretty brown eyes filling up with tears. She sniffed. "If anyone finds out I talked to you it's going to be my job." A flicker of defiance hardened her pretty Mediterranean features.

"I don't care," she said. "I only stayed on here because of Richard . . . Mr. Amber."

"What happened Wednesday, Rhoda?" I prodded. Gently. I knew she was hurting, and she wouldn't even have the solace of a funeral and somber-faced friends and relatives telling her how sorry they all were.

"Wednesday . . . Mr. Amber had the biggest fight with Mr. Stendall."

"What about?"

"The Deming account," she said. "I couldn't hear all of it, because they only started shouting at the end. It was unusual. Mr. Amber was usually so soft-spoken and sweet."

"How did it turn out?"

"It ended up Mr. Stendall said something like, 'It's my name on the door of this goddamn shop, and you'll do it my way or not at all!' Something like that."

"And what did Mr. Amber say?"

"Nothing. He just stalked out the door." She almost smiled with the remembrance. "Slammed it hard, too."

"What time was this?"

"At the end of the day. Stendall wanted to talk to Richard . . . Mr. Amber . . . about the meeting with Mr. Deming the next morning. And it turned into a shouting match."

"Who won the match?"

She smiled adoringly, looking up into the gray-blue skies as if she were speaking of James Dean. "Mr. Stendall screamed the loudest, but Mr. Amber showed what a classy gentleman he really is." The smile flickered and faded. "Was," she amended, and then she started to cry again, leaning her head against my chest. I put my arms around her awkwardly, feeling the sharp points of her shoulder blades beneath my hands, and waited until she sobbed it all out. When she finished there was a wet spot from tears on my car coat.

She rather fussily pulled herself together with the aid of a wadded-up tissue, not the last one she'd use up before this business was done. Then she looked at me seriously. "I suppose you can guess how I felt about him. But there was never anything between us. After all those years nothing ever went on." She tried another sad smile but it didn't work too well. "I guess that's really why I'm crying," she said.

"Rhoda, you're a very nice woman," I said. "I appreciate your talking to me. I'll keep it confidential, you can depend on it."

"Without Richard here, it's . . . just a job. I can always get another." She turned, hugging herself against the cold, and started back into the building. "Get this killer, will you? So maybe I can sleep nights?" She cast a smile over her shoulder. "Give me a couple of minutes before you come back up."

I waited about five minutes, watching my breath freeze in front of my face, and then I went back upstairs.

I entered Stendall's office without knocking and he looked up, annoyed. I decided we'd have it out before things got totally out of hand.

"What's your problem, Jerry?" I said. "You and I don't have to hold hands, but it seems to me you'd be falling all over yourself to help. Is it something about my personality?"

He iced me with a stare. "I'm not used to murder and detectives," he said. "I don't like it. I don't like it in the office. Richard is dead and the police are looking into it and I don't see where you have any right here, especially asking questions and making innuendoes."

"I don't remember any innuendoes."

"Look, the people in this shop are good people. Most of them have worked a lot of years to get where they are today. Advertising is a tough business—"

"Oh, bullshit!" I said. "I'm tired of everyone whining to me how tough the advertising business is. You don't like it, open a hardware store! Otherwise get off the pot. Every business is tough, including law enforcement, and we're all extremely impressed with your success, but now it's time to talk about other things. You can talk to me or to the police. I know a deputy chief by the name of Kemp who wouldn't take five minutes to get you singing 'Ave Maria.'"

That shook him up, but to his credit he decided to tough it out a while longer. "You're kind of feisty this morning, aren't you, Jacovich?"

"Damn right I am," I said. "There's a man dead, and he didn't die pretty, and all I'm getting from everyone here is a song and dance."

"I've never lied to you."

"You've never told me the whole truth, either. The fact is you and Richard didn't get along at all, did you? You saw him as a threat, and he saw you as . . . a nephew."

"I'm going to ask you to leave, Jacovich."

"Ask away, but I want some straight talk from you, and if I don't get it Chief Kemp is going to be up here so fast you won't have time to lock yourself into the executive washroom."

He began fingering his nostril again. Evidently that's what he did when he was thinking things over. Then he said, "I've already told you everything I know."

"You and Amber were at each other's throats. You and he had quite a set-to on Wednesday before closing time."

"How did you—"

"And four hours later he was gone, and a week after that he floats down the river like a dead tree branch. Now it seems to me you have some heavy talking to do."

"So what that we argued? People argue in this office all the time. It's nothing to get excited about."

"Isn't it? Then why didn't you tell me about it a week ago?"

"It was none of your—"

"Maybe because you knew he was dead and you didn't want a lot of questions from the police?"

"That's slander!" he said.

"Brush up on your law, it's nothing of the kind. We aren't screwing around anymore, Jerry, this is murder, and you can talk to me or the police. What's it going to be?"

He gnawed on the inside of his cheek for a while. If looks could kill there would be a *missa solemnis* for me in the morning. Finally he grumbled, "All right. But there's nothing to tell you that you don't already know."

"Tell me again. Just for fun."

He sighed heavily. "I didn't like Richard, and Richard didn't like me, okay?"

"Why not?"

He didn't answer for a moment, and then the floodgates of resentment opened up and I was afraid I'd never get him to stop. "He was the fair-haired boy around here, and I was damned sick of it from the time my uncle brought me aboard. Richard is so talented, Richard is such an asset to this agency, without Richard we wouldn't have Deming Steel, without Richard we'd be just another seat-of-the-pants shop scrabbling for pizzeria and carpet-cleaner clients. Richard knows the governor, Richard knows the mayor, Richard is well-connected, Richard this, Richard that. Well, fuck Richard! I know what people think of me, that I'm damned lucky I'm John's nephew, but I can't help it that I am, and I can't help it I didn't marry a goddamn gold mine, and I can't help it that I'm the president of this agency, but I would have been one dumb bunny not to have jumped at it when it was offered."

He paused for a huge gulp of air as though he'd just run the hundred, and went on, "And don't think the resentment went just one way, either. Richard was jealous of me because he thought *he* should have gotten the presidency. Richard had all these polished manners and quite a way with clients, quite a way with women, quite a way with everyone. But he never got over the fact that he'd had to work for it while everyone else seemed to be born rich. He resented it, he resented me, and he never missed an opportunity to cut me down in front of my uncle or damned near anyone else. When Walter Deming was around he treated me like a goddamn office boy instead of the president of this agency. I'd ask someone to do something around here and Richard would tell them never mind, what *he* wanted was more important. I didn't get respect from anybody, and it was all because Richard thought he was some sort of golden boy. I think he enjoyed my discomfort, because God knows he caused enough of it. Yes, we fought all the time, and yes, we fought the afternoon he disappeared. I thought he was an arrogant prick. But this agency needed him and that means I needed him, so if you're thinking I killed him you're just crazy, that's all. Just crazy!"

I waited to see if any further eruptions were forthcoming. He was making a superhuman effort to get himself and his emotions under a tight rein, and when he'd just about managed it, I said, "I'm sorry, Jerry."

He waited until he stopped hyperventilating and the flush receded from his face. "And if I had killed him I sure as shit wouldn't have tortured him to death. I probably would have brained him with a one-iron." He smiled wryly. "That's about the only thing a one-iron is good for anyway—and it would have probably taken me three strokes."

I had to give him credit. He pulled himself out of his funk pretty quickly, and Jerry Stendall was probably not the kind of guy who lost it that often. I knew he was telling the truth about his feelings for Amber, because from the beginning I'd thought of him as a flunky myself. It couldn't have been easy for him, working at the pleasure of his uncle in the shadow of a supernova like Richard Amber while everyone else in the small world of Cleveland business snickered at him behind their hands, or sometimes openly. It never ceases to amaze me what some people will do for money. Stendall earned in the low six figures per year, but he had to eat a mile of shit every morning to get it; it may have been worth it to him.

I stopped off at Jeff Monaghan's office. He was on the phone but waved me into a chair. He was arguing with someone about a line of copy having to do with used cars. "'Previously owned' is a bullshit expression," he was saying, "and it doesn't fool anybody. If it's a fucking used car, say it's a fucking used car." He went on that way for a few minutes, and my mind drifted.

I was more sure than ever that Amber had been killed because someone was trying to get him to tell them something, and that the break-in at his home was connected. Until I found what that something was, I still had no straight edge, no framework within which I could maneuver. All I had was an abused and frozen corpse, and everyone in town mad at me, including some very rough guys with bent noses and bulges under their jackets.

Finally Monaghan hung up on his caller and gave me his full attention. "Well, my favorite shamus," he said.

"Is your ad copy as corny as that, too? How's your cold, Mr. Monaghan?"

"Well, I can breathe through my nose most of the time now," he said, "but I have a hell of a night cough. These things just have to run their course. Are you still poking around about Richard?"

"Still poking around," I said.

"Jesus, I can't get over it. He was my best friend, my mentor. What can you say about a man like that?"

"It's a tragedy," I agreed.

"I hope like hell you find the bastard that did this. I'd like about twenty minutes with him before you take him downtown. I don't suppose that's possible, though."

"Not very."

"You have to hate someone an awful lot to do that kind of a thing to him. I'm really sick over it. Sick."

"Are you planning on staying with the agency now that Richard's gone?"

He shook his head and threw up his hands. "Who knows? I haven't given it much thought. I suppose I will, for a while. It depends."

"On what?"

"I don't know what, I'm just talking. Christ, I'm really upset."

"I can see that," I said.

"I'll tell you one thing, though, pal. This has taught me a good lesson. I mean, Richard was the greatest guy I ever knew, and on the surface you'd think he didn't have a care in the world. But just look at the pressure he was under, giving him a heart condition, for Christ's sake. That's not for me. I'd just as soon take a couple bucks fewer and not kick off twenty years before my time."

"I think it's only fair to point out that Amber was murdered," I said, "which has very little to do with job stress."

He shook his head, coughed into his fist. "The principle remains," he said.

"I don't suppose you've had any brainstorms about this killing?"

"If I did, buddy, I'd tell you in a flash. Jesus, what a grotesque thing!"

"I'll be in touch," I said.

My last stop was at Charlie Dodge's office. He was just staring out the window at the traffic passing on Chagrin Boulevard.

"This is it for me," he said after the usual amenities and going over how terrible it was what had happened to Richard Amber. Everybody in the world was just sick about it, it seemed.

"How do you mean?"

"They'll be giving me notice anytime now, as soon as the shock wears off. I was here because of Richard. Now that he's gone . . ." He trailed off, still looking out the window at the cars. There were more of them now, close as it was getting to going-home time, their tires hissing in the slush.

"What will you do?"

"I don't know," he said. "I'm just a tired, funny-looking old fart. Know anyone looking for one of those?"

I was sure the question was rhetorical.

"I know that everyone wondered why a high-powered ad agency like this one had someone as dull as me up front. It doesn't matter that I'm good at my job. What matters is the bells and whistles, and I'm not very good at that. So I'm just waiting for the guillotine to drop."

"You have any idea who would have done this, Charlie? Anyone who might have wanted to?"

"It's incomprehensible to me," he said. "I made a list of reasons why Richard would have taken off the way we thought he did, and none of them made any sense. None of this makes any sense, either."

I couldn't believe my ears. "You made a list?"

He smiled sheepishly. "I make lists of everything, Mr. Jacovich. That's what I do. See all these papers on my desk, in my files, hanging on the wall? They're all lists. I even make lists of the lists I've made. I can't afford any mistakes or forget to do something or tell someone something, because I've been hanging on with my fingernails all my life. Other people are brilliant, witty, innovative, flashy, creative. I'm efficient. I make lists. It's just about all I have to offer. And few people besides Amber could see that. Now that he's gone—I expect I will be, too. Very shortly. They're going to be tightening belts around here anyway, and it doesn't take a crystal ball to see who'll get it first."

"Don't lay down and die until you have to, Charlie. For God's sake, anything can happen. Don't give up!" I didn't know why it was so important to me. I just never understand the thinking of people who always perceive themselves as victims. It's a self-fulfilling prophecy, it seems to me; a snake that runs up its own ass.

"Maybe so," he said, not meaning it. "You can say it, Jacovich, you're your own boss."

"We're all captains of our own souls, Charlie."

He smiled sadly. "The amazing part of it is," he said, "I think you're dumb enough to actually believe that shit."

I stopped off at Noggin's on Warrensville Road and had a beer. Then I decided I'd get something to eat. Noggin's was Yuppie heaven, and I didn't feel terribly comfortable there among people I didn't understand and couldn't talk to, but the food was decent. They also had one of the best wine lists in Cleveland, but I wasn't about to order a ten-dollar bottle of wine to accompany a mush-room-onion burger and a salad. I had another Stroh's. Something was bothering me, something I couldn't seem to get at, and it had little to do with the onions I was eating. I knew I was close, that somewhere I had a key to the answer, and I was going to chew on it until I found it. Or until Ethan Kemp found it.

Kemp was a strange guy, but I liked him somehow. I also thought he was a pretty good cop. Whatever reasons he had for walking around like a movie gunslinger were his own, but there was an intelligence working there, a never-miss-a-trick canni-ness that can normally only be spotted by another cop—or ex-cop. And I definitely didn't ever want to run afoul of that intelli-gence, never wanted to get Ethan Kemp mad at me. I wasn't sure

I'd survive it intact. I hoped I could give him something on the Amber case, because I not only wanted to help him, but I desperately wanted to crack it. I had been beaten up, shot at, followed, jerked around, and this was one I didn't want to lose.

I finished my dinner and had some coffee. Then I called Mary Soderberg.

She didn't sound good. "This has been a rough day," she said. "I'm trying to sort out my feelings, but it's not easy."

"I know," I said.

"It's not that Richard and I had anything left between us. We didn't. We hardly had any contact at all the last few years. But you're not a woman, you wouldn't understand. He was in my life, in my bed—and for him to die that way—it's just messing me up. Badly."

"I understand," I said, and I really did, but it didn't keep it from hurting. I found myself resenting Richard Amber as much as everyone else seemed to. The difference was that I knew I hadn't killed him.

I promised I'd call her tomorrow and went back up to the bar and had another beer. There were two young men on the stools to my left wearing dark three-piece suits and almost identical red ties. They looked like a vaudeville dance act and were earnestly discussing mainframe computers and flow charts and marketing trends. I think they were networking. I tuned out quickly.

When it got dark I left Noggin's and drove east on Chagrin to Pepper Pike. I was careful to hold my speed to at least two miles under the limit, because I was no longer on salary or expense money. But I had some things to say to Judith Amber, some more questions to ask, and I didn't much care whether or not I was getting paid. What else did I have to do, anyway?

The Amber house on S.O.M. Center Road was lighted up as if for a party. There were several highway patrol cars parked up and down the street, and I had a moment of panic that the prowler had broken in again and hurt someone. But my fears were allayed when I saw the black stretch limo in the driveway in front of the front door and the two giant-sized state cops standing near it.

I parked my car and was stopped by three people between the curb and the front door who wanted to know who I was and what my business was. I finally told one of the two state troopers at the door that I wasn't leaving until they let Mrs. Amber know I was here. He went inside for a few moments, and then reappeared with Judith Amber behind him. She was wearing a wine-colored knit—hardly deep mourning.

"I thought we'd finished our business together," she said.

"We did," I admitted, "but there are some things I have to ask you."

"You've come at a bad time," she said. "There are people here."

I looked around at the array of law enforcement. "No kidding?"

"Call me tomorrow."

"Tomorrow may be too late, Mrs. Amber. I'll talk to you or the police will talk to you. This is a homicide now; no one cares about your influential friends."

She looked nervously over her shoulder into the house and put her fingernail gently between her teeth. Then she said, "You're inopportune, Mr. Jacovich. Come in."

The trooper stood aside and I walked into the living room and stopped cold, staring at the two men sitting on the sofa. "Good evening, Mr. Deming," I said, and then turned to the other. "Good evening, Governor."

CHAPTER SIXTEEN

I don't know whether the American public tends to only elect to high office those who are well-turned-out and charismatic and have that special starry glow to them, or whether it's something that one automatically acquires after the election, but whatever the case George Kinnick had it to spare. Tall and trim, with a body that looked as if it treated itself to twenty laps in the pool, ten minutes on the tanning bed, and a game of racquetball each morning before breakfast, he was one of those people whose occupation could easily be guessed by a television celebrity panel. If not a successful politician he would have to be a high-powered industrialist or possibly the CEO of a major film studio. He had the look. Born to moderate wealth, he had breezed through a prep school education, gone to the state university and thence to Yale for a law degree, and had climbed the political ladder from mayor of Cincinnati to state auditor to the governor's mansion with hardly a snag. And if he often overlooked the problems of the hardscrabble dirt farmers of Ohio in favor of the big-city fat-cat business interests, well, what the hell, you can't have everything, and though the farmers had no fewer votes than the businessmen, it was the corporate world that filled the drawers of his war chest and eventually hoped to send him to Washington. So much for the midwestern populist movement.

"It's a pleasure to meet you, Mr. Jacovich," the governor said, taking great care to pronounce my name in exactly the way it had been spoken to him, wringing my hand with such sincerity that I thought he would break into weeping with the thrill of knowing me. "I only wish it were under happier circumstances. Mrs. Kinnick and myself have known Richard and Judith since we were all in school."

Walter Deming nodded curtly in my direction. He was smoking one of his cigars, probably the only man in the world nervy enough to foul the air in Judith Amber's otherwise pristine living room. Another man stood near the wall, and the governor identified him as "My aide, Steve Smith." Steve Smith was very tall, rather fat, and had a silly black mustache and an almost puppylike expression telling everyone how much he needed to be liked.

Judith said, "I've explained to Mr. Jacovich that it might be better if he came back tomorrow, but—"

"Not at all," the governor said. "If he was a friend of Richard's—"

"Actually," I said, "I'm not—"

Judith Amber interrupted me. "Mr. Jacovich is the detective I hired to try and find Richard. I can't imagine what he's doing here tonight, however."

"Just a few loose ends," I said. "I didn't mean to intrude, Governor Kinnick."

"Would you like some coffee, Mr. Jacovich?" the governor said, and Steve Smith stood up a little straighter, ready to fetch it.

"No, sir, thank you," I said. "I just had to talk with Mrs. Amber very briefly."

"You know, Mr. Jacovich, a thing like this just makes everyone soberly reflect on his own mortality, doesn't it? It's a sad thing when a citizen of the greatest state in the Union can't walk his own streets with impunity. I'm looking into putting together a task force to deal with street crime on the state level. This has got to stop!"

"Looking into putting together." Campaign rhetoric at a wake. Making an empty political promise over the body of a longtime friend. Five-hundred-dollar suit notwithstanding, George Kinnick was a cheap pol. I'd no doubt he'd go far.

"It had to be some wacko," His Excellency was saying. "No one who knew Richard would ever do such a terrible thing, would they, Mr. Jacovich?"

"In all my dealings with him," I said truthfully, "there was never so much as a discouraging word between us."

"Steve," the governor said, turning so quickly that Smith almost lost his balance and fell over, "I want to put together an open letter to all the law enforcement people in the state, the top guys. We can't have our community leaders like Richard come floating . . ." He glanced up at Richard's widow and rethought his statement.

Walter Deming worked his cigar, shifting it from one side of his mouth to the other, looking like a guy who managed middle-weights. "Jacovich, this is an occasion of family grief. We appreciate your coming by to pay your respects, but perhaps . . ."

I was being dismissed. Or at least that's what Walter Deming thought. I said, "If I could have just a few moments of Mrs. Amber's time in private—"

"Maybe tomorrow," Deming said.

"Maybe just a few minutes tonight," I said, and took Judith Amber's arm. "If the governor will excuse us?"

Kinnick looked at me strangely. He had obviously picked up from Walter Deming that I wasn't anyone particularly important, and if I wasn't, what in hell was I doing going into the kitchen with Judith Amber and leaving the governor of Ohio cooling his heels on the sofa?

"Really, Mr. Jacovich," Judith said when we were in the kitchen out of earshot, "this is awfully embarrassing."

"Your husband was tortured to death, Mrs. Amber. Do you want to catch the man responsible or do you want to make nice with the governor? Just let me know."

"You're not working for me anymore," she said. "This is a police matter."

"I'm working for me now," I said. "I've been beaten up by mob punks and shot at by a sniper and squeezed by the police and snubbed by a bunch of agency types and now patronized by the governor. I'm no more out of this case than you are, and I want a few simple answers."

She leaned against the tile counter, her small, well-formed breasts pushing against the knit dress. "Well?"

"Well. When I was searching the house I noticed a lot of bottles of pills and vitamins and things in that cabinet over there. Are they yours or your husband's?"

"They're all Richard's," she said. "He was very into vitamins and health foods and prevention and all that sort of thing. I keep a bottle of iron tabs in my purse and that's all I take."

"I didn't notice anything in there that would be used by a man with a heart condition."

She shook her head. "Richard didn't have a heart condition. Well, obviously he did have, but he didn't know about it. He'd never had any problems along those lines at all that I knew about. He was always . . . healthy."

I wandered over to the cabinet and opened it. All the bottles and jars were still there, of course. I closed the door and turned back to her. "You never told me if you found anything unusual in the safe deposit boxes."

"That's because I didn't. Everything there was supposed to be. Oh, there were a few things—"

"What things?"

"A cameo brooch," she said. "A beautiful cameo brooch that I'd never seen before. I suppose it was destined for someone else's throat, not mine, because Richard saw fit to hide it. It looked extremely expensive."

"What did you do with it?"

"I left it there," she said. "It didn't belong to me."

"Anything else?"

"Well, yes," she said. "A manila envelope stuffed with papers."

"And?"

"I couldn't make head or tail out of it. It was all in Richard's handwriting, but it seemed to have something to do with betting on football games and things."

"Did you leave that there, too?"

"No," she said. "I brought it home with me. But I never had a chance to tell you because Richard . . ." Her eyes filled up, and I thought she was finally going to crack, but she did yeoman service in maintaining her ice-princess image.

"Can I see the envelope?" I said gently.

"Now? Can't you come back in the—"

"Now, Mrs. Amber. Right now."

She shrugged, martyred, and disappeared for a few minutes. There was half a pot of coffee in the coffee maker, and I poured myself some in a cup I'd gotten from another cupboard. I'd been through this kitchen stem to stern, and I knew where everything was.

She came back carrying an eight-by-ten envelope that looked well-used and handed it to me.

"Thank you," I said. "I'll just sit here and look at it."

She glanced again at the door. "Why don't you take it home with you?"

"Go on back out to your guests, Mrs. Amber. Can't keep Governor George waiting."

"You're an impossible person," she said, and went out through the swinging oaken door. I sat down on one of the stools at the counter and removed the contents of the envelope.

There were several sheets of lined yellow paper inside, all full of figures and calculations, and a cardboard schedule of all the NFL football games for the season just past. There was also a Day-Glo green spiral notebook, the kind stenographers use. I had a feeling it had been pilfered from the supply cabinet at Marbury-Stendall Advertising. Probably more money is lost each year due to employees taking home pens, paper clips, and stationery than to all the car thieves and hoodlums who knock over 7-11 Stores combined.

I flipped open the notebook. On the first page was a date, evidently a Sunday from the past September, written in Richard Amber's precise hand with a brown felt pen. Listed on the page were two football games, and for each matchup one of the teams had a plus sign or minus sign with a number next to it. Written underneath each set in green ink was what I took to be the actual score of the game. Then in blue ink at the bottom of the page was another plus sign in front of the figure $2,500. That had evidently been a good day for Richard Amber. There was also a set of initials at the top of the page, written in brown. I assumed those belonged to the person with whom he'd placed his bet.

On each successive page was the same pattern, only the date was seven or eight days past the previous one (he'd obviously bet a few Monday-night games as well as Sunday-afternoon contests); the numbers and the teams were different but the ink colors and the patterns were the same. And on each successive page the amount wagered was higher. As the season progressed Richard Amber had obviously lost more heavily. The last page was dated January 11 and dealt with just one game, the Browns vs. the Denver Broncos. In brown ink it said "Cleve + 2" and underneath it in green was the final score of the game, which the Browns had lost by three points. At the bottom of the page in blue a figure was scrawled in a shaky hand: −$30,000.

I riffled the pages, doing quick math in my head, and figured that Amber had lost somewhere in the vicinity of $38,000 over the course of the season, not counting the vigorish on the bets. That was a lot of money even for the prodigal son of Ohio advertising.

The notebook didn't tell me very much I hadn't already known except that Amber's loss on the Browns-Broncos game was not a momentary aberration but an ingrained habit. It was interesting to me that Amber was such a methodical fellow he would write so careful a record of his stupidity. Maybe he'd been hanging around Charlie Dodge and his voluminous lists for too long and some of it had rubbed off.

Steve Smith came through the door with two cups and saucers. He looked startled to see me, as though he'd forgotten I was there.

"Oh," he said. "Hello."

"Hello, Mr. Smith," I said.

"I came for some coffee."

"Yes, I see."

"You know, this is a terrific shock for the governor," he said. "He and Mr. Amber were such good friends."

"It's a shock for everyone."

He began pouring coffee. "You're in an interesting line of work," he said.

"It has its moments."

"I'd like to have a chat with you sometime. Pick your brain, so to speak."

"About what?"

He set down the coffeepot and put one foot up on the rung of a stool. "Well, you've been looking for Mr. Amber for some time now, and I imagine you've discovered a lot of interesting things."

"So?"

"So, maybe if we put our heads together we can figure out who did this terrible thing."

"I didn't know the governor's office was in the law enforcement business."

"We're not," said Smith, casting a nervous eye on the door. "I just thought a meeting might be mutually beneficial." He took a business card from his wallet and gave it to me. It identified him as the governor's "legislative assistant." He said, "We're staying in Cleveland tonight but we'll head back to Columbus in the morning. Why don't you give me a ring, say, tomorrow afternoon?"

"Forgive me, Mr. Smith," I said, "but I'm private. I don't share information with anyone but my clients, and the police when it becomes necessary. And as far as our getting our heads together, I don't see the benefit to me because you haven't got anything to trade. You can tell the governor that as of yet I haven't found anything in the course of this investigation to make him nervous. And you can also tell him that whatever else I do find I have no intention of suppressing if it has any bearing on Amber's killing."

Smith's eyes, small for the size of his face to begin with, had shrunk to glittering points. He said, "You know, Jacovich, private investigators' licenses come up for renewal. I'd hate to think anything would get in the way of your making an honest living."

"Mr. Smith," I said, "the governor's coffee is getting cold."

Politicians were all alike, I thought. In his great grief for his friend, all the governor and his legislative assistant could think of was that somewhere in the dark corners of Richard Amber's life he had been doing something like dealing smack or selling eight-year-old boys to pederasts or bilking old ladies out of their life's savings, something that would embarrass the governor and put a dangerous curve in his road to Washington. Well, if that were the case they would damn well have to find it out for themselves. I wasn't interested in George Kinnick's career. I wasn't even that interested in mine. I was looking for a killer.

I began looking through the sheets of legal-sized yellow paper Amber had left in his safe deposit box. Again they were very carefully dated, starting on May 12 of last year. Beneath each date, written in Amber's favorite brown ink, was a set of six numbers. Directly below, in green ink, was another set of six. Each piece of paper held four dates, with a green-ink line separating them, and each date was precisely seven days later than the one before. No Monday-night games here. The last date was last week's—February 11. And for that date there was no green-ink entry—just the one set of numbers, carefully written with a brown felt pen.

Twenty-one. Thirty-four. Thirty-three. Fourteen. Twenty-six. Two.

I felt an adrenaline rush so strong that it made me dizzy. I carefully folded the papers and put them in my jacket pocket. Then I went back out into the living room.

Steve Smith was again standing by the wall, now looking at me as though he'd asked me to dance and I'd rejected him in front of all the other guys. Deming was most of the way through his cigar, and the governor was sitting next to Judith Amber holding her hand and speaking in soothing whispers.

Deming said, "Aren't you finished yet, Jacovich?"

"Just about," I said. "Excuse me, Governor?"

He looked up pleasantly. After all, I was a registered voter. "You and Mr. Amber went to Ohio State together, didn't you?"

"Right," he said. "Class of '56."

"Do you happen to remember what his major was?"

"Certainly. He was a business major, and I was pre-law. We used to joke that I'd be his attorney when he became a millionaire."

"Did he have a minor?"

The governor smiled easily. He had no way of knowing the results of my conversation in the kitchen with his dog-robber. "Ah, that's where Richard really missed his calling. He minored in mathematics. He was an absolute whiz with figures and formulas and advanced calculus. It was way beyond me, I'll tell you, but he did have a way with numbers."

Judith Amber and her uncle were looking at me as if I'd lost my mind, probably because I had broken into a grin. I couldn't believe it—but I had just found my straight edge.

CHAPTER SEVENTEEN

For a community that had been founded by and named after a religious sect that observed a doctrine of celibacy and common property, Shaker Heights had come a long way, and in the postwar prosperity years of the forties and fifties had occupied the enviable position of being the richest suburb, per capita, in the United States. And although it had lately been superseded by such nouveau riche enclaves as Palm Beach and Bel-Air and Grosse Pointe, there were still few poverty pockets within its boundaries. Jerry Stendall's house, just a block off Shaker Boulevard, was similar in feeling and design to Richard Amber's, except it was smaller and looked more lived-in, probably due to the presence of children. There was a rusty basketball hoop mounted on the garage above the door, and a Volkswagen Rabbit parked in the driveway, undoubtedly the property of the eldest of the Stendall progeny.

My ring was answered by a well-dressed, angular woman in her late thirties. She peered at me through glasses framed in pink plastic with wings that swooped up to her eyebrows. "Yes?" she said. The way she said it wasn't unpleasant, but if she had been auditioning for Welcome Wagon Lady she'd never have made the cut.

"Mrs. Stendall? My name is Milan Jacovich. I wonder if I might have a word with your husband?"

She looked over her shoulder at not much of anything and said, "We're just finishing up dinner," one of those non sequiturs that keep the world turning.

"It's rather important," I said.

"You're not a salesman, are you? Jerry hates to be disturbed by salesmen."

I gave her my card, and she regarded it as if it were made of Kryptonite. I said, "It's about Richard Amber."

She lost what little color there was in her face. "Just a moment," she said, and closed the door, leaving me standing out on the front porch in the cold. I felt like having a cigarette but I didn't know how long I was going to be out there.

After about a minute and a half Jerry Stendall came to the door and stepped out onto the porch with me. He was wearing the trousers to the suit he'd had on at the office, and the same shirt, but was now tieless and wore a nondescript cardigan sweater. Get him out of the office and he was just as homey as an old shoe.

"I really resent this," he said. "This is my damned home! I don't do business at my home."

"This isn't business, Jerry, and I don't care if you resent it or not. Now we can talk here, or at any one of a number of depressing police stations in the area with an audience, and that includes several guys on the other side of a two-way mirror. But I think you might be in over your head, and we'd better talk about it now. Privately."

He hunched his shoulders, whether against the icy temperature or the vicissitudes of fate, I couldn't tell. He finally said, "All right, come inside."

The furnishings in the Stendall home didn't match the image of ad agency president, but then again neither did Jerry Stendall. He led us past the dining room, where Mrs. Stendall was nervously twisting her napkin in the company of two teenaged boys. I recognized them as the ugly children in the photograph in Stendall's office. They had become ugly adolescents.

"Under no circumstances do I want to be disturbed," Jerry told his family, and led me into the kitchen, where we sat at a breakfast nook. There must be something about me that I keep wind-ing up in people's kitchens. The same something must keep those people from offering me anything to eat or drink.

"What's on your mind, Jacovich?" he said.

"Murder."

He shook his head and ran a hand over his face. "That's awfully damned melodramatic. What's the bottom line?"

I said, "What did Richard Amber say to you when he called you the night he disappeared?"

Under the health-club tan Jerry blanched, and his lips all but disappeared. "I don't know what you're talking about," he sput-tered. At least that's what he meant to say, but it came out in a series of herky-jerky, saliva-filled sounds that had little relation to human speech.

I said, "Since you're having a little trouble talking, Jerry, why not let me talk and you just shake your head yes or no?"

He gripped the edge of the table so hard that his knuckles whitened. "My family—" he said.

"No trouble, Jerry. Just talk. Somewhere between seven-thirty and eight o'clock on the Wednesday night he disappeared, Rich-ard Amber called you on the phone, didn't he?"

Stendall didn't want to answer that, but after thinking it over he decided he'd better. He simply nodded his head.

"And he told you, in so many words, to take his job and shove it? Just like that?"

His eyes widened, wondering at me as if I were clairvoyant. I went on, "He also probably told you exactly what he thought of you, and it wasn't terribly flattering."

"How did you . . . My God!" He put his face in his hands.

"It just makes sense, Jerry. The pieces fit."

"I never told a soul about it, I swear! You're right, he called me up and quit, effective immediately—but I never told anyone."

"Did he happen to tell you why he was quitting, Jerry?"

He shook his head, his face still buried in his own fingers, and when he spoke it was hard to understand him. "I couldn't—figure it out—so sudden—"

"Why didn't you tell me this when I talked to you the next day?"

His eyes appeared between his fingers, beseeching, but I wasn't about to stop.

"Maybe because you were hoping it was a temporary aberration of his, that he'd come to his senses in a day or two and come back to work the way he did several years ago when he just bugged out and went to Indiana."

"I didn't want John to know," he muttered. "I would have been blamed."

"I understand all that. But then when Richard's body was found you still didn't speak out about the phone call. That's called withholding evidence, Jerry, and the police don't like it much in a murder case."

He put his hands back on the edge of the table and leaned forward, his voice high-pitched, whispering, intense, just next door to hysteria. "By then I couldn't," he hissed. "I was afraid."

"I don't blame you," I said. "So what happened after he told you on the phone to go fuck yourself, Jerry? You got in your car and went over there—"

"No!" he said so loudly that it echoed in the kitchen and we both looked to the door to see if it would bring Mrs. Stendall or the boys running.

"Why not? If Richard Amber left the agency because of you, your uncle would have had your skin hanging on the wall. You had to stop him from quitting, so you went over there and tried to talk him out of it, and when you couldn't, you killed him."

"No, I swear to God!" he said, and started to cry, his head down on his arms on the tabletop. He sobbed softly for quite a while, and I just let him. Finally I took out a cigarette just to have something to do.

The spasms subsided finally and he raised a ravaged, tearstained face to me. "Do I look like I could kill anyone that way?" he said.

"Desperation makes people do strange things. If Amber quits, he takes the Deming account with him, there are massive cutbacks at the agency to take up the slack, and the most obvious one is the guy who makes the second-biggest salary and does the least. But if Amber dies there's still a chance that Walter Deming will hang in there with Marbury-Stendall. That translates into a pretty good motive for you, Jerry."

"I swear to God," he said again, and then we both looked up as the larger of the two Stendall teenagers walked into the kitchen. His hair was dark brown and about as long as Veronica Lake wore hers in *The Blue Dahlia*.

"I'm just getting some ice cream—" he began.

His father shrieked, "Get out, goddammit!" and the boy did, less out of fear than puzzlement. I don't think his father was capable of inspiring fear in him, or anyone else for that matter, and I suddenly realized that all Jerry Stendall's protestations to the deity were for real—he hadn't killed Richard Amber.

I waited until the disturbed vibrations from his outburst had been laid, and then said, "Didn't you call him back or go out to Pepper Pike and try and talk him out of it?"

"I couldn't talk Richard Amber out of a second cup of coffee," he said. "He had no respect for me, he didn't like me, he only spoke to me when it was absolutely necessary. I told you, he treated me like shit."

"I'm sure you didn't just go back to watching television after that call, Jerry."

"Of course not," he said, self-disgust coating his words. "I called his best friend to try to talk some sense into him."

"Who was that?"

He stared at me, unbelieving that there was anyone in the world not *au courant* with the office politics at Marbury-Stendall. "Jeff Monaghan," he said.

It took several rings of the bell before Jeff Monaghan answered the door. He was also wearing a baggy cardigan sweater over an open white shirt—it seemed to be the outfit of choice for off-duty Marbury-Stendall executives. He didn't look happy to see me.

"Why don't you give it a rest, Jacovich?" he said. "From how I understand it, private eyes don't investigate murders. You're a little out of your area, aren't you?"

"Maybe," I said. "But I'd like to come in anyway."

He hulked in the doorway like a bouncer in a country-western nightclub, but he wasn't big enough to pull it off. He finally stood aside. "Come on in," he said.

This time he ushered me into the living room, asked me to take off my coat and sit down on the sofa, and excused himself for a moment. He came back shortly and sat down opposite me in a modernistic butterfly chair. At least we weren't in the kitchen.

"Jacovich, I'm tired," he said. "I'm tired of this whole Richard Amber business. I've done my grieving for my friend and now it's time to get on with my own life."

"Pretty cold, isn't it?"

He shrugged. "It's how I am. I've got a very orderly mind, a very orderly way of doing things, and that's how I survive in my business. So I don't really think we have anything to say to each other."

"Why didn't you tell me Jerry Stendall called you the night Amber disappeared and told you he'd just quit?"

It's easy to tell how shaken up someone is by watching their eyes. Monaghan's pupils became so wide for a moment it seemed there was no other color to the eyeball, and they shifted from one side of the room to the other as though looking for the nearest exit. He got them under control and said, "I assumed Jerry had told you."

I smiled. "You know what happens when we assume?"

"Don't patronize me, Jacovich, I don't like it. Okay, Jerry called me, very upset, and told me Richard had just called him up and quit on the spot without giving a reason. Just quit, cold. Jerry never cut much ice with Richard, so he asked me to give Richard a ring, find out what the trouble was, and try to talk him out of it. Frankly, I didn't want to get involved, but Richard had been very good to me so I thought I'd give it a shot. I called, but there was no answer."

I raised my eyebrows. "The machine wasn't on?"

"Oh, yeah, sure—but there was no one home."

"Why didn't you leave a message, Mr. Monaghan?"

"Hey, what is this? I don't like being rousted."

"Rousted? Where the hell did you hear that, on television someplace? If you're going to use underworld slang, use it right, okay?"

He sat back in his chair and jammed his fists into the pockets of his sweater. "I used to like you—sort of. I guess I was wrong."

"You must have been weakened by that cold of yours. So now tell me. You called, got the machine, elected not to leave a message—and then what?"

"Then I called Jerry back, told him Richard wasn't there, or at least wasn't answering his phone, and I said I'd call him in the morning, and I went back to reading."

"What were you reading, Mr. Monaghan?"

"How the hell do I remember? Look at all these books—pick one you like. What were *you* reading nine days ago?"

"As a matter of fact," I said, "it was a biography of Lyndon Johnson, and I was reading it because I was too disgusted with the Cavs getting slaughtered by the Celtics to finish watching the game. And then Richard Amber called me and asked me to come out and be his bodyguard, and when I did he was gone."

"There, you see?"

"The trouble is, Mr. Monaghan, he called Jerry Stendall after seven-thirty, and he called Karen Wilde just before eight, and he called me at nine. So you see, he was home until at least nine o'clock, maybe longer. And Jerry Stendall says you called him back to tell him Amber wasn't home just after eight o'clock."

"I don't see your point, I don't think you have a point, and it's starting to piss me off."

"I don't mean to piss you off," I said, "but I'd like your opinion on something."

"What's that?"

"Why do you suppose he needed a bodyguard anyway?"

"I don't know," Monaghan said. "You're the detective. You tell me."

"All right, I will," I said. "What Amber didn't tell me because I was a stranger he wasn't sure he could trust, what he didn't tell Stendall because he wanted him to stew in his own juice overnight, what he didn't tell Karen because he wanted it to be a surprise—was some good news that he had. But he finally couldn't stand it anymore, he just had to tell someone. So he told his best friend. You."

"I'm telling you I never talked to him that night!"

"That's what you're telling me. It ain't necessarily so."

"Why would I lie?"

"I don't know, Jeff. To beat a murder rap?"

His face got tight like a woman's leather clutch purse that had been stuffed too full with makeup and cigarettes and tampons and address books. "Take a hike, Jacovich, I don't have to put up with this crap."

"You know Amber was a business genius, don't you? You worked with him and for him long enough. But what you might not have known was that he was a mathematical genius as well."

"Richard was always good with figures—it helped him out with client presentations."

"There are figures and figures, Jeff. Amber was a whiz when it came to the science of mathematical probabilities and percentages. At least that's what his good friend and former school chum Governor Kinnick says."

"Jesus, you've even bothered the governor with this? You've got the balls of a brass monkey."

"And the persistence of a bulldog, the courage of a terrier—if you write copy the way you talk, no wonder Marbury-Stendall is in trouble. I'll bet your dictionary of American clichés is falling apart from overuse."

"Fuck you, get out of here," he said.

"In time. First, back to Richard and his nimble fingers on the calculator keys. Sure, it made him a good living, but lots of people make a good living. Richard wanted to write without any downgrade of his lifestyle—and he had to figure out ways to do that without having to put up with the likes of John Marbury and

Walter Deming and Jerry Stendall. So he got out his calculator and his slide rule and went at it.

"At first it didn't work out very well, and then it started paying off a little bit—during the football season, when Richard began betting on his calculations. It's amazing how a mathematical mind can take twenty-two guys wearing cleats and shoulder pads and feed them into a computer and it spits out the probability of a football score. But the computer doesn't take into consideration a quarterback with a hangover or a nose guard who's injured or a tailback who has the trots from eating too much soul food. And Richard started *not* doing so well—until finally when the Brownies got to the playoffs he went off the deep end to a bunch of guys whose names are all Knuckles and Spike and Carmine."

"I didn't know—" Monaghan said slowly.

"Well, it's not really important, Jeff, other than background. Because he was doing other calculations, too, based on mathematical probabilities. Lots of people do them, and then sell their findings by mail order for forty or fifty bucks. Richard played his—he developed a numerical system for doping out the winning numbers on the lottery."

Monaghan cleared the frog out of his throat without opening his lips. It sounded ever so genteel.

"He kept coming closer and closer, every week. And every week he'd write down the winning combination and how close he'd come. Even picked up about three grand or so last October, but to a man making six figures and married to Judith Amber that was chicken feed. Guess what happened then, Jeff?"

He glared at me. "You're a very childish man, Jacovich."

"Call me Milan," I said, "all my friends do."

"I doubt you have any."

I smiled. "You're getting better, Jeffrey. Well, sir, come last Wednesday night, and son of a bitch if those six numbers didn't come up ! Twenty-seven million bucks on a one-dollar investment. Of course as it turned out two other people had those numbers, too, so it would have only worked out to nine million—but Richard didn't know that. He was nervous about sitting there with a negotiable piece of paper worth a sizable fortune, so he called an acquaintance of his at the Cleveland P.D., one Marko Meglich, and asked him to recommend a bodyguard. Marko and I went to high school together in Slavic Town, so he recommended me. Talk about your old-boy network!"

The only color left in Monaghan's face was the red and flaky skin around his nostrils that comes with blowing your nose all day for a week trying to shake a cold. The rest of him looked like Lincoln's granite face on Mount Rushmore, stark white and immobile.

"So the first thing he did, Jeff, was call Jerry Stendall and tender his resignation, with instructions, without giving him a reason. Then he called Karen Wilde and out of the blue asked her to marry him. You see, he didn't need the job anymore, and he didn't need Judith's money. He was rich in his own right, rich enough, certainly, to settle down with the woman he loved and write his great American whatever."

"You ought to be the writer," Jeff said, "with an imagination like that."

"In the meantime Jerry calls you, whining that Richard has quit on him, and asks if you can call Richard to find out what's up—but you didn't get an answering machine, Jeff, you got your best friend on the phone and out of sheer joy and exuberance he gives you the wonderful news.

"So you say congratulations and God bless, Richard, and then you hang up, call Stendall back and tell him Richard is gone and get dressed and drive out to Pepper Pike, where your pal and benefactor lets you in the door, maybe for a celebration drink, and you whack him on the head and tie him up so he can't stop you while you look for that lottery ticket. When you don't find it in the den, you march Richard out to your car and take him someplace— maybe out in the woods where no one can hear him scream and beg—and you use your best powers of persuasion to get him to tell you where he's hidden it. A creative guy like you should have been able to come up with something a little classier than a beating and lighted cigarettes on the feet, but I realize this was a spur-of-the-moment thing with you and you had to improvise."

He tried to laugh but it came out a seal's bark. "You are so full of shit it would be funny if it weren't so serious. You're looking at a lawsuit it'll take you several lifetimes to pay off."

"Don't get litigious on me, Jeff, it scares me silly. Now, where were we? Oh yes, torturing our best friend. But maybe you got a little too frisky, or maybe it was just one of those things, but all of a sudden the fear or the pain got to be too much for Richard, and he died on you. Heart went like that!" I snapped my fingers and he jumped. "And there you are with a corpse on your hands in the middle of one of the coldest nights of the year out in the uncharted woodlands of northern Ohio. So you did what anyone with an intelligent mind would do under the circumstances—you dumped him into a hole in the ice over the Chagrin River and he disappears until spring. How'm I doing so far?"

"So far it's a book club alternate selection," he said. "Tell me more."

"You probably had a bit of a cold when you started, Jeff, but spending several hours out in the woods savaging someone to death and then sticking him under the ice aggravated it so you couldn't make it to work the next morning. You really ought to take better care of yourself."

"I'm going to, starting right now, when I throw you the hell out of here and call my lawyer."

"Not ready to go just yet. Of course you had no way of knowing Richard had called me. You lucked out—if I'd gotten there a few minutes sooner I might have found Richard all tied up and you methodically looking in his den. You started getting nervous, though, that Judith might turn up, and figured it was easier to squeeze the ticket's location out of him. That cost him his life.

"When you found out I was in the picture it didn't bother you much at first. You even told me all about Richard's little flings with Karen Wilde and Mary Soderberg to throw me off the track. You waited until Judith went out for her regular Friday-night slap-and-tickle, and you busted into the house and trashed the den looking for what you now knew was a nine-million-dollar ticket to Fantasyland. I'm a bit curious, though—did you find it?"

"*If* I'd killed Richard and *if* I'd broken into the house that night and *if* I'd found the ticket, do you think I'd be sitting here putting up with the ravings of a Yugoslavian lunatic? I'd be on my way to Switzerland or Costa Rica to live in luxury for the rest of my life. You're crazy, Milan Jacovich."

I nodded. "You're right. You didn't find the ticket. And when you didn't, you got jittery again. You knew the police weren't looking for Amber yet—just me. So the next day you tailed me out to the Valley Gun Club. A good job, too, for an amateur. I never even noticed you. Then you slashed my tires so you'd have a more or less stationary target, hid in the trees across the river—poor bastard, it must have played hell with your cold—and took a shot at me with a deer rifle."

"I don't own a deer rifle. I hate hunting."

"Maybe you do. But somewhere between Wednesday night and Saturday afternoon you purchased one. I'll be willing to bet that somewhere way downstream of Gates Mills that rifle is now rusting in the river. Damn shame to throw away a brand-new gun like that, wasn't it, Jeff? And I'm also willing to bet that if the police get really interested in this story they'll do some checking and find a gun shop or sporting goods outlet somewhere within a two-hundred-mile radius that sold you a .30-.30. Is that a bet you'd like to cover?"

His voice was shaky. "If this little farce has even a nodding acquaintance with reality, why didn't I go back and search the rest of the house for the ticket?"

I smiled. "Only the killer would know that no one has tried to break in again."

He didn't say anything. His left foot was wiggling as though he had to go to the bathroom. I don't know, maybe he did.

I said, "You're right, though, Jeff—nobody searched the house again. Maybe because when you went back there you were astute enough to see a goon in a black Olds 98 keeping watch over the house, so you decided to be discreet and wait until the heat died down. But you had plenty of time—no one knew there was a lottery ticket to look for, at least not at the Amber household. All of Ohio is wondering where the third winner is, but it never occurred to anyone that it might be the missing advertising executive. Men like Amber don't play the lottery. It's always guys with blue work shirts and polyester leisure suits and greasy dirt that'll never come out from under their fingernails. So you figured that when the brouhaha about Richard's disappearance was over and the gunny in the Olds stopped watching, you could go back at your own time and try again. Nine million bucks was worth waiting for—if Judith Amber didn't find the ticket first. Of course, not being a trained meteorologist you had no way of knowing we were going to break all existing temperature records for February, the ice was going to melt, the river would begin moving again, and Richard's body would come floating downstream like an Indian war canoe. I don't have much of a scenario after that because we're just about up to date."

I took a cigarette out of my pocket and lighted it, leaning back in the chair comfortably. "How'd I do?" I said. "Miss anything?"

"You forgot about pinning the Lindbergh kidnapping on me," he said.

"No, I didn't—but that's not my case."

"Jacovich, I am absolutely fascinated by this little wet dream of yours. It shows imagination, style, and flair. You ever think about becoming a copywriter?"

"You're the second one to offer me a job in advertising today."

"You should have accepted. It would save you your license and a lot of other legal grief."

"It won't fly, Jeff."

"Sure it will. Because Richard could have called anybody else and told them the glad news, including the governor himself, the mayor, and about a hundred of his nearest and dearest friends. You haven't a shred of proof it was me."

"I've got a shred, Jeff."

He frowned, his shoulders still hunched, his fists still hidden in the pockets of his cable-knit cardigan.

"When I visited you in your office today, you made all the right noises of sympathy, and it sounded great—saying that the pressures of the business had given Richard a heart condition and that wasn't for you anymore."

"It's true."

"Yes, it is," I said. "Except that until the moment of his death no one knew Richard Amber had a weak heart—not even his wife—and the only thing released to the news media was that the cause of death was under investigation. Only the killer would know that cause was a coronary. You screwed up, buddy."

Jeff Monaghan's mouth started working, as if he were trying to isolate an errant fish bone between his incisors, and his face, deathly pale up until now, began to redden. Then he broke into a painful grimace, and he took his hands out of his sweater pockets and there was a 9-mm Luger in the right one.

"You fucker!" he said.

I looked at the gun. "Did you go and get that right after I came in, Jeff, or have you been sitting here with it in your pocket all evening?"

"You're one smart son of a bitch, aren't you?"

I didn't agree. I felt like one dumb son of a bitch, thinking I could just walk in here and accuse him of murder when I knew he had been desperate enough to kill one man and attempt to kill me, as well. The gun looked like a cannon pointing right at my head. If I didn't play this carefully I was not going to live through the night.

"I just put pieces together once I had a framework," I said. "Didn't take a rocket scientist."

"You have most of it just about the way it happened, Jacovich, except for one thing. I hated Richard Amber's guts!"

"Why?"

"Because I carried him for years. Who do you think came up with all the creative stuff, all the campaigns, who worked far into the night to do his presentations, who whispered every fucking idea he ever had into his ear? *I* was the genius in that shop, not Richard. He was just a highly paid cocktail hostess! A whore! All charm and nothing underneath. He got the dinners with the governor, he got the party invitations and the committee bids, he got to fuck all the pretty ladies, he got the salary and the stock options and all the perks that come with a high-visibility job, and every year when he collected all the awards for great commercials and great campaigns, he'd say how he'd like to thank his creative team, especially Jeffrey Monaghan. There wasn't a day in the past five years that I didn't want to kill the sonofabitch, but I never had the guts before."

"It's amazing how nine million dollars can buy you a set of balls," I said. "And after all that trouble, after catching a bad cold from staying out in the snow all night, you didn't even get the money."

"I'll get it," he said. "My plans haven't changed a bit—except for killing you."

"Go ahead," I said. "But I just came from Jerry Stendall's house, and he knows where I was headed. Besides, I should warn you, I'm a bleeder. You kill me here and I'll bleed all over your chair, your rug. If I disappear the police will undoubtedly check, since this was my destination and since Jerry and I had a long chat about it. You'll have a tough time convincing them you just happened to be butchering hogs in the living room."

"You don't think I'm stupid enough to kill you here?" he said.

"You have another place all picked out? The same place you took Richard, maybe? Jeff, you're getting really experienced at this."

He stood up, the gun pointed at my head. "Get up, Jacovich. "

I felt the sweat rolling down my back. I don't like guns pointed at me, especially by desperate men. But I also knew I was dealing with an amateur. I had to throw him off balance, but not so much so that he'd pull the trigger.

"No," I said easily.

The gun wavered in front of my face. "What?" he said with disbelief.

"No, I'm not going to get up and go with you so you can kill me someplace convenient. When you want something, Jeff, you have to work for it."

He brandished the gun, trying to look tough. "I said get up!"

"What are you going to do if I don't? Shoot me?"

He was nonplussed for a moment. This wasn't how it happened on television. You point a gun at somebody, and they do what you tell them to, that was the rule. But when they know they're going to get it anyway, there's not much else you can threaten them with and your gun becomes meaningless as an instrument of persuasion. Then he became enraged, and I watched his eyes and thought maybe he was going to do just that, shoot me, and I felt my throat closing up with fear, with a panic that I wasn't ready to die just yet, that I wanted to see my kids again. I took a big chance, and I said, "You've had it, Jeff. You gave it a good try, but you're an amateur and you made a few mistakes. Pointing that thing at me was your worst one."

He realized he was out of options and he lost it; something snapped behind his eyes and he swung the gun at my face. I turned my head aside at the last moment, and it hit me on the left cheekbone, and I heard the bone crack and all the fireworks on all the Fourth of Julys in history went off behind my eyes, sparklers and cherry bombs and pinwheels and rockets and the kind that explode and then turn into the American flag up in the sky, and I thought I was going to faint from the pain and then some dim instinct for survival told me if I did that I was dead, and I opened my eyes and saw him swing the gun again, and I caught his wrist and twisted.

The momentum of his swing took him off his feet, yet I was so dizzy and in such pain I couldn't do much about it but hang on, and then he was swarming all over me, grunting like a professional wrestler on TV and trying to wrench his wrist from my grip, and I hung on even though he was all knees and elbows and feet and fingernails, battering at my rib cage and my shoulders and my thighs, and scratching at my face. We tussled on the couch like a teenaged boy and his recalcitrant date, and finally his cheek was up near mine, and I could feel his scratchy beard on my face and idly wondered, despite the agony that was caroming through my face and head, why women ever liked to kiss men with beards, and I looked in his eyes and saw the desperation there, a dread that slowly metamorphosed into madness as he gritted his teeth and struggled, mucus bubbling out his nostrils. He brought his knee up between my legs and the pain shot to the top of my head, even worse than the broken cheekbone, and I made a superhuman effort to get up or at least get into a better position so he couldn't do that again, and with my greater weight I managed to wrestle him down onto the floor and smother him with my bulk. But his fear gave him abnormal strength, and he began thrashing around underneath me the way no woman ever had, and then there was a muffled explosion and I felt the recoil against me and the sudden heat between my body and his, and smelled the cordite and the burning fabric, and he loosened his grip and relaxed, and I sat up and saw the bullet hole about two inches below his navel; we both saw it, only he was staring at it dully, the shock already numbing him. He'd awakened from a nightmare only to find out he wasn't dreaming at all.

I got up from the floor heavily, waves of dizziness crashing against the shore of my brain, and took a pen from my shirt pocket and stuck it through the trigger guard and gently lifted the gun out of his now limp fingers. The anguish in my cheek was white hot, and I thought I was going to pass out right on top of him. I swayed until I regained my equilibrium, and I looked down at him and he was staring up at me and silently mouthing the words "Help . . . me," like those childhood dreams where you open your mouth to scream and no sound comes out, only this time I was trapped in somebody else's nightmare, and that didn't make it any easier.

"Help . . . me," he mouthed again. And so I did.

I called the police.

CHAPTER EIGHTEEN

It has occurred to me on more than one occasion to find another line of work. If I were a rack jobber, or a middle-management executive with a small electronics firm, or a typist, or a greengrocer, or the guy who solicits subscriptions to the *Plain Dealer* over the telephone, I wouldn't have felt as bad as I was feeling on this cold, bright Saturday, with my ribs aching, my head throbbing, and the left side of my face swollen to twice its normal size so that I had to peer out over my own cheekbone like a little old man trying to see over the too-high dashboard of a Cadillac. Civil service workers whose disdain chills the state unemployment offices, window dressers at Higbee's, private snow removal crews, corporate attorneys, and waiters in smart little cafes off University Circle probably were beaten up and shot at rarely, if at all, and then it was usually not job-related. I was glumly staring out the window at the people having lunch in the front window of the Mad Greek or coming out of the fancy grocery store with brown paper bags full of arugula and wild rice and shiitake mushrooms and herb teas and balsamic vinegars, thinking to myself that Aunt Branka was possibly right and that I should get a real job. I was hoping that by the next day, Sunday, I would be at least healed enough to go back out to Euclid and dine with her and her daughter and son-in-law, even though I dreaded the questions that were sure to accompany dinner. I was hoping that by the time the sun went down this evening the pain would have subsided enough for me to get some sleep.

I'm sure my pain was nothing to Jeff Monaghan's. He'd had extensive surgery to remove the 9-mm bullet from his intestine and was on a steady morphine regimen for a while. Recovering from a stomach wound was not exactly a day at the beach. After he was well enough to get around, the district attorney was planning to seek an indictment for him to stand trial for the murder of Richard Amber.

Ten days after Monaghan's arrest I received a letter of appreciation from the governor's office. I hoped it wouldn't destroy Governor Kinnick to know that I neither framed it nor kept it in an album, but left it on my desk for three days and then threw it away at the same moment I decided the ashtrays were too full.

Deputy Police Chief Ethan Kemp, to show his appreciation, had rescinded the order to stay out of his territory and had even invited me to dinner with him "and the little woman" as soon as my face healed. He was the first to admit I'd made him and his department look pretty good, and for a small-town cop that's just about the nicest thing one can do. Jerry Stendall wasn't talking to me anymore and said he didn't like my attitude. John Marbury didn't talk to me, either, but he was far too busy dancing Walter Deming around to bother with anyone as unimportant as a Slovenian private detective, and I guess he knew what he was doing at that, because as things turned out Deming stayed with the agency after making a deal with the U.S. government for a federal loan and another one for a rather lucrative contract. Of course that probably had nothing to do with twelve thousand five hundred shares of Marbury-Stendall Advertising being transferred to the name of Judith Marie Amber. Marbury did say that anytime I wanted them his season tickets to the Indians' games were available to me—except on weekends.

Both Rudy Dolsak and Ed Stahl were willing to wait until I felt better to cash in on their luncheon dates with me, and Marko Meglich was once more reminding me of how high my star might have risen had I stayed in harness on the force. Karen Wilde was going into rehearsal for a revival of *Twentieth Century* at the Playhouse, and Charlie Dodge was keeping a low profile and hoping the powers-that-be at Marbury-Stendall would forget he was there until he was ready to retire. Rhoda Young gave the agency two weeks' notice.

Victor Gaimari sent a bottle of champagne with a note expressing hope for my quick recovery and saying he'd "still like to work" with me sometime, so I assumed I wasn't going to have to deal with Sunglasses and his pals for a while. I'm not sure what they did about the forty-five thousand dollars Richard Amber owed them. I couldn't quite see them leaning on the widow, especially under the circumstances. But if Giancarlo D'Allessandro decided that's what he wanted to do I'm sure Gaimari would simply go along with it. One didn't get to Gaimari's position in an organization such as D'Allessandro's by letting a little thing like sentiment stand in the way of business and honor. Dues must be paid in such a family.

As it turned out, though, Judith Amber could have paid her late husband's gambling losses without having to pawn her jewelry or get a part-time job. After taking a vacation to "get away" from things for a while, a trip that took her to London, Paris, Rome, and the Greek islands for almost two months, she returned home, and in the course of reorganizing her life she was disposing of her husband's personal effects, the memories being too painful for her to live with. His clothing went to Goodwill, his books and papers were presented to Ohio State University, and his Cadillac was used as a trade-in for Mrs. Amber's new Ferrari. And while she was clearing out the kitchen cupboard where Amber had stashed his vitamins, his acidophilus and his kelp, and his garlic tablets and his digestive enzymes, she happened to notice, through the brown glass of a bottle of tocopherol tablets that, taken as directed, supplied one hundred percent of the minimum daily requirement of Vitamin E, a wadded-up piece of paper. She opened the bottle, removed the paper, and found it to be a ticket from the Ohio lottery bearing the numbers twenty-one, thirty-four, thirty-three, fourteen, twenty-six, and two, which was worth a bit more than nine million dollars, payable in equal increments annually for twenty years. Judith told the press, which descended on her home with cameras and microphones and notepads at the ready, that the money wasn't going to change her lifestyle that much.

The Cavaliers continued to lose on the road.

But this was the Saturday after Richard Amber's body had been found, and I had the stereo playing, mainly because my face hurt too much to watch TV or read, and absolute silence in my apartment would have been unbearable. I was smoking a lot, between two and three packs a day, and though it was only just past one in the afternoon I was working on my second six-pack of Stroh's because it dulled the pain and because I couldn't think of a single reason not to.

And then one rang the doorbell.

"You're only the second man that's ever stood me up," Mary Soderberg said, "and the first one was in junior high school. How are you feeling?"

I was so happy that she'd come to see me I didn't even answer. It wasn't easy to talk. It had been less easy for the past few days eating pudding and Jell-O and soft-cooked scrambled eggs. I had called to cancel our museum date, explaining what had happened, and she had been sympathetic and understanding, although at that point I think she was still too shaken up about Richard Amber's death to care about our date one way or the other. But here she was, dressed in faded, form-fitting jeans and a short suede coat, with a blue scarf around her neck that highlighted her eyes, carrying a little bouquet of flowers "because I thought you could use some cheering up," and all at once my drab apartment was brightened and lightened by a special face.

"Does it hurt a lot?" she said.

"You've obviously never had a broken cheekbone or you wouldn't ask." The thought of anything happening to those exquisite cheekbones was very distressing. "Do you want some coffee or a beer or something?"

She pushed me down into my overstuffed chair. "Don't wait on me," she said, "you're the convalescent." She went into the kitchen and managed to discover where I kept the beer.

"This stuff is murder for you," she said, handing me one only reluctantly. "You ought to be drinking fruit juice."

"Don't make me smile, it hurts."

It delighted me that Mary drank the beer straight from the bottle like some sort of curvaceous cowboy, and I let her know it.

"I told you I was a no-frills lady," she said. "The guys in the three-piece suits drink Pimm's Number One cups. I figured a private detective was a straight-from-the-bottle guy. And so am I. I guess that's why I'm here. Or maybe not, maybe I have another reason, one that kind of scared me this past week. I can be pretty tough and up-front when I want to be, but sometimes I get feelings that scare me."

"I'm glad you're here, for whatever reason," I said. "You're what I needed to make me forget how lousy I feel—and to forget how lousy the world is sometimes."

"Is it always this way, Milan? Your getting shot at and beaten up and stuff?"

"Not always," I said. "Just often enough to make life interesting. Most of the time it's just a job."

She half-smiled. "Is that your idea of making life interesting? Hoodlums and killers and crooks?"

"Oh, my!" I said. "Hoodlums and killers and crooks, oh, my!"

She said, "You've been leading a very sheltered life if you call that interesting." She put down her beer and came over and sat on my lap and gave me one of the ten best kisses of the twentieth century, even if it did taste like Stroh's. When we finally came up for air she said, "I'm sorry if I was a little distant on the phone this week. When I heard about Richard—well, I just had to sort out my feelings."

"That's fair," I said. "And did you?"

She answered me by wriggling around on my lap deliciously and giving me another kiss, which promptly knocked the previous one out of the top ten. When you don't do it for a while you forget just how much fun necking can be.

When we grew dangerously close to permanent fusion at the lips and broke apart, she opened her eyes and frowned. "I have to tell you I'm not sure where this is all going," she said.

"Me, neither. What if it only goes partway?"

"Partway where?"

I shrugged. "I don't know, it's your metaphor."

"Nut," she said, and gave me a loud, wet kiss, then pulled back, looking at my cheek with motherly concern. "Does that hurt?" she said. "When we kiss, I mean?"

"A little."

"We'll stop, then."

"Good idea," I said. "You have about three hours. There are some things you can't just quit cold turkey, you know."

"I know," she said. "I'm sorry. Well, how about that? Does that hurt? Or this? This doesn't hurt, does it? Oh, no, that feels good. Tell me if this hurts, Milan . . ."

It wasn't long before the issue of what hurt and what didn't became moot. And afterward, after we had moved into the adjoining room for reasons of comfort and greater maneuverability, and we were each smoking a cigarette and sharing a Stroh's, I couldn't help reflecting on the nature of the universe, and how from death comes life, from destruction comes rebirth, and from a particularly messy and brutal case that had pretty much destroyed my faith in human nature came my first moment of real peace and happiness in a long time.

And maybe, just maybe, it might not have happened to a greengrocer or a rack jobber or the guy who sells ads on the phone for the *Plain Dealer*. And that made it all okay.

A NOTE FROM LES ROBERTS . . .

Thanks for joining Milan Jacovich's ongoing adventures at the beginning.

When I started Pepper Pike, I had no way of knowing if there would be another Milan novel. I just hoped the character--and the city--would catch on with readers. If you had told me back in 1987 when I began writing it that there would be thirteen Milan adventures in all, I would have asked for a hit on whatever it was you were smoking.

The next book in the series is Full Cleveland. I loved the title, but because I still lived in Los Angeles at the time, I had no idea Clevelanders find the term offensive. It didn't seem to bother anyone, though, because the book became a regional bestseller.

The story of Full Cleveland is based on an actual experience of my own, when I was "hired" to edit a magazine that turned out to be a scam. The experience cost me quite a bit of time and money, so I was glad to be able to earn a little of it back by writing a book about it. No good writer wastes anything; we're like the American Indians carving up a buffalo and using every scrap.

A major scene in the novel takes place in one of Cleveland's downtown architectural jewels, the Old Arcade. I had a wonderful time describing the place, never knowing that fifteen years later I would be taping my own radio show out of a studio on the Arcade's second level. Life can be circular, don't you think?

-- Les Roberts

Now available in quality paperback:
the Milan Jacovich mystery series . . .

PEPPER PIKE
Introducing Milan Jacovich, the private investigator with a master's degree, a taste for klobasa sandwiches, and a knack for finding trouble. A cryptic late-night phone call from a high-powered advertising executive leads Milan through the haunts of one of Cleveland's richest suburbs and into the den of Cleveland mob kingpin Don Giancarlo D'Allessandro   1-59851-001-0

FULL CLEVELAND
Someone's scamming Cleveland businessmen by selling ads in a magazine that doesn't exist. But the dollar amount hardly seems worth the number of bodies that Milan soon turns up. And why is Milan being shadowed at every turn by a leisure-suited mob flunky? One thing's certain: Buddy Bustamente's fashion sense isn't the only thing about him that's lethal.   1-59851-002-9

DEEP SHAKER
Ever loyal, Milan Jacovich has no choice but to help when a grade-school chum worries his son might be selling drugs. The investigation uncovers a brutal murder and a particularly savage drug gang—and leads Milan to a relic from every Clevelander's childhood that proves to be deadly.   1-59851-003-7

THE CLEVELAND CONNECTION
The Serbs and the Slovenians traditionally don't get along too well, but Milan Jacovich makes inroads into Cleveland's Serbian community when an appealing young woman convinces him to help search for her missing grandfather. Hatreds that have simmered for fifty years eventually explode as Milan takes on one of his most challenging cases.   1-59851-004-5

THE LAKE EFFECT

Milan owes a favor and agrees to serve as bodyguard for a suburban mayoral candidate—but these politics lead to murder. And the other candidate has hired Milan's old nemesis, disgraced ex-cop Al Drago, who carries a grudge a mile wide.   1-59851-005-3

THE DUKE OF CLEVELAND

Milan dives into the cutthroat world of fine art when a slumming young heiress hires him to find her most recent boyfriend, a potter, who has absconded with $18,000 of her trust-fund money. Turns out truth and beauty don't always mix well—at least in the art business.   1-59851-006-1

COLLISION BEND

Milan goes behind the scenes to uncover scandal, ambition, and intrigue at one of Cleveland's top TV stations as he hunts down the stalker and murderer of a beautiful local television anchor.   1-59851-007-X

THE CLEVELAND LOCAL

Milan Jacovich is hired to find out who murdered a hotshot young Cleveland lawyer vacationing in the Caribbean. Back in Cleveland, he runs afoul of both a Cleveland mob boss and a world-famous labor attorney—and is dealt a tragic personal loss that will alter his life forever.   1-59851-008-8

A SHOOT IN CLEVELAND

Milan accepts an "easy" job baby-sitting a notorious Hollywood bad-boy who's in Cleveland for a movie shoot. But keeping Darren Anderson out of trouble is like keeping your hat dry during a downpour. And when trouble leads to murder, Milan finds himself in the middle of it all.   1-59851-009-6

Get them at your favorite bookstore!